THE BLAZING SEA

Also by Tim Hodkinson

The Whale Road Chronicles
Odin's Game
The Raven Banner
The Wolf Hunt
The Serpent King
The Bear's Blade
Blood Eagle
Eye of the Raven
The Blazing Sea

The Knight Templar Richard Savage Series
Lions of the Grail
The Waste Land

Other Titles
The Spear of Crom
Sword of the War God

THE BLAZING SEA

The Whale Road Chronicles: VIII

TIM HODKINSON

An Aries Book

First published in the UK in 2025 by Head of Zeus,
part of Bloomsbury Publishing Plc

Copyright © Tim Hodkinson, 2025

The moral right of Tim Hodkinson to be identified
as the author of this work has been asserted in accordance with
the Copyright, Designs and Patents Act of 1988.

All rights reserved. No part of this publication may be: i) reproduced or transmitted in any form, electronic or mechanical, including photocopying, recording or by means of any information storage or retrieval system without prior permission in writing from the publishers; or ii) used or reproduced in any way for the training, development or operation of artificial intelligence (AI) technologies, including generative AI technologies. The rights holders expressly reserve this publication from the text and data mining exception as per Article 4(3) of the Digital Single Market Directive (EU) 2019/790.

This is a work of fiction. All characters, organizations, and events portrayed in this novel are either products of the author's imagination or are used fictitiously.

9 7 5 3 1 2 4 6 8

A catalogue record for this book is available from the British Library.

ISBN (PB): 9781804540701
ISBN (ePub): 9781804540688

Cover design: Simon Michele/Head of Zeus
Typeset by Siliconchips Services Ltd UK

Printed and bound in Great Britain by
Clays Ltd, Popson Street, Bungay, NR35 1ED

Bloomsbury Publishing Plc
50 Bedford Square, London, WC1B 3DP, UK
Bloomsbury Publishing Ireland Limited,
29 Earlsfort Terrace, Dublin 2, D02 AY28, Ireland

HEAD OF ZEUS LTD
5–8 Hardwick Street
London, EC1R 4RG

To find out more about our authors and books
visit www.headofzeus.com

For product safety related questions contact productsafety@bloomsbury.com

For Trudy, Emily, Clara and Alice

Sól tér sortna, sígr fold í mar,
hverfa af himni heiðar stjǫrnur;
geisar eimi við aldnara,
leikr hár hiti við himin sjálfan

The Sun turns black, the earth sinks into the sea
The bright stars disappear from the heavens
Smoke swirls around the ancient tree
High heat plays against the sky itself

Völuspá, 'The foretelling of the seeress', verse 55

One

Mālaqah – Fort City in the Caliphate of Al-Andalus
AD 938

Einar Thorfinnsson took off his helmet. He wiped the back of his hand across his brow. Sweat was already making his eyes sting. It was early morning, but the heat was already overbearing. Not for the first time he cursed the weather and wondered how folk endured living in these southern lands. There were no pleasant breezes. No snow, no ice. Just bright blue seas and blazing sunshine.

At first he and the others had found the warmth pleasant, a welcome change to the bleak winters of the north. The further they sailed south, however, the hotter it grew until it became almost unbearable. Like the other Norsemen in the crew, his skin blistered and his hair and clothes began to stink of sweat all the time.

This was not helped at that moment by his being dressed in his full war gear. Despite the fact that they were supposed to be in Mālaqah for trading, Ulrich had insisted they arm themselves for battle. They were in a strange land, among strange people whose customs were unknown and the little leader of the Wolf Coat crew wanted his men ready for any eventuality.

Ulrich himself, as well as Skarphedinn – Skar to his friends – stood on the stone quay of the port, awaiting the master of the harbour who they were told was on his way. The short, smooth-chinned Ulrich, his hair receding from his forehead, was a sharp contrast to the towering giant Skar who was his right-hand man and the *stafn-búi*, the prowman of the crew.

Beside them stood Thord, a Rus merchant adventurer who Ulrich had decided to become a trading partner with. Like most of the Norsemen who came from the realms of the *Austr-vegr*, the Eastern Way, his long hair was swept back and braided, and every scrap of visible skin on his face and the burly arms that rested across his chest was covered in blue-black and dark green tattoos that looked like the endless branches of a tree in winter.

Surt was on the quay too. The big, black-skinned man was grinning like a fool. His obvious happiness at returning to his homelands after so many years had increased with every league they sailed southward. All the way, the usually taciturn former ring fighter had chattered, regaling the rest of the crew with tales of his young days and the wonders they would see once they reached the place he called 'civilisation'. Now they had finally arrived in Al-Andalus, it was his job to act as interpreter between the Norsemen and the Serks – as the Norsemen called the local people of Surt's faith – in trade negotiations that Ulrich had promised would make them all rich.

Those on the quay were dressed in their best clothes – light, expensive shirts and britches. Einar envied his leaders' light clothing. The leather shirt he wore was thick and its weight was increased by the *brynja* he wore over it. The sun heated the metal rings of that mail shirt so it felt like he was encased in a coat of fire. His maimed right hand was girded in his *járngreipr*, his fighting glove. This was the iron and leather gauntlet that allowed him to hold a sword as steadfastly as any other warrior, despite missing the little finger and part of the palm of his right hand. Even though the gauntlet had been fashioned by a craftsman so skilled some thought he was a wizard, wearing it in this heat made Einar's skin itch. He replaced his helmet and beneath its visor his nostrils filled with the smell of hot metal. Sweat once more dribbled in a continual stream down his cheeks and into his beard.

Einar cast another nervous glance at the twin cargos of slaves, one in the belly of Thord's *knarr*, a wide-bodied trading vessel, and the other in the Wolf Coats' *snekkja* longship. They were young – fit, strong lads and good-looking women – destined for sale in Al-Andalus. For most of the voyage their faces had borne the usual bleak, hopeless expressions that were common to the enslaved. Now those looks were replaced with anxious watchfulness as they realised they had reached the place where they would most likely spend the rest of their days.

Einar could not blame them for their anxiety. They were Slavs, taken from their native forests and villages in Pulinaland or the Dnieper river by raiders. The scorching heat and blinding sunshine of this foreign land discomfited their pale skins as much as it did the Norsemen who now enthralled them.

Ulrich had run into Thord in a tavern in Hedeby, the great Norse market town on the edge of Denmark. The trader had convinced Ulrich to go into business with him to take slaves to Al-Andalus. For some reason the Serks of that land had a huge appetite for Slavs and Thord had promised Ulrich he could double his money if they made the trip a joint venture. Einar had watched in dismay as Ulrich had handed over the hoard of silver they had stolen from King Aethelstan, but he also understood that the venture made sense from a practical point of view and, if everything went to plan, they would end up doubling or perhaps tripling their wealth.

Ulrich's *úlfhéðnar* had managed to get on the wrong side of nearly every king in the northern world, so they were planning to sail southwards anyway, ostensibly at the urging of Surt, who wanted to go home. Why not make the trip a profitable one as well? For his part, Thord welcomed the extra protection a ship full of úlfhéðnar would provide. So everyone was happy. Well, everyone except for the slaves.

Einar checked his weapons. His mouth was dry and not just from the heat. Now they had arrived in the Al-Andalusian port, it was the most risky part of the journey. The slaves were chained to the rowing benches but would have to be unfettered to move them off the ships. If any of them decided to take their only chance to escape, the Wolf Coats could probably contain a few of them, but not if they all decided to run at once. If the locals decided to cause trouble as well, the situation would be hopeless.

The two longships were docked nose-on to the quay, so the only way off was by their narrow prows. This was deliberate, forming choke points in case any of the slaves did try to make a run for it. Einar was positioned at the prow as further discouragement. Affreca was at the stern of the snekkja beside the wizened little figure of Roan, the skipper, who manned the steering oar. She held her bow in a nonchalant way but Einar could see she had an arrow notched and knew that at the first sign of trouble she would draw and not hesitate to shoot. The remaining members of the company – Sigurd, Kari, Starkad and the Saxon Wulfhelm – were positioned around the edges of the deck. They all kept wary eyes on the human cargo. On the next ship along, Thord's own warriors stood a similar guard.

The harbour around them was packed. The longships were just two of many vessels of all shapes and sizes from all over the known world and beyond, docked along the two quays that formed a stone ring. It was broken by a gap at the harbour mouth, narrow enough to allow only one ship of reasonable size to pass through at a time. Inland from the harbour rose a bustling town over which brooded the stark, stone walls of a great fortress. The cries of seabirds mingled with the noise of the busy harbour as crews loaded or unloaded cargo, laughed, sang or shouted in a myriad of tongues. Through it all Einar perceived a steady beat, the unmistakable tramp of men marching in unison.

A band of warriors pushed through the throng in the harbour and began to file along the quay. At their head was a big man dressed in white. The glitter of jewels and gleam of gold that emanated from all over him announced that this was an important man. His dress and that of the warriors who accompanied him seemed quite outlandish to Einar, though he reasoned that as he was in a foreign land, this was only to be expected.

'Right, lads,' Skar said over his shoulder to the Wolf Coats in the ship. 'This looks like the harbour master so it's time to start trading. Be ready for anything.'

Two

The harbour master regarded the Norsemen and Surt on the quay with a look of disdain.

He was tall and heavy and his prodigious belly was swathed in rolls of white linen. He wore a strange headdress that as far as Einar could work out had been made by winding a long strip of white cloth around his head many times, finished off with a few laps of his neck and chin. His skin was dark, though not as dark as Surt's, and a long, bushy moustache – not unlike those worn by the Saxons of Britain – bristled beneath his nose. A sword with a jewelled hilt and a strange, curved blade was sheathed at his belt. Rings of gold and silver circled his wrist and fingers.

The twenty warriors who accompanied him were dressed in mail coats, polished so they gleamed like silver in the bright sunlight. They had metal caps that shone like gold and carried spears and round shields painted in bright colours. Einar noted that unlike the Norsemen whose shields bore the images of battle beasts or magical creatures like the wolf, the bear, the dragon or the eagle, the Serks' shields had no pictures painted on them, just squiggly lines in black that looked like some form of foreign runes.

Shading his eyes with his palm, Einar surveyed the Serk

warriors, trying to look as nonchalant as possible while assessing what threat they posed. They were well armed and equipped, and Einar began to play through different possibilities in his mind: what he would do in each possible situation that might arise if there was trouble. The narrowness of the quay meant the Serks had to file into a column, so at most they would have to fight them three at a time, which was to the Wolf Coats' advantage. On the other hand, the Serks were on home ground. If they called for help, then in a short time there could be a lot more of them.

As Einar mused, he realised that over half the warriors and most of the people in the port were dark-skinned, their complexions ranging from light brown to as dark as Surt's. In the northern realms, Surt had stood out like a lump of charcoal in a snow field. Here it was Einar and his fellow Norsemen who were the obvious foreigners.

The harbour master barked some words. Surt replied. Both spoke words in a tongue Einar did not understand and guessed that it was that of the Serks. The harbour master's eyebrows shot upwards and he shook his head. Then turned to Ulrich, Thord and Skar.

'I have no need of an interpreter,' he said, speaking in a high voice and, to all the vikings' surprise, in the Norse tongue, albeit with an accent. 'I am the master of a harbour where ships from all over the world come. I speak many tongues, including barbarian ones. Like yours.'

Ulrich and Skar folded their arms.

'You bring slaves?' the harbour master said.

Thord moved his arm in a sweeping gesture across both longships tied to the quay, both their holds thronged with human cargo.

'Only the best,' he said, grinning.

'They are all *Saqaliba*?' the harbour master said, his eyes glittering.

'Slavs? Of course,' Thord said. 'I know the emir is hungry for them.'

'The men will swell his army,' the harbour master said. 'And the women will fill our harems.'

'The emir is using foreign slaves in his armies?' Surt said, frowning.

The harbour master scowled, as if the question annoyed him like a horsefly.

'How is it that you know our tongue?' he said, eyes narrowing.

Surt's chest swelled. He hooked his thumbs into his belt.

'This is my home, brother,' he said. 'I am returning after many years. You can tell Emir Abdullah ibn Muhammad that Sayf al-Din is back. He will be most pleased to see me I assure you.'

The harbour master's bushy eyebrows shot upwards again.

'You knew the emir Abdullah ibn Muhammad?'

'I was once the commander of his personal guard,' Surt said, his mouth breaking open in a grin. 'I saved his life twice.'

'And now you trade slaves with barbarians?' The harbour master's nostrils wrinkled.

'No,' Surt said. 'I was taken captive and sold into slavery myself. I was traded into the far north.'

'One moment,' the harbour master said.

He turned and walked back a few steps towards the first of the warriors who stood behind him. He then began talking to the man.

'He's probably telling his men that Sayf al-Din has returned,' Surt said to Ulrich and Skar. 'You wait and see. When the emir hears I am back we will be treated like kings. Prepare yourselves for luxury beyond your wildest dreams.'

'I have some pretty wild dreams my friend,' Skar said, smiling.

Einar, watching from the prow of the longship, felt a prickling feeling down the back of his neck that had nothing to do with the heat. There was something about the way the harbour master was speaking to his lead warriors that made Einar uneasy. He was leaning close to them, speaking low so those in the longships could not overhear and all the while flicking his eyes back towards Surt.

The harbour master turned and strode back towards the longships. His warriors followed, filing into a column two abreast, which was all they could manage on the crowded, narrow quay.

Einar spotted two archers near the back of the column. They swept bows out from under long linen cloaks and though they pointed them towards the ground, their arrows were notched.

He whistled through his teeth. Ulrich shot a glance towards him. Einar cocked his head towards the approaching archers. The expression on his face told Einar that Ulrich understood the danger straight away.

'You must have been away for a long time, friend.' the harbour master said to Surt. 'Times have changed here. Al-Andalus has no emir. It is now a caliphate and our caliphe is Abd al-Rahman. He overthrew Abdullah ibn Muhammad and now rules in his place. The old fool lost his head. If you were as close to him as you say, that makes you an enemy of the caliphe. You are all now prisoners.'

Three

'Wait!' Thord was indignant. 'This has nothing to do with me. I'm just here to trade slaves.'

Einar dipped to a crouch and felt with his left hand for a spear that he had placed on the deck earlier, close to the side of the prow. All the while he never took his eyes off the men on the quay above.

'Your goods are seized,' the harbour master said to Thord. 'This man is an enemy of the caliphe and you consort with him. You are therefore as guilty as he is. Your slaves now belong to the caliphe and, as his representative...'

He flashed a most unpleasant grin at Thord, revealing several gold teeth.

'To me.'

'Can't we work this out, friend?' Skar said. He held both hands up before his chest, palms outwards. 'Perhaps we can do some sort of deal?'

The harbour master sighed and shook his head. He opened his mouth to speak but before his words came out, Skar lunged forwards. His hands that had been in a gesture of surrender reached out and grabbed the voluminous material of the harbour master's robes. Skar wrenched the man towards him while at the same time powering his own head forwards. With a sickening crunch of bone he head-butted the harbour master full in the face.

Einar's fingers found the spear on the deck. They closed around it and he surged back to his feet. He hurled the spear at the leading Serk warrior on the quay who was lowering his own spear to charge at Ulrich. He was perhaps ten paces away and Einar's spear hit him hard, dead centre in the chest. The rings of his mail shirt saved him but the impact sent him staggering backwards into the man behind him, clutching at his chest as he struggled to regain the wind that had been knocked out of his lungs.

The archers Einar had spotted loosed their bows. The harbour master, either unconscious or stunned, dropped to his knees, blood dribbling from his ruined nose and smashed mouth. Skar caught him under both arms and hauled him back up. The harbour master was a big man but Skar was bigger. Ulrich's prowman pulled the Serk up and held him before him, using his fat body as a shield. It jerked as one of the Serk archers' arrows thudded into their own commander's back.

The second arrow was aimed at Ulrich. Unarmed and with no armour, if it struck him he would not stand a chance. Einar launched himself up and out of the ship. As he ran he twisted to face Ulrich, so the shield still strapped to his back came between the archer and both himself and Ulrich's unprotected chest.

Einar's body rocked as the arrow thudded into the wood of his shield, the impact hard enough to make him stagger a couple of steps. He was still recovering as Ulrich scrambled onto the ship, grabbing the dragon head on the prow in both hands and swinging himself onto the deck.

The rest of the Serk warriors came forwards, though they were hampered by their numbers on the narrow quay. Einar drew his sword but knew he had no time to fix it properly in his fighting glove before the Serks were upon them.

One of the Serk archers jerked as an arrow from Affreca's bow hit him in the throat, transfixing it from front to back. He had drawn his bow for another shot but his arrow now went high, sailing towards the blazing sun instead of at Skar and Einar. The archer, eyes wide and choking for breath, dropped his bow, both hands going to the arrow in his neck as he crashed to his knees then fell onto his side.

Skar hurled the arrow-stuck body of the harbour master towards the nearest Serk warrior. The impact of the dead man's weight made the charging warrior stumble and they both crashed to the stones of the quay in an entangled heap. The warrior charging close behind, either to avoid the fallen men or out of some sort of fear or respect for the harbour master, leapt aside, only to find he had run out of room on the narrow quay. His legs still pumping and arms wheeling, the warrior tumbled into the sea between the moored ships, sending up a terrific splash.

This created a little space between the Norsemen and the approaching Serks. Einar glanced up to see what the other Serk archer was doing. He saw that the man had wheeled to confront the threat of Affreca and her bow. Both were still notching arrows. It was a race to see who would draw, aim and shoot first.

The Serk had a slight edge as he had shot his previous arrow before Affreca. He was first to be ready but Einar could see panic on his face as he loosed his bow. He had rushed his shot. Affreca did not flinch as his arrow went wide of her. It thudded into the raised stern of the ship about an arm's length from her head.

The Serk archer's panicked expression turned to one of horror as Affreca raised her bow and took aim in one measured, unhurried movement. He was still turning to run away when she shot him through the chest.

'Into the ship,' Skar shouted to Einar, emphasising his words with a hard shove.

Half under his own volition and half propelled by Skar's push, Einar tumbled back onto the longship. Thord leapt into his own ship at the same time. Skar jumped after Einar. He landed on the deck. The ship's planks reverberated from the impact of the big man. The prowman took Einar's sword, plucking it with ease from Einar's weakened grasp. He slashed the ropes that tethered the ship to the quay, the taut lines parting with a loud twang.

Einar and Skar, one on either side of the dragon-carved prow, each placed one foot on the wall of the quay and shoved with all their might. The boat began to slide backwards into the harbour.

'Oars!' Ulrich screamed. 'Get those oars in!'

The slaves were still chained in their places on the rowing benches. Dumbfounded at the sudden change of events, they did nothing, no doubt reluctant to help those who were in league with Thord who had enslaved them.

On the way into the harbour, the Wolf Coats had stashed weapons under the strakes on the prow. Einar thanked Ulrich's always suspicious nature as he and Skar grabbed a spear each. They hurled them at the Serks on the quay. Their casts, along with another arrow from Affreca, made the charging warriors pause for another moment to take cover. It was a small respite but they needed to get moving soon or all would be lost.

'Get those oars in the water, you sons of hounds,' Kari was yelling at the slaves. 'Do you think the Serks will treat you any better than us?'

He brandished his drawn sword at them but still none of them moved.

'If you get us out of here, you will all have your freedom,' Einar shouted.

'What?!' Ulrich said, glaring at Einar with an expression of incomprehension.

The slaves looked at each other, their expressions a mixture of sudden hope and uncertainty whether they should trust a Norseman or not.

'You have my word,' Einar said.

The slaves decided to take their chances. Dropping to the rowing benches, they began sliding the oars into the water.

'They're no use to us anyway if we're all dead,' Einar said to Ulrich. 'Right now we just need to get away.'

Ulrich shook his head but said no more as the slaves began pulling on the oars and the ship surged backwards, picking up speed as it pulled away from the quay. In a moment they were too far away for the Serks to reach them, even if they jumped.

Thord was not so lucky. His prowman was still trying to undo the ropes as the Serk warriors reached their ship and poured on board.

The Wolf Coats' snekkja was now clear of the rear end of Thord's ship and heading backwards fast towards the ships docked at the quay opposite.

'Forwards!' Ulrich screamed at the slaves on the benches.

The slaves changed the direction of their rowing. The water churned and surged around the ship as it halted, then began to move forwards. Roan, the wizened old skipper, slammed the steering oar to the side, turning the dragon prow towards the mouth of the harbour.

Einar could hear warning bells ringing and whistles being blown all around the harbour. The sailors on the surrounding ships stared in surprise at the events unfolding around them as more Serk warriors, their bronzed helms flashing in the sun, began pouring into the harbour and fanning out along the horseshoe of the quays. Einar cursed their luck that Mālaqah was a port large enough to have garrison – and a large one at that.

The Wolf Coats' longship was now surging towards the harbour entrance, a small gap where the two curved quays almost met that was only wide enough for one ship to pass through at a time. There was no chain guarding the entrance – they had checked on the way in – so if they made it there, there was nothing to stop them escaping into the open sea beyond. Then they would hoist the sail and nothing would be able to catch their sleek, fast warship.

A Serk ran to the stern of Thord's ship and hurled a spear as the snekkja glided past. It struck one of the slaves on the last rowing bench, hitting him in the back just below his left shoulder. The man cried out, slumping forwards over his oar as Affreca levelled her bow and shot back. Her arrow struck the Serk who had cast the spear in the centre of his chest, sending him staggering backwards into the side of Thord's ship. Then he toppled over it and into the water.

The ship was only a few lengths from the harbour entrance now. There were Serk warriors pounding along the quays on either side, almost level with them, but Einar knew there was little they could do. Once the ship made it to the entrance, they would be free.

Then the entrance to the harbour darkened. As Einar watched, a massive ship moved across it from the outside. It was the biggest vessel Einar had ever seen, taller than the walls of the quay and with two rows of oars and two masts. That it was a warship there was little doubt. Not only did its deck throng with warriors but it also had what looked like a wooden fort built in front of the masts. As the prow passed the harbour entrance he could see a huge spike protruding from it, its tip sheathed in metal and designed for plunging into the guts of other ships and ripping them open. Its own sides were sheeted with metal to stop the same thing happening to it.

The huge ship hove to a stop, chains rattling as anchors dropped into the water. It now blocked the exit to the harbour with its massive hull. Ranks of archers lined its deck. All had bows drawn and aimed down at the crew of the snekkja. In a moment they could unleash a torrent of arrows that would annihilate everyone on board.

'Stop!' Ulrich shouted, following it with a curse through his teeth. Ramming the big ship would have been futile. In all likelihood the much smaller snekkja would simply have been splintered to matchwood against the other vessel's armoured side.

The slaves dug their oars in, reversing their direction once again, and the ship slowed to a mere drift. The warriors on the quays on both sides gathered at the edge, raising their spears.

Another tall Serk in flowing white robes with an air of command about him strode to the edge of the quay to the right.

'If you don't want to die, turn this ship around and go back to the dock,' he ordered. 'You are prisoners of the caliphe.'

Four

If Einar had found the heat outdoors hard to bear, it was nothing to what the night brought in the cramped, stinking cell in the stifling prison he and the others ended up in.

After their foiled escape attempt, the Wolf Coats had been manhandled at spear and blade point off their ship to join Thord and his warriors who were already captives on the quay. The slaves were all unloaded and marched off to their miserable fates in the service of the Serks, then the Norsemen were disarmed, kicked, punched and shoved out of the harbour and up a narrow, winding street to the fortress Einar had spotted earlier, glowering over the town.

Despite the perilous situation they were in, Einar could not help feeling a sense of amazement at how much of the town of Mālaqah was built of stone. Unlike the daub, wattle, timber and turf buildings of Jorvik, Dublin, Hedeby or the other cities of the northern realms he had visited, the houses and merchants' shops here were constructed of a pale, reddish stone. This could only mean the Romans had been here too, he reasoned. No one else he knew of had the wisdom for how to build with stone with such skill. Either that or the Serks had learned the craft of stone building from them.

The streets were cobbled with paving stones as well, in contrast to the wooden-planked walkways that floored those in the cities of the north. The same foul-smelling filth flowed down the sides of the streets, however, the effluence of kitchens, butchers and the rest of the detritus that exudes from having so many folk live so close together.

After a short journey they reached the stone tower that marked the gates to the fortress. Once inside they passed through two more stone walls that surrounded the inner block of the fort. There were armed warriors everywhere, outnumbering the Wolf Coats many times over. These harsh odds daunted any thoughts they might have of escape.

Once inside the main building, they were led up four flights of stairs, something that made Einar's head swim a little. He hated heights and being in buildings constructed with more than one storey made his guts churn and his balls crawl. It was not natural and he spent every minute inside one in stressed anticipation of it collapsing under its own weight or himself somehow tumbling out of it to fall, arms and legs flailing, to death far below.

The air inside the stone building was hot and stinking. It was thick with the odour of many bodies crushed into a small space: sour sweat, vomit and the reek of piss. Every room they passed was a cell, with doors made of iron bars and miserable prisoners jammed inside, watching the new captives as they passed with baleful, hopeless eyes.

At the top of the last flight of stairs, they were marched along a narrow corridor with three cells that was thankfully, from Einar's point of view, lacking in windows except for one at the far end. The Wolf Coats and Thord's crew were then jammed into a cell and the iron barred door slammed shut behind them. With a rattling of keys the door was locked and then, safe in the knowledge that the Norsemen were now secured behind bars, the company of Serk warriors left, posting five guards outside to watch the corridor.

The cell, like the fortress, had stone walls and one small window that was criss-crossed by iron bars. There was barely room for ten people in it and altogether the Wolf Coats and Thord's men came to twenty-eight. Jammed into the confined space, they jostled and pressed against each other. The heat was appalling, as was the stench in the cell, and at first Einar thought he was going to faint.

'What if we need a piss?' Starkad said.

Skar pointed at a channel in the floor that ran along the back wall of the room. The wall itself was coated with a foul green slime.

'I'd say that's what that wall's for,' he said.

'I'm not pissing against a wall in front of this lot,' Affreca said. There was anger in her voice.

'Well you'll just have to cross your legs, princess,' Ulrich said. 'It's not our fault the Serks didn't realise you were a woman. Maybe if you didn't wear men's britches they might have. I doubt you'd be any better off if they did, mind you.'

'I don't see how they could make that mistake,' Einar said. 'I mean, you're obviously a woman. You're beautiful...'

The words were out of his mouth before he realised it. He trailed off, Affreca's green eyes were boring into his, reproach burning in her gaze. Skar, Ulrich and Kari were all looking at him askance, smirks on their faces despite the dangerous situation they were in.

'I was just saying!' Einar protested. 'I mean it's obvious she's a woman!'

Eager to change the subject, he continued: 'What sort of ship was that? I've never seen anything that size before.'

'That, my northern friend, was a *shini*, a galley,' Surt said, laying a hand on Einar's shoulder. There was a note of pride in his voice. 'The galleys of Al-Andalus are some of the largest ships to ply the Middle Sea. If it had hit the snekkja with its ram, there would be nothing left of our vessel but splinters.'

'We checked for a chain protecting the harbour,' Skar said with a tut. 'But never thought they would have a ship big enough to close the entrance.'

'Well we know it's there now,' Ulrich said. 'Let's not forget.'

There was one small window and the Norsemen took turns to place their faces against the bars and suck in air from outside. Even though it was heated by the blazing sun outside, it felt like the coolest of mountain breezes compared to the thick, hot air inside the stifling oven they were packed into. Some men managed to sit on the floor, their backs to the walls, but they had to hug their shins close to their chests to avoid getting their lower legs inadvertently stamped on by their standing comrades. Others leaned against each other for support, trying to stop themselves from passing out in the heat.

As the day wound towards night, they found to their dismay that the heat did not fade with the setting sun. Instead it seemed to grow ever more oppressive as if the stones all around them had sucked the warmth of the sun into them and now breathed it all out into the night.

'I thought you were supposed to be an important man here?' Ulrich said to Surt.

The black-skinned man sighed. 'I was,' he said. 'But the man I served has been usurped. I remember that snivelling little wretch, his grandson: the man who now rules here. He was not to be trusted. I never did.'

'No doubt you made that very clear too,' Skar said. 'Which is why we're now all locked in here.'

'You know yourself,' Surt said, shaking his head, 'when a king falls, the last people the man who takes his throne wants near him are those who were loyal to the man he usurped. We're a danger to him.'

'Well it's not a great start to our plan to get rich here,' Skar commented. 'I doubt we'll see those slaves again.'

'He was going to give them their freedom,' Ulrich said, looking at Einar, his face a mask of disbelief and disappointment.

'It got them to start rowing, Ulrich,' Einar said. 'Sometimes you need to give men encouragement, something to aim for. Not just shout at them and order them about.'

Ulrich cocked his head. 'Oh, do I? So the lad is suddenly an expert in how to lead men, is he? Well, let me tell you this, son: I led this crew long before you joined it and have led it ever since. The day I need your advice will be the day I am no longer fit to call myself leader.'

Einar sighed and turned away. There was little point arguing with Ulrich. Their dire situation and the unbearable heat meant everyone's tempers were frayed. On top of that, Einar could not help the suspicion that Ulrich had never really forgiven him for leaving the company in Francia. He had been allowed to rejoin, but it was because the others had insisted. Had it been left up to Ulrich, Einar wondered if he would still be a lone wolf.

'What do you think they'll do to us?' Skar said to Surt.

Surt pursed his lips and for a moment considered things.

'You, I don't know,' he said. 'Maybe they'll kill you for what happened to the harbour master. Maybe you'll end up slaves. They said the new emir is making an army of foreign slaves. There will be a terrible price to pay if that is your fate though.'

He glanced down then quickly looked away. Einar was about to ask what he meant when he began talking again.

'I'm a dead man, though. Once the emir hears I am back, I doubt if I'll live past the morning.'

Einar saw the big man's eyes become glassy.

'I'm glad I made it home,' he said, his voice cracking a little. 'If only I could have seen my family one last time. If any of them still live.'

A sullen mood settled over everyone as the futility of their situation sank in. Regardless of what their fate was to be, there was nothing to do now but wait for it.

A terrible thirst beset them. Einar felt like his mouth was full of sand. Surt went to the bars of the door and began shouting out to the guards in the corridor outside. He used the Serk tongue so the others in the cell did not understand what he said. Einar surmised he was asking for water because after a short time one of the guards approached and shoved a skin bag through the bars. It was plump with liquid inside but there would be barely enough for one man in this heat, never mind twenty-eight. Surt shouted what sounded like a complaint to the guard as he held it up. The guard just gave a contempt-laden sneer and walked away again.

'Well it looks like this is it,' Surt said, looking ruefully at the bag.

'Everyone take one sip each. Try not to gulp,' Ulrich said.

'Fuck you,' one of Thord's warriors said. He was a tall, gangly man whose lank black hair was thinning on top but long around the sides. He had braided the bones of small animals – birds and mice – through it. Einar recognised him from times the crew had mingled during several stops on the voyage south. He was from the Southern Isles off the coast of Scotland, a product of the mixing of Norsemen and celts: a *Gall-Gáidhil* in the tongue of the Scots or a *vikingr-scotti* in Norse. His name was Thjódrík but was better known as Fisk: the Fish. From his previous encounters with him, Einar judged this nickname was due to the amount of ale he liked to down.

Fisk began shoving himself through the throng to get closer.

'I'm taking that,' he said.

'Ulrich's right, Thjódrík,' Thord said. 'If everyone takes one drink then more of us may survive. We've more chance to escape if there's a crowd of us. If one person drinks it all, they'll survive the night but others will surely die in this heat.'

'The way I see it,' Thjódrík, or Fisk, said, 'that one person may as well be me.'

Ulrich said nothing. He just took the skin from Surt and held it in one hand, regarding Thord's warrior with a look almost as contemptuous as the Serk guard's.

'Are you going to stop me, wee man?' Fisk said, now having pushed his way almost to the door.

Thord's face fell in dismay.

'This is Ulrich Rognisson, Fisk!' the merchant said. 'These men are úlfhéðnar! Mind your tongue when you speak to them.'

Einar, who had seen Ulrich rip out the throat of much bigger men than Fisk with his bare teeth, moved his feet into a fighting position but for the moment contented himself to just watch and see what happened.

'So you say,' Fisk said. He spoke the Norse tongue with the brogue it had taken on from living close to the Gaels. 'But I've seen fuck all of their vaunted prowess the whole of this voyage. They've fought no one. If there was any sign of trouble they skulked around it. They were supposed to be guarding us and look—'

He moved his head around the room.

'We're all stuck in here,' Fisk continued. 'Now give me that skin, wee man, or I'll break your ugly wee face.'

He reached out, fingers outstretched to grab the water skin.

With his right hand, Ulrich tossed the skin to Skar, who caught it on instinct. At the same instant, Ulrich's left hand flashed forwards and caught Fisk's extended right. He grabbed the bigger man's index and middle fingers and pushed them backwards, bending his whole hand back at the wrist.

With a yelp of surprise and pain, Fisk had no choice but to halt his advance. If he did not, his fingers and perhaps his wrist would snap. Ulrich pushed forward, bending Fisk's hand back more and forcing him to twist his body beneath it in a desperate attempt to avoid having his bones broken. In a moment he was almost on his knees, looking up at Ulrich, his mouth fixed in a grimace of agony, his eyes wide with panic.

Ulrich drove his right fist into Fisk's upturned chin. The big man's eyes rolled up into his head and he pitched sideways. He was unconscious but the press of the others around him held him in a kneeling position. Ulrich let go of his now senseless left hand.

'Anyone else want to drink all the water themselves?' Ulrich said, surveying the now silent crowd around him with one raised eyebrow. 'No? Good.'

Einar looked around as well. Part of him was amused at what Ulrich had just done but another cursed his wiry little leader for his recklessness. The faces of Thord's men were fearful, but also bore looks of sullen resentment. They outnumbered the Wolf Coat crew more than two to one. If they decided to take Fisk's side then, úlfhéðnar or not, stuck in this little cell Einar and the others would be in trouble.

Then there was a rattling of keys in the door. Everyone turned to see a man outside in long, white, official-looking robes.

'I believe we are about to learn our fate,' Surt said.

Five

The door swung open. The guards outside stood in a semicircle around the newcomer, spears lowered and feet braced to deter anyone inside the cell from thoughts of escape. Their eyes were wide, teeth bared and they shouted what could only be threats.

'Why don't we rush them?' Starkad said, glaring at the guards. 'There's more of us. We could take them.'

'The first five of us – at least – would die,' Ulrich said. 'Do you want to be one of the first?'

'I was thinking more we send Thord's men first,' Starkad said, a half-sheepish grin on his face.

'Then we'd have to fight our way down the stairs and out of this fortress,' Skar said. 'With only the weapons we can pull from those five guards.'

'*A corpse is no use to anyone*,' Ulrich said, quoting the words of Odin. 'We wait until we see a decent chance to escape, one with lower odds that we all end up dead.'

'I hope that chance comes,' Starkad said.

The official-looking man was dressed in flowing white robes that reminded Einar of a rich woman's dress, and a tall, red headdress. He looked like a Serk but Einar was surprised to see he had piercing blue eyes instead of their usual brown or black. He had a large, bushy beard and stood with his thumbs hooked into his wide leather belt.

He pointed to Surt and spoke some words in the Serk tongue. He was tall and broad-chested but Einar was surprised at how high the man's voice was.

'Abd al-Malik!' Surt said.

There was a look of surprise on his face as the nearest guards grabbed him and hauled him out of the cell. They then prodded the Norsemen behind him back with their spears and slammed the cell door shut again.

Einar pressed himself to the little barred window in the door.

'Surt knew that man,' Ulrich said. 'What's going on?'

'They're walking down the corridor,' Einar reported, pushing his face against the bars so he could see more outside. 'The way they're talking, it looks like they know each other well. Surt is very serious.'

'So the other fellow hasn't killed him?' Ulrich said. 'At least that's a good sign.'

Einar heard a shout from one of the guards outside. Its tone was angry and full of reproach and Einar just had time to pull back from the little barred window before the guard poked the sharp end of his spear through it.

'I think he wants me to mind my own business,' Einar said.

They waited for a little more, then the lock in the door rattled and Surt was shoved back inside. Seeing the questioning looks from all around him, he gave Ulrich a knowing look and began pushing himself through the crush of bodies in the cell, away from the door and towards the back wall. Ulrich, Skar and Thord followed him. Curiosity getting the better of him, Einar pushed his way after them.

When there were four or five packed bodies between them

and the door, Surt stopped. Affreca pushed her way through to stand beside them as well.

'Well?' Ulrich said. 'Who was that man?'

Surt's face was grave. Einar could see the hurt on it.

'He brought news of my family,' Surt said, speaking in a low voice. 'My wife is dead.'

'Did this new caliphe kill her?' Einar asked.

Surt shook his head.

'She died many years ago of sickness,' he said. 'I was King Harald's slave for so many years. I was a fool to think I could be away for so long and everything would be the same when I returned. My children are grown but fled when the new caliphe took over. Having me as a father put them in danger. All but my youngest daughter, that is. She did not escape—'

His voice caught in a barely concealed sob.

'She is now a slave like I was,' Surt said. 'Sold to the Emir of Frumentaria.'

Einar and the others dropped their eyes, feeling awkward and unsure how to react to Surt's emotion.

'You know him, right?' Ulrich asked, attempting to change the subject.

Surt nodded.

'There is still honour in Al-Andalus, it seems,' he said, the look in his now glassy eyes hardening. 'That was Abd al-Malik. He was one of the last emir's generals. I saved his life once as well. Two assassins stole into the palace in the middle of the night. They got as far as Abd al-Malik's bedchamber. I was on guard duty that night. I killed one with my sword but it stuck in his corpse. I had to kill the other one with my bare hands.'

'You were quite the bodyguard,' Skar said, a look of genuine respect on his face.

'I was good, in my day,' Surt said, now smiling.

'If you don't mind me saying,' Einar began. He was hesitant, unsure how to broach the subject to the dark-skinned Surt. 'He did not look like you. Or a Serk.'

'Ah you mean his blue eyes?' Surt said. 'Al-Andalus is a place of many peoples, bound together by one faith. The men you call *Serks* are Moors, whose forefathers came from Mauritania in North Africa. I myself come from Africa beyond the great sand sea. Before our people came to Al-Andalus the people who lived here were Visigoths, a people who once came from the north like you.'

Ulrich nodded. 'They are cousins of the Geats,' he said. 'They moved south with other clans during the Age of Great Wanderings when the Romans still ruled much of the world.'

Einar frowned. Here was another piece of the great tale of the world he did not know. There was so much still to learn.

'Our people conquered the Visigoths, but we allowed them to remain,' Surt said. 'Provided they took on our faith in Allah. Some have done well, like Abd al-Malik, though adopting the beliefs of new rulers is sometimes not enough by itself if you want to fit in. He dyes his blond beard black and I know, because I was his bodyguard, that he paints his face so it looks darker. He can't hide those blue eyes though.'

'If he served the former emir, like you did,' Ulrich said, 'how come he is still alive?'

'When a new emir takes over, it's wise to get rid of the old emir's trusted men,' Surt said with a shrug. 'New bodyguards – even good ones like me – can be found easily enough. There are others who have talents and skills that are harder to come across. Abd al-Malik is a superb general. He defeated two rebellions in my time. He is a man of real genius in war. The new emir allowed him to live and continue to lead his armies.'

'Lucky him,' Ulrich said.

'Lucky? Some might not agree,' Surt said. 'He paid a terrible price to keep his life. Caliphe Abd al-Rahman made him a eunuch.'

'A what?' Einar said.

'My people believe that what drives every action of a man is his balls,' Surt said.

Einar spotted Affreca nodding.

'So if you want to control a man, you cut them off,' Surt said.

Ulrich, Skar and Einar winced.

'Without his balls a man no longer has loyalty to his family, the army, his homeland,' Surt continued. 'Therefore, for a man like Abd al-Rahman, a eunuch can be trusted more than others who may care more about their wife and children or their own ambitions.'

'So do you think you can still trust this... man?' Ulrich said.

'He may have lost his balls, but he has not lost his honour,' Surt said. 'Some things are not forgotten by honourable men. I saved the last emir's life once, it is true, but I saved Abd al-Malik's twice. Also two of his children were in the palace that night and would have shared his fate if those assassins had succeeded. When he heard I had returned and was prisoner here, he came to tell me he will help.'

'How will that work?' Ulrich said. 'The guards saw him talking to you.'

'He is still an important man here,' Surt said. 'He told the guards he wanted to question me to see what threat I posed. They dare not question his motives.'

'But he's gone,' Skar said. 'And you're back in here with us.'

'He can't just let us out,' Surt explained. 'This is the Al Qasba fortress. It is not just a prison. The town's garrison is also based in this building. We are on the top floor. Do you expect to just walk out past them all unchallenged?'

'So what do we do?' Ulrich asked.

'Have patience,' Surt said. 'We must wait until the darkest hour of the night. Abd al-Malik assures me he will have our means of escape waiting outside. We just need to deal with the guards.'

'There's also the small problem of being locked in this cell,' Ulrich said, raising one eyebrow.

Surt opened his fist, revealing a large iron key in his palm.

'Abd al-Malik also gave me this,' he said.

They all locked eyes and nodded. There followed a hurried conversation in low voices as they worked out a plan, then there was nothing to do but wait.

Six

The night drew on, and they all did their best to stay alive and conscious in the oven-like heat of the cell. Several of Thord's men did not manage this and passed out. Einar knew if he did not find a way to cope with the temperature, he would join them. He closed his eyes and forced himself to breath in a regular way, in through his nose and out through his mouth. It was a craft Ulrich had taught all the Wolf Coats to do when they found themselves in an intolerable situation they could do nothing about.

This was how Ragnar Loðbrók was able to sing in the snake pit, even while he was dying, Ulrich had said.

Recalling these words. Einar began chanting in his own mind the words of the *Ragnarsdrápa*, the ancient poem said to be composed for Ragnar himself. For a while he became unaware of the discomfort and danger around as he fell into the strange trance that overcame a skald when in the midst of recitation.

After a long time his reverie was interrupted by a tap on his arm. Einar opened his eyes to see it was Skar who had touched him. The big man flicked his eyes to Ulrich and Surt, who now stood beside the door.

The time had come.

Einar and Skar joined Ulrich and Surt at the door. Thord's men let them through. It was evident that they did so because they had no desire to be among the first through the door. The Norsemen in the cell outnumbered the five guards outside, but they were unarmed while their captors had swords, knives, spears and body protection. It was only the úlfhéðnar crew who surrounded the door but Einar was happy with that. He knew every one of those who would be first out the door with him were well trained, highly skilled and deadly.

He could also now see through the little barred window in the door. This revealed to him that one of the guards was lounging backwards on a chair, his feet up on a wooden table that stood a little way along the corridor. He looked like he was dozing. Another three squatted on their haunches, engaged in a game of dice between them while the final guard stood above them, watching. All had rested their spears against the wall, safe in the knowledge that the prisoners were securely locked away and that all the guards would have to fight with during these long hours of the night was boredom.

Surt slid the key into the lock, taking extreme care that it did not rattle. Then, he began to turn it. He moved with exquisite slowness, his skin slick with sweat, as he rotated the key little by little until it had turned full circle. A click that sounded loud as thunder to those in the cell announced the door was now unlocked.

Holding their breath, they all fixed their eyes on the guards outside. Einar was sure they must have heard the noise of the lock but no, the guards continued with their game, oblivious of the new threat that had just arisen.

Ulrich looked at the Wolf Coats surrounding him, an expression on his face that posed the question without the need for words: *Ready?*

They all nodded. Ulrich shoved open the door.

The Wolf Coats swept out of the cell. Each one had their own target set by Ulrich. There were ten paces from the cell to where the guards were, but they crossed it in a flash. They were silent, knowing that shouts or war cries would alert other guards from downstairs and send reinforcements charging up to help their comrades. The Wolf Coats also knew that the same danger would arise if they let the guards cry out in alarm. All depended on how swift they could be.

The three crouching guards looked up, expressions of horror flooding onto all their faces to see the cell door open and the prisoners in their wolfskin cloaks rushing towards them. The guard who had been watching the gamblers had his back to the cell and was only starting to turn around when Skar rammed his shoulder into the man's back. The big man threw his considerable weight into it, which drove the guard flying towards the wall. Skar grasped the back of the other man's skull in the outstretched palm of his right hand, propelling his face hard into the stones of the wall at the same time his body collided with it. There was a sickening crunch of bones and teeth. The only sound the guard managed to make was a grunt as all the air was driven from his lungs by the impact.

Kari, Sigurd and Einar dived on one of the crouching guards each. Each fell on their man, one hand clamping down hard on the guard's mouth to stop him uttering any cry, the other grabbing the back of his neck and using the force of their own impact and the guards' already unstable squatting positions to knock them to the floor.

Almost the moment they hit the stones of the floor, Affreca, Wulfhelm and Surt fell on the now prone guards, tore their own knives from their sheathes and sliced the men's throats. The baking night air was filled with the metallic stench of hot blood as the guards' life blood surged from the wounds in their necks over the floor.

Ulrich, the slightest built and the swiftest of foot in the company, made it to the guard at the table in the same moment. The guard tried to scramble out of his lounging position but in his panic lost his balance instead. The stool he was leaning back on toppled beneath him, sending him crashing to the floor, his feet still up on the table.

Ulrich delivered a swift kick to the guard's face, which sent his eyes rolling into his head. Then the little Wolf Coat leader dropped onto the guard, drew the man's knife and drove it into the slot at the bottom of the guard's throat. The blade sliced through his flesh and arteries into his heart and at the same time severed the bottom of his windpipe. The dying guard's body jerked and convulsed in silence several times then went completely still.

Surt slammed the head of the man he had driven into the wall into it one more time for good measure. There was no real need, however. The guard was already limp and hung in the powerful grasp of the prowman like a scarecrow. Surt let him go and he dropped to the floor, either unconscious or dead.

For a moment there was a silence as the Wolf Coats strained their ears for any possible sound from down the stairs that might herald that either more guards were coming or the alarm had been raised. They could hear voices on the floors below but no one was shouting or speaking in agitated tones. There were no clattering footsteps on the stone stairs. The only sound apart from the Wolf Coats' heavy breathing from the sudden action was a long, slow fart that came from one of the dead guards as his bowels emptied.

Skar wrinkled his nose.

'There's never much dignity in death,' he said. 'Take good

note of that. Starkad, Kari and Wulfhelm: grab those spears and guard the top of the stairs. If anyone comes up, kill them.'

Surt took one of the dead guard's daggers and went over to the guard Skar had dealt with. He crouched beside him and slid the knife into his throat, releasing a torrent of dark blood.

'He wasn't exactly a danger,' Einar said. 'Was there any need for that?'

'I promised Abd al-Malik,' Surt said, rising to his feet and wiping the blade on his britches. 'They saw him on this floor of the fort. We can leave no one who can tell tales of that.'

Thord's men were now coming out of the cell. Fisk, who Ulrich had knocked out earlier, was now recovered and looked at the carnage in the corridor with sheepish astonishment. This second display in one night of the undoubted prowess of the Wolf Coats made him uncomfortable that he had previously doubted it.

'Staunch that blood before it starts to run down the stairs,' Ulrich said to Thord's men in general. 'Use the guard's clothes.'

'Do what he says, lads,' Thord said, speaking in a very low voice. 'Well done, Ulrich. I'm so glad to be out of that cell. I feel like I can breathe again.'

'Well, we're out,' Skar said. 'But now what? We're on the top floor of a fortress filled with Serk warriors. We can't just walk down the stairs.'

'We don't go down,' Surt said. 'We go up.'

Seven

Halfway along the corridor there was a trapdoor in the ceiling. At Surt's instruction, several of the Norsemen moved the table the guard had been lounging on underneath it. Surt climbed onto it. Ulrich clambered onto his shoulders and pushed the trapdoor up. It opened, revealing the night sky above.

'It leads to the roof,' Surt explained.

Ulrich scrambled up through the door. Skar clambered onto Surt's shoulders next then on up onto the roof. Thord went next. Then they reached down and hauled Surt up between them.

The Norsemen formed a queue and began to move in this fashion up through the trapdoor until there was only Starkad, Kari and Wulfhelm left guarding the staircase. With one final look down to check no one was coming, they then left their post and followed the others.

Einar found himself in a flat area that covered the whole of the roof and was surrounded by a waist-high wall. Standing up he crossed to the wall and looked around.

The view was amazing. The almost full moon glared its silver light all around, showing the fortress they were in, the buildings of the town that surrounded it and the harbour down the slope below. Here and there torches burned in brackets adding detail to the parts of the streets that were mostly sunk into the shadows of the buildings that lined them. Einar noticed that, like the one they now stood on, the roofs of most of the buildings of the town were flat and covered with clay tiles, a stark contrast to the high-ridged, thatched roofs of the buildings of the northern realms. In the harbour and the sea beyond, the moonlight shattered into countless diamond-like shards by the chops of the waves on the water surface.

'At least the ship's still there,' Ulrich said, peering down to see the Wolf Coats' snekkja bobbing in the water of the harbour, tethered to the stone quay.

'Ours too,' Thord said.

They looked down. Einar swallowed hard, fighting the queasy feeling the plunging height of the building they stood on provoked in his guts. Below them the double walls of the fortress ringed the central building they now stood on. There were torches and braziers set at regular intervals and even in the middle of the night, they could see Serk warriors patrolling the ramparts. Thankfully, they were all looking outwards, scanning the darkness for any potential attack from the direction it was most likely to come from, and paying no attention to the roof of the building right at the heart of their own fort. They outnumbered the Norsemen many times and it was obvious there would be no way out by trying to cross through the walls – the way they had come in.

'Now all we need to do is get to the ships,' Ulrich said. He turned to Surt. 'How do we do that? Fly?'

Surt made a face then went to the wall at the opposite side of the roof. Ulrich, Einar and Skar followed him. Surt scanned the darkened town below, looking for something. After a few moments he stopped.

'There,' he said, pointing towards a building outside the

fortress walls and about halfway down the short slope to the harbour. Einar looked. All the buildings were much smaller downhill to the towering fort they now stood on, and he and the others looked down on their flat roofs.

On the roof of the one Surt pointed at, Einar could see three figures in the moonlight, one dressed in white flowing robes.

'There are no guards on this side of the walls,' Surt said, moving his hand to indicate the ramparts below which were empty of Serk warriors. 'Why would there be? It's the city side and the fortress is here to protect the city.'

He raised his arms above his head and waved them back and forth. Einar saw the figure in the white robes on the rooftop below respond with the same gesture.

'It's Abd al-Malik, all right,' Surt said. 'Now stand back.'

They moved away from the wall at the edge. As they did so one of the figures on the other roof raised a bow, aimed it upwards then loosed it. The archer's arrow sailed high into the night sky, disappearing for a moment into the darkness above. Then Einar caught sight of it again as it slowed down until it almost halted in the air, all its energy now spent. Then it turned downwards and fell towards the roof where he stood.

The arrow landed with a rattle on the flagstones beneath the rooftop. Surt dashed forward to grab it. Einar saw that there was a very thin rope tied to the shaft – little more than a string – which trailed off over the edge of the roof and back through the air towards the other building where the arrow had been shot from.

'Come on,' Surt said, passing the arrow and the rope end to Einar. 'Let's get this hauled in.'

Surt and Ulrich joined them and they began pulling the rope, hand over hand. Einar found it was surprisingly heavy. Then he saw as they pulled more and more of it onto the roof, that the smaller rope, which was light enough to not stop the arrow in its flight, had been the means to send a much thicker, heavier one which was tied to the end of it, to their rooftop.

After some time of hauling, they pulled the end of the thicker rope over the wall at the edge of the roof, leaving the rest stretched across the night air downwards at a slant to the top of the other building where Abd al-Malik, the archer and the third man stood.

'Pull it taut and tie the end around the flagpoles,' Surt said. 'Make sure you tie it well. Our lives will depend on it.'

Einar and the others nodded and set to work fastening the thick rope to the flagpoles.

'Use ship knots,' Ulrich said. 'We want them as fast as possible. So no slip knots.'

As they completed the task, Einar felt his stomach tightening as much as the rope. The plan was obvious: they were going to have to clamber down the rope, suspended over the dizzying height, one slip away from certain death.

When they had finished and the rope was secure, the others ran back to the edge of the roof where the rope trailed off into the night. Einar stayed behind to give the knots one last check and to haul on the rope to see what effect it had on the flagpoles. They were made of stout wood and barely flexed at his pulling, but all the same Einar offered a silent prayer to red-bearded Thor that the flagpoles would be able to bear the weight of the Norsemen who would soon be suspended from the rope.

Then he went to join the others. Kari was already over the edge of the roof, legs crossed over the rope, arms grasping it while he dangled out over nothing but air. Moving hand over hand he began a rapid descent along the slanting rope to the roof of the other building below. Thord followed him and before long there was a line of Norsemen dangling below the rope, making their way down it.

Einar knew they had little time to get away. At any moment more guards might come up the stairs below and find them gone from their cell and their comrades dead. Then it would not be long before they would put two and two together and be up on the roof. Or a rampart patrol could complete their circuit of the walls below and return to this side of the fortress. Then all they had to do was look up and the alarm would be raised.

All the same, he found he was in no rush to launch himself out over the edge of the roof and into space. He had no qualms with fighting men twice his size – in fact he had done just that several times – but there was something about heights that made his guts churn and his balls threaten to crawl up inside his body. This made him hang back a little, not joining the line to clamber onto the rope until he was one of the last and there was nothing else for it, if he did not want to stay behind.

Einar waited for his turn, doing his best to steel his nerves for what was to come. He took deep breaths through his nose as he stood in line, painfully aware of how little the others around him seemed to show any signs of fear at the test of nerves and strength they would soon go through. He wiped his hands across his chest, aware of how sweaty they had become and dreading the thought that their potential slippiness could make him lose his grip once on the rope.

At last it was his turn. Einar gripped the rope in both hands before he planted his feet on top of the low wall that surrounded the roof. Thanking the gods that he at least did not have to go head first, he leaned backwards and hauled his right leg up, hooking it over the rope at the bend of his knee. Then he crossed his left foot over his right ankle above the rope.

He closed his eyes for a moment, trying to find the inner calm he had achieved in the cell earlier, trying to quiet his heart that thudded in his chest, its wild beating thundering in his ears.

It was time to go.

At first the going was easy enough. He slid his legs and moved hand over hand, the pull induced on his body by the slant of the rope doing much of the work. Above him was the endless darkness of the star-splattered sky. This filled his vision. The sheer drop that lay under him was invisible to him. The air was warm but compared to the stifling heat of the cell, almost refreshing.

The more he moved away from the roof of the fort the stronger the wind felt. The rope bucked and bounced as each man moved down it. Einar knew he would have to tear his gaze away from the stars and look down and ahead to check he was not about to collide with the man in front, possibly sending them both flailing downwards to their doom.

Gritting his teeth, Einar looked down. He was still a body length away from the next man but he felt his stomach lurch as he caught sight of the rampart of the fort, falling away beneath him into darkness. There were no guards on it, which was a relief, but it seemed a very long way down. His shoulders and thighs were starting to ache from the effort and the roughness of the rope chafed his thighs and arms through his clothes.

He was about halfway down when he heard the shouting.

Voices were raised on the rooftop of the fort, cries in the Serk tongue of alarm and anger. This could only mean the guards had discovered the Norsemen's escape. In his mind's eye Einar envisaged Serk guards pouring onto the roof through the trapdoor, looking around and seeing the rope trailing over the edge into the darkness.

'Go! Go!' the man behind Einar shouted.

All the men on the rope began scrambling as fast as they were able. Then Einar felt a rhythmic thumping begin to vibrate down the rope.

'They're cutting the rope,' someone cried from ahead.

Panic spurred them on even faster but Einar knew they would never make it at the rate they were going. The men in front must have realised this too as they halted their measured descents, hooked their elbows over the rope and just let themselves slide.

Einar did the same. In an instant the breeze that had been buffeting him became a roaring wind in his ears as he hurtled down the slanted rope towards the other rooftop. The rope felt red hot as his arms and thighs scored along it.

He saw the men in front landing on the other rooftop. They were going so fast they were unable to stop themselves and as they let go of the rope went sprawling on their faces, backs or bellies. There were four men in front of him, then three, then two. All landed in a tangled heap at the end of the rope. He was almost there.

Just as his feet crossed the low wall that lined the second rooftop, Einar felt the rope go slack. He dropped like a stone, half on and half off the roof. All the air was driven from his chest. Terror and dismay gripped him as he felt himself toppling backwards, out and off the rooftop that was to have been his salvation. It was not as high as the fort they had come from, but it was still too tall to survive a fall from the top.

Einar felt hands as strong as iron gripping his shins and thighs.

'Where do you think you're going, lad?' Skar said.

Einar looked up and saw Skar, Starkad and Wulfhelm had caught him.

Screams made him look up. The Serks on the fort had finished cutting the rope and it was now falling into the streets behind him. Two Norsemen were still on it, clinging in vain as they hurtled down into the darkness of the streets below. Their cries halted abruptly in sickening, wet crunches.

The others hauled Einar onto the rooftop. He wanted to throw his arms around all of them but relief, tension and receding terror held him in an iron vice. The most he could manage was to pat their shoulders. The others nodded, understanding the gesture. There would be time to thank everyone later. Now they had to get off this second rooftop before the Serks caught up with them again.

Eight

Einar scrambled to his feet and looked around, checking for the others. As well as the three who had caught him he spotted Affreca and Ulrich. Roan the skipper was rubbing his scrawny arms, trying to dispel the rope burn that now troubled his skin. Surt was talking in an earnest way to Abd al-Malik. There was no sign of Sigurd or Kari.

Dismay flooding his heart, he looked back into the darkened streets, the vision of the two men who had been on the rope behind him dropping to their deaths still burned into his memory. In the darkness he hadn't been able to make out who they were. Could they have been the other two members of Ulrich's crew?

'Relax,' Skar said, somehow reading his thoughts. 'Those must have been two of Thord's men. Sigurd and Kari are already gone. Ulrich sent them on ahead to make sure we get away.'

Ulrich looked around, checking the rest of his company were now on the roof.

'Let's go,' he said. 'Fast as you can back to the ship. If anyone's not there when the ship pulls away they'll be left behind. Is that clear?'

They all nodded. Then they started running. A door led from the roof to stairs. The Norsemen thundered down these as fast as was prudent in the gloom of what looked very like a darkened house. Einar briefly wondered who lived there as they descended two flights of steps, passing four closed doors on the way.

At the door of the house they nodded their thanks to Abd al-Malik who then hurried off with his two men up the street. The Norsemen began running in the opposite direction, downhill towards the harbour. Einar was relieved to find that once in the streets, what had looked from above like pitch-black caverns between the buildings had enough ambient light from the moon and stars above to make it along them at a decent pace. They could hear shouting behind them from the direction of the fortress, as well as the alarm bells ringing and whistles blowing. The streets they charged through were quiet though. There were none of the taverns or other dens of disrepute that could waylay travellers until the early hours of the morning, and every door remained closed. No one peeked out to see what the commotion outside was, and Einar wondered what sort of a city Mālaqah was where people did not dare to look outside their doors when a band of strange men came tramping past in the night.

It was a short distance to the harbour and it did not take long to get there. To everyone's relief the quays were as dark and quiet as the streets. They jogged along the stone quay towards their ships, all the while aware of the shouting of the Serk guards from the fortress that sounded like they were getting ever closer.

Like rats running along the harbour wall, the Norsemen scurried down the dark and empty quay, skirting barrels of goods, chests and pallets either waiting to be loaded onto vessels in the morning or picked up by merchants when the sun rose.

The ships were still tied up where they last saw them. Like the other ships in the harbour they were dark, quiet and empty, though the crews of all the others were in inns and the like in town rather than imprisoned.

Thord took his men to his ship while Ulrich and the Wolf Coat crew scrambled onto the snekkja. The skipper, Roan, took his place at the steering oar while Skar began to untie the ropes that fastened the ship to the quay. Einar, Wulfhelm, Starkad and Surt took their places on the rowing benches and lifted their oars. To Einar's surprise and not a little consternation, Ulrich and Affreca began fumbling with some boards on the deck near the prow. These, he knew, covered a secret compartment the Wolf Coats used to hide war gear for situations like this one. After a moment's work, Ulrich and Affreca pulled the planks aside and the moonlight glinted on weapons, helms and other equipment underneath.

'The Serks didn't find it,' Ulrich said with a grin. 'Excellent.'

'I know they took our weapons when we were captured,' Einar said. 'But right now would we not be better working on trying to get away?'

He shot a nervous glance towards the street they came from only a little time before. Already he could hear the stomping feet of running Serk warriors and see the light of flaming torches that were approaching all too fast.

'There will be too many of them to fight,' he added.

Ignoring him, Affreca lifted a bow from the hiding place. There was a spark of light and Einar saw Ulrich had struck the flint in the small metal fire starter box from the hidden hoard.

'We don't need more light,' Einar said. 'There is enough from the moon.'

Skar shoved the quay with his considerable strength and the ship slid away into the black, smooth water of the harbour. The big man then skipped across to a rowing bench in front of Einar and grabbed an oar.

'Let's get her going, eh?' Skar said, dipping his oar into the water.

Einar and the others followed his lead. They strained their backs and the boat began to move towards the harbour mouth. There were no slaves to row now and there were only five on the oars so the work was hard. Einar's shoulders and back felt the strain straight away.

Affreca had wrapped cloth around the top of an arrow. She touched it to the wood shavings that now glowed alight in the fire starter box. From the way the cloth leapt into flame at the touch of the fire it must have been soaked in some sort of oil. There were all sorts of weapons in the hiding place and the fact that they included fire arrows was no surprise to Einar. What puzzled him though was what Affreca intended to do with her now flaming arrow.

This time Thord's ship was in front of theirs. He had more men at the oars and even though it was bigger it got going faster and was already nearing the harbour mouth. There was only room for one ship at a time to leave the harbour so the snekkja fell in behind it.

Einar, facing back towards the town, cursed as he saw the first Serk warriors burst from the street and begin pouring into the harbour.

Whistles and shouting began but this time it was from a lot closer and Einar realised it was from the far side of the quay. With a surge of dismay he realised the noises must be coming from the huge galley that had barred their escape earlier. The crew must have heard the alarms and no doubt were rushing to move the ship forward to block the harbour entrance once again.

Once more Einar and the others would be trapped. He

doubted that this time their captors would be so lenient as to let them live long enough to try another escape.

A loud wolf whistle came from the end of the quay beside the harbour mouth. Einar swivelled his head. He managed to see a tall figure standing on a stack of barrels on the quay, outlined against the moon behind him. Einar knew it could only be Sigurd or Kari: two triangular points stood up from the man's head – the ears of a wolf from the hood of his skin cloak. Whichever one it was, he was waving his arms above his head in the direction of the snekkja.

Ulrich nodded to Affreca. She drew the bow, blazing arrow notched, and tilted her aim to the sky. Affreca loosed the bow, sending the arrow almost straight up, high into the air above the quay. The rush of the air it shot through caused its flames to roar and burn ever brighter.

When it lost its momentum, the arrow stopped and began to fall, the light of its fire carving an arc through the darkness of the night. It fell towards the far side of the quay and disappeared from view.

'Well that was a waste of an—' Einar began to say.

Then the night exploded into light. It looked like the sun was rising behind the quay, blotting out the moon in the sky. A great wave of hot wind swept over the deck of the snekkja.

'Row, you bastards, row!' Ulrich shouted as he and Affreca grabbed oars and joined the others on the benches.

Thord's ship slid through the harbour mouth and the snekkja followed it. As they passed the end of the quay Sigurd and Kari jumped down onto the deck. They rushed to take their places on the rowing benches, took an oar each and straight away the ship increased in speed.

As they emerged from the harbour mouth, a great breath of heat swept over them. Most of the deck of the huge galley that had guarded the harbour entrance was ablaze. Flames were already licking upwards on all of its three masts. There were men in the water – crew who must have jumped off to save their lives. Four other unfortunate crew members were staggering through the inferno on the deck, little more than walking bonfires themselves, beating in vain with flailing arms at the flames that engulfed them. Reaching the edge they toppled over, hitting the sea with massive splashes that both swallowed their bodies and quenched the flames that tortured them.

'You found something that burns then?' Ulrich said over his shoulder to Kari.

'Aye.' Kari was grinning from ear to ear, delighted at the carnage he and Sigurd had created. 'That's the beauty of a harbour. With cargoes and ship supplies stacked all over the quays, there's always a lot of stuff like barrels of oil just sitting around, waiting to be used. We found a stash quite near the galley, broke open a few barrels and emptied them over the deck. All we needed was fire to light it and Affreca sent that.'

'Good work,' Ulrich said. 'Now let's get away from here. Put your backs into it.'

They all heaved on the oars, sending the ship ever faster out into the darkness of the open sea. Behind them, in the light of the blazing galley they could see many Serks swarming around the end of the quays.

'Do you think they'll come after us?' Einar wondered aloud.

'I'd say they will be too busy trying to put that fire out,' Ulrich said. 'Even if they do, they may have bigger ships but they can't match us for speed.'

It seemed Ulrich was correct. As Mālaqah slipped further and further away behind them, they saw no sign of any ships leaving its harbour to come after them.

'There's a decent wind,' Roan shouted from his post at the

steering oar at the stern. 'Why don't we get the sails unfurled? Unless you lot enjoy rowing, that is.'

Starkad left his rowing bench and shinned up the mast. He untied the ropes that kept the large square woollen sail rolled on the cross-beam. Einar and Skar grabbed the ropes at its bottom corners and made them fast on the sides of the ship. The wind caught the sail, it billowed forward then went taut. The ropes that held it creaked and the ship surged through the waves even faster.

Now there was no more need to row, the rest pulled their oars in and stood up from the benches, stretching stiff backs and rubbing sore muscles. The excitement of the chase was fast draining away from them, leaving a leaden-limbed tiredness that promised sleep would not be hard to fend off for long.

'Well?' Roan said. 'Where to now? I need to set a course.'

For a moment Ulrich looked at a loss. Then he said: 'East.'

'What's there?' Skar said.

'I don't know,' Ulrich said. 'We've lost pretty much everything but our shirts and some old weapons. We're not welcome every land north and west of here. Now we've been chased from Mālaqah too. South is more Serk lands. I don't know what lies to the east, but right now this is the only way we have left to go.'

Nine

The blazing sun woke Einar. He had been dead to the world, flat on his back inside his leather sleeping bag, oblivious to the hard, flat planks of the deck he lay on. He woke from a dream where he had been walking in the cool, sweet-smelling shade of a forest of great pine trees. He had been chasing a mysterious, elf-born ball of fire that seemed to have a life of its own. As soon as he got close to it, the fire skittered away from him like a playful dog, leading him further and deeper into the woods. What it was he had no idea. All he knew in the dream was he needed to catch this strange fire.

He woke before he managed to. Still wondering what the dream meant, Einar sat up. He had slept long into the morning and the sun was already high in the sky above. Perhaps it had been the scorching heat that beat down from it, or memories of the blazing ship the night before that had provoked his strange reverie.

The burning ship must indeed have kept the Serks of Mālaqah busy as no vessels had given chase to the fleeing Norsemen. When it became clear they had escaped for sure, those not unlucky enough to get a spell on watch or at the steering oar crawled with thanks to the gods into their sleeping bags and, exhausted by the exploits of the day and night before, went straight to sleep.

Einar looked around. Most of the others still slept. Roan – who never seemed to need rest – stood at the steering oar, guiding the ship over the white-topped, impossibly blue waters of the Great Middle Sea. Affreca was awake too. She stood at the prow, her gaze turned to the sea ahead.

The sail was full and the warm wind drove them eastward. The ship surged and fell in rhythm with the waves it cut through, each one thumping against the prow then hissing spray over the dragon-carved post. Affreca must have been getting soaked by this, but she did not move. It was an experience that, since arriving in these hot realms, most of the crew had found was refreshing. It was one of the few ways to get welcome relief from the relentless heat of the sun.

Einar scrambled out of his sleeping bag and stood up. He stretched, wincing at the jolts of pain that jabbed his bones and muscles at various parts of his body. He was not an old man, at his own reckoning he had now lived through twenty-one winters, but that meant he was also now far from a youth. The years of hard, relentless toil and several serious injuries were starting to take their toll. Sleeping on the flat, hard wood of the deck did not help much either.

He strolled down the deck to join Affreca. She nodded to acknowledge him when he reached the prow, then turned her attention back to the sea.

'Beautiful, isn't it?' Einar said.

Thord's longship cut through the waters a little way behind them. Einar could not stop marvelling at the colour of the water in the Great Middle Sea. He had not seen anything close to it apart from some of the seas around the land of the Scots and north Ireland where white sandy beaches merged with clear waters. That water was freezing cold, however. Einar knew that if he jumped off the ship here the water would be almost as warm as that in one of the hot spring baths back home in Iceland.

Not that jumping off the ship at the moment would be a good idea. They were well out in the open sea and there was no sight of land anywhere on the horizon. The ship was also going faster than a man could swim. They had caught sight of some huge creatures in the waters too, whether they were fishes or monsters – *nicors* or water dragons – they could not tell. They were for certain unlike any whales Einar had ever seen.

'Where do you think we'll end up this time?' Einar said as he joined Affreca at the prow. He closed his eyes and turned his face to the spray, enjoying the cooling feel of the water as it misted them both. He was soaked in moments but did not mind. It was the closest he had come to a bath in days.

Affreca shrugged. 'There is much to the east,' she said. 'Rome. Miklagard. Jorsalaborg.'

'Where?' Einar said with a frown.

'The Christians call it Jerusalem,' Affreca said. 'It's their holy city. Their God walked the earth there.'

'Like they say Thor did at the rivers Körmt and Örmt?' Einar said, turning down the corners of his mouth. 'I thought the Christian holy city was Rome?'

'They have several,' Affreca said. 'The Irish would talk about it a lot. Their All Father lives in Rome.'

'Do you believe the gods really walk the earth?' Einar said.

'I don't know about the gods,' she said. 'But it looks like we're doomed to wander the earth for some time.'

There was a short silence as they both contemplated the situation they were now in.

'Half the world is still open to us,' Einar said. 'West and south.'

'South?' Affreca made a face. 'You think it's warm here? When you travel south from here it just gets hotter and hotter. There is more Serkland, then a great sea of sand, then who knows what?'

'The lore of our folk says Muspelheim lies that way,' Einar said. 'The glowing land of fire where *jötnar* dwell. Where the world began and where its end will come from. On the last day, at Ragnarök, the great fire giant Surt will come from there, do battle with the gods and burn up the whole world with his fiery sword.'

'I don't know about myths and legends,' Affreca said, wiping the gathering sweat from her forehead, 'but I could certainly believe there is a land of fire somewhere not far away. The very wind seems heated here. There's no relief from it. I never thought I'd say this, but some days I long for the bogs and rain of Ireland.'

'I wonder how our own Surt is doing?' Einar said, glancing round at the black man who still slept on the deck.

'It must be hard on him,' Affreca said. 'To spend all those years a slave, forced to kill people as a ring fighter. The one thing that must have kept him going was the hope he would one day return home and be reunited with his family. Then when he finally achieves that he finds he has lost them too.'

Einar nodded. For a moment both lapsed into silence at the sombre thought.

'Imagine if we went to Rome, though,' Einar said, trying to lighten the mood. A faraway look of wonder spread across his face at the thought of it. 'Imagine what it will look like! You've seen all those amazing stone buildings the Romans left all over the world. What must their home city look like?'

'Surt says Rome is just a lot of crumbling old ruins,' Affreca said. 'Miklagard is much more impressive. I had an uncle went there to fight for the King of the Greeks. You know they think of themselves as Romans, don't you?'

Einar frowned and shook his head.

'I'm surprised at that,' Affreca said. 'What with you thinking the Romans are so great.'

'Morning, lovebirds.'

Ulrich's voice made them both turn around. The Wolf Coat leader was swaggering down the deck towards them.

'Why don't you two just get married?' Ulrich said as he joined them at the prow. 'You're always nattering away together like an old married couple.'

Affreca shot him a look that would have made milk curdle.

'You better watch yourselves,' Ulrich went on. 'I don't want any babies on this ship. It's bad enough having a woman on board but one of those nasty, smelly, wailing creatures would be too much. If I ever see you with one I'll throw it straight over the side.'

'Piss off, Ulrich,' Affreca said. 'You're not funny.'

'I asked her to marry me once,' Einar said, folding his arms. 'She turned me down. Even though I was trying to help her out.'

'I did not turn you down,' Affreca said. 'I said I wouldn't even think about it until you were Jarl of Orkney.' Now Affreca was smiling too.

Einar's own grin faded as another thought came to his mind.

'That might have been a step closer if we hadn't spent all Aethelstan's silver on those slaves,' he said. 'Now we've lost everything! I could have used that silver to buy warriors and ships to take Orkney back.'

Ulrich's smile faded a little. Einar swallowed, realising too late he had drifted perilously close to criticising Ulrich's leadership.

'Eirik Bloody Axe was King of Norway,' Ulrich said. 'He took an army with him to Orkney and a fleet of a hundred ships or more to take the earldom that was your birthright. There was a lot of silver in those chests we took from Aethelstan, lad, but nowhere near enough to pay for sufficient men to retake Jarls Gard. Your uncle's fortress is all but impregnable.'

'We broke into it once,' Einar said.

'It was all but empty,' Ulrich said. 'And as Ulrich always says, a small company can slip unnoticed where an army can't go. They can't hold a large fortress by themselves though. You would need an army as big as Eirik's to take Jarls Gard and keep it. Maybe bigger.'

'Well one day I shall get that army,' Einar said, knitting his brows. 'And I will lead them to the gates of Jarls Gard and take back what is mine.'

Both Ulrich and Affreca exchanged glances. There were barely concealed half-smirks on their faces.

'You may lead them, Einar,' Ulrich said. 'But will they follow you? It takes more than silver to get men to charge into battle. You can't just walk in front of them and think they'll be ready to fight – to perhaps die – for you.'

'I led a company of men in Britain!' Einar blurted out. 'Aethelstan entrusted me with a war band of my own.'

'Saxons?' Ulrich said with a grunt. 'They're like ducklings. They'll follow anyone with a shiny helmet.'

'Do you think this too?' Einar turned to Affreca who was standing, arms folded across her chest, smiling at his annoyance. 'You do! Why couldn't I? Why not?'

'Some men are just born to lead great armies,' Affreca said. 'It's bred into them from an early age. Others...' She stopped for a moment, as if trying to find the words. 'Others are born to follow.'

'Oh, is *that* it?' Einar felt his cheeks flushing. 'You think I'm just a follower, do you?' He glared at Ulrich. 'That's what you think too, isn't it?'

'No, Einar, I don't,' Ulrich said. He was all of a sudden serious again. 'There are some men born to lead. Some born to follow. There are others who just go their own way no matter what direction anyone tries to point them in. Such men choose their own path. But they walk it alone.'

'An *eingangr maðr*?' Einar said, not sure if the accusation made him feel more angry. In the tight-knit community in Iceland he had grown up in, everyone was expected to be able to look after themselves but everyone also knew that they had to pull together as a folk – kith, kin and neighbours – if they were to survive the winters, gather in their crops, haul in the herring catch or land a great shark. An eingangr maðr – a man who walked alone – was regarded as an outcast. An outsider who did not fit in. An unlucky man who others sometimes feared to associate with.

He looked at Affreca who still smiled. She leaned towards him and tapped him with her elbow.

'Right,' she said. 'You are the perfect example of an eingangr maðr.'

'Now will you stop distracting Affreca?' Ulrich said to Einar. 'She's supposed to be on watch.'

'Don't worry,' Einar said. 'I'm not getting in her way.'

'Really?' Ulrich said. 'Well, she's missed that. You all have.'

They looked past the prow, in the direction Ulrich was pointing.

There was a ship ahead. It was coming straight for them.

Ten

The ship was smaller than Thord's but larger than the snekkja. It had a single bank of oars on each side, which were extended and rippled in and out of the water like waves. Like the longships, rows of shields lined the sides of the ship, providing protection from arrows or spears for the rowers who sat on the rowing benches behind them. This detail alone was enough to tell Einar it was some sort of warship. Unlike the Norsemen's single-masted vessels with their square sails, the new ship had two masts, and its triangular sails – filled by the wind – added to the propulsion of the oarsmen. The sails were dyed a bright blue, almost the same colour as the sea. There was some sort of wooden tower built up over the prow that looked like a little fortress. The tower had a rectangular hole in its wall, about halfway up its height. It looked like a vantage point that someone could fire arrows or other missiles from inside while remaining protected by the wooden sides. The front wall of the tower, which had the opening in it, was sheeted with metal to add extra shielding.

The ship was still sailing straight towards them.

Surt and Skar, now awake also, came jogging down the deck to join the others at the prow.

'What do you think?' Ulrich said to Skar.

'They seem intent on meeting us,' Skar said.

'That's an imperial galea,' Surt said. He pointed to the banner that fluttered above the wooden tower on the prow of the approaching ship. Einar squinted and made out some sort of bird with spread wings embroidered on it. 'A Roman navy scout ship from Constantinopolis.'

A horn sounded above the hissing of the spray and crashing of the waves. It came from Thord's ship, which was pulling closer alongside the snekkja. Einar saw Thord himself was on the prow. He was dressed for war in helmet and mail, which meant he too must have hidden weapons on board his vessel. Einar saw that others of Thord's crew behind him were likewise armed.

'Ulrich!' Thord shouted. 'Let's take this ship. The booty will make up for some of our losses.'

Ulrich pursed his lips.

'Surt says that's a ship of the imperial navy,' he shouted back. 'Perhaps the smart thing is to avoid it?'

'It's smaller than my ship and we outnumber them,' Thord yelled. There was anger in his voice. 'We can take it easily. I'm attacking with or without you. If you don't want a share of the booty then so be it!'

His ship veered away from the snekkja again and began to aim directly for the approaching galea.

'What do you think?' Skar said.

'Those slaves were worth a small fortune,' Ulrich said. 'Now they are lost, I think Thord might be worried his own men are going to throw him over the side if he doesn't start making good for that. That is perhaps pushing him to make rash decisions.'

'We can't just let them fight alone,' Skar said. 'And what if that ship turns out to be laden with gold and silver: taxes collected for the emperor?'

'Get the rest up,' Ulrich said. 'Everyone arm themselves.'

Ulrich did not shout, nor was he excited, though he had become deadly serious. Einar and the others reacted in a similar way. Without over-haste or panic, they went into action. Affreca, Kari, Surt and Einar opened the hiding place in the hold and began retrieving weapons and helmets while Skar returned to where Sigurd, Wulfhelm and Starkad still slept to shake them awake.

The weapons were spares so not the best or the most ostentatious, but they were functional and each of them got a spear and sword, except Affreca who took the bow and slung the bag of arrows over her shoulder. All their shields had been taken by the Serks and there were only two coats of mail. There were enough thick leather jerkins for all of them though and battered and old though they were, there was also a helmet for everyone.

When each Wolf Coat was ready, they pulled up the hoods of their wolfskin cloaks. These were the garments that gave the warriors their name. They were made from the skin of a wolf each one of them had personally killed as part of their initiation ritual. The hood was formed by the heads of the beasts and when pulled up over their helms the ears stuck up and the snout ran down over their forehead like a crest. Each one of them looked half-man, half-wolf.

All except Wulfhelm and Surt. They were valued members of the crew but would not forsake their own Christ God, which meant they could not be one of Odin's own warriors.

By the time they were ready, the ships had almost closed on each other. Any doubt that the new vessel was a warship was dispelled by the sight of a band of archers, maybe five or six, who had climbed to the top of the wooden tower at its front.

Ulrich nodded to Affreca. It was all the order she needed to hurry back to the centre of the ship. There she took up a position just behind the mast. The thick wood of the mast would give her protection from the enemy archers while still allowing her to duck round it and – the plan was – return arrows that could pick them off one by one. It was a tactic that had worked many times in the past.

The rest of the Norsemen gathered behind Skar at the prow. In sea fighting, this area of the ship was crucial. It was the point where either the enemy was most likely to attempt to board, or else if the chance arose the Wolf Coats would launch their own boarding attack on the enemy. Skar the stafn-búi, the prowman of the crew – the biggest, meanest warrior on the ship who was either first to meet anyone trying to board or first onto an enemy's ship – took up his position right behind the carved dragon.

Now there was little to do but wait. For the first time nerves began to slosh in Einar's guts. To distract himself he checked the straps of his helmet and those on his fighting glove that secured his sword hilt to his hand, pulling them tight as he could manage to bear.

Skar cursed and Einar looked up to see that Thord's ship had swerved in front of the Wolf Coats' snekkja, cutting into its path and leaving so little space between the stern of one ship and the prow of the other that Einar feared they were going to collide. Roan saw this too and slammed the steering oar to the side, turning the agile snekkja and just avoiding ramming into the back of the other longship.

'That fool Thord must be desperate for whatever plunder he can get from that galea,' Ulrich said through clenched teeth. 'Let him and his men go first then. They can do half the fighting for us.'

'We need loot too, Ulrich,' Sigurd said. 'We've lost everything we had in Mālaqah as well, remember?'

Thord's ship closed with the imperial vessel. Both ships were on a collision course and most of Thord's warriors crouched in a huddle at the prow, weapons ready, preparing to leap into the enemy ship as soon at the two vessels hit each other.

At the very last moment the imperial ship turned aside. Einar noticed that a strange-looking hollow metal tube now extended from the rectangular hole in the front of the tower that he had thought was for protecting archers. The tube looked like it was made of brass and it slid sideways until the open end of it pointed towards the prow of Thord's ship. A loud hissing noise started up from somewhere inside the tower that quickly turned to a roar like a howling wind on a mountain top.

'What's that?' Einar said, pointing at the odd device.

Surt let out a cry in his own tongue that Einar could not understand, but by its tone he guessed it was some sort of alarm. His eyes were wide and round. His jaw hung open in an expression that to Einar's surprise spoke of sheer terror.

'Everyone get down!' Surt shouted, now speaking in the Norse tongue. 'Find shelter! Your lives depend on it.'

As he spoke, a jet of fire shot from the metal tube. It was not a mere tongue of fire but a torrent of liquid flame like burning oil that surged through the air and splattered across the prow of Thord's ship. Everywhere it landed it set ablaze. The men crouching at the prow, ready to attack, were engulfed by the inferno. Their agonised screams tore the air as the imperial ship carried on its path alongside Thord's longship, the brass tube continuing to spew the blazing liquid over the deck for the rest of its length. The remainder of Thord's crew had gathered along the side, waiting to follow the others onto the imperial galea, but instead they too were now turned into human torches as the fire sprayed over them. In an instant the whole deck was ablaze. Men ablaze stumbled this way and that across it, colliding with each other or the side, screaming in agony and desperation as they tried escape the flames that engulfed them.

The Wolf Coats dived behind the sides of their ship in the yearning hope that it would somehow save them from the flames coming their way. Einar glared in horror at the sight, unable to tear his eyes away or move. He saw Thord, his brynja ablaze and with flames spewing from the eye holes of his helmet visor, staggering around in circles as he beat at his body in a vain attempt to put out the fire. Several of Thord's warriors went over the side, either by accident or by jumping. They landed in the sea with huge splashes. To Einar's astonishment the sea did not quench the fires. He could see the flames under the surface as the men continued to burn despite being in the water. Likewise, in places where the burning liquid dribbled off Thord's ship or splashed into the sea, it sat on the surface, still ablaze.

'This must be witchcraft,' he said, his voice not much more than a coarse whisper.

The imperial ship had almost gone the length of Thord's ship now and having drenched it in fire was about to reach the prow of the snekkja.

'Find shelter, you fool!' Surt cried to Einar. 'That's Greek Fire. You don't stand a hope if it lands on you!'

He lashed out with his foot from where he crouched, striking Einar on the shin. The blow was enough to wake Einar from his astonished stupor.

He looked around, desperate to find somewhere that might provide safety from the jet of fire that drew remorselessly ever closer, spewing burning liquid that set ablaze the very sea between the stern of Thord's ship and the prow of the snekkja.

Eleven

Affreca, who had been at the mast, ran towards the stern where Roan still gripped the steering oar, resolute to stay at his post until the last. Without thinking Einar ran towards them. He had no idea what he was doing, but something inside him urged him to get to her.

As he sprinted along the deck he was painfully aware of how exposed he was. With each step his skin itched with anticipation that the next one would bring the agony of the burning liquid as it spread its inferno over the snekkja.

He made it to the stern, however. To his surprise Affreca had an indignant look on her face.

'What are you doing?' she said. 'You could have been killed, you idiot.'

Einar opened his mouth but could not explain his actions even to himself.

'I was going to tell you to jump over the side before the fire comes,' he said instead.

'I could have worked that out for myself,' Affreca said. 'And it looks like there may be no need.'

Einar turned around, realising that he was not dead nor was the ship on fire. The imperial ship was still bearing down on them but the awful howling from the front tower subsided back to a hiss and the jet of burning liquid petered out first to a dribble that left several spots of burning sea, then it stopped altogether.

The rest of the Wolf Coats at the prow popped their heads up from behind the sides of the ship to see what was going on. Seeing the fire had stopped, they rose to their feet.

The deck of the other ship bristled with warriors. They were all clad in body armour consisting of jerkins dyed as blue as the sails, over which were sewed many small, rectangular pieces of shining metal that overlapped like the scales of a snake. Their heads were protected by tall, conical helmets with long nasal guards and they wore short skirts that left their lower legs bare in the manner Einar had seen some of the Gaels of Scotland and Ireland wear. These garments, however, also had long leather strips hanging all around to add extra protection to their lower limbs.

Six of the warriors on the other ship hurled grappling hocks at the Wolf Coats' snekkja. They sailed through the air over the sea then landed with a clatter, their iron claws digging into the wood of the deck or the sides of the longship.

Ulrich, Skar and the others at the prow charged towards the hooks that were nearest to them, intent on prying free the hooks' grasp. Before they could reach them a shower of arrows shot by the archers on the imperial ship thudded into the deck between the embedded hooks and the three running Wolf Coats. They halted.

Imperial warriors began hauling on the ropes that trailed from the hooks, drawing the ships closer together. The archers levelled arrows at the Wolf Coats, the message that they should leave the hooks alone clear.

The prow of the galea crashed into the side of the longship just behind the mast, sending a shudder through the deck of the

Norsemen's vessel and sending it slewing round. Everyone on board went staggering. Einar grabbed the side of the ship, trying to steady himself.

As he did so he was surprised to hear a shout from behind him, over the side of the ship. Confused, he turned and saw a man clinging to the side. The man looked up and Einar saw it was one of Thord's crew, the big man from the Southern Isles known as Fisk: the Fish. The man had somehow managed to escape the inferno that engulfed Thord's longship.

Einar reached his arm down over the side and Fisk grabbed it. He winced as the full weight of the big man almost dragged him over the side but managed to brace himself, allowing Fisk to clamber on board.

'I thought they called you the Fish because of the amount of ale you drank,' Einar said. 'But maybe you're actually half fish?'

He nodded at the sea, referring to the impressive feat of strength Fisk had just performed in managing to swim to the snekkja, not only fully dressed but also wearing a mail shirt.

'I thought I was lucky getting off our ship,' Fisk said, panting. 'But it looks like you lot are equally fucked.'

Affreca was running to join the others. Fisk and Einar followed her. As the two ships clunked together, the imperial warriors began to clamber over the sides. The Wolf Coat crew did their best to create a defensive line. With no shields they could not call it a shield wall.

As he took his place, Einar felt almost naked with nothing to shelter behind. A quick count of the warriors boarding told Einar there were about sixty of them, which meant the Wolf Coats were outnumbered by around seven to one.

Affreca raised her bow and took aim at one of the archers on the other ship, but Ulrich laid his sword blade on her forearm, prompting her to lower it.

'What are you doing?' Affreca looked at Ulrich, astonishment on her face. 'I could kill at least a couple of them.'

'They could have shot us all already,' Ulrich said. 'They deliberately missed and shot warning arrows instead. They did not burn us like they did to Thord either. Let's see why.'

'We can't just stand here and let them climb aboard,' Sigurd said through clenched teeth. 'We might not have enough men to win this fight but let's at least take a few of the bastards with us.'

'They might have other intentions,' Ulrich said. 'Yes, we could kill some of them but they'll kill all of us. As Odin himself teaches us: *A lame man can ride, a handless man drive sheep, a deaf man can fight. A corpse is of no use to anyone.* Why die if we don't have to?'

Sigurd spat his disgust but nevertheless held his position and did not rush forwards to attack the imperial soldiers who continued to board the snekkja.

Thord's ship was now engulfed in fire and billowing smoke. It drifted sideways, aimless and unguided. There was no movement among the inferno and the only sound was the roar and crackle of the flames. As he smelt the terrible stench of roasting flesh drifting across the sea air, Einar hoped Ulrich was right and the warriors now boarding them weren't saving the Norsemen for a similar, horrible fate.

The imperial warriors fanned out across the deck. Every man wore identical armour and uniform but Einar was surprised at how different the men themselves were. They appeared to come from all sorts of folk. Some were dark-haired, a couple were blond. Many had olive skin, some dark brown and two were black-skinned like Surt. They formed into a disciplined line facing the Wolf Coats then locked their shields side by side to form a continual barrier. Each soldier slid a heavy fighting spear over the top of the shield, points towards their enemy, eyes levelled, narrow and cold.

The Wolf Coats glared back. Sigurd, Kari and Starkad bared their teeth in snarls while Ulrich curled his lip in a dismissive sneer.

Unarmed men with the look of slaves about them began fastening the sides of the ships together with ropes to prevent them sliding apart. Then behind the ranks of warriors facing them the same menials placed a boarding plank between the two ships and lashed it into position. When it was steady, two more men walked across it from the imperial galea onto the snekkja.

Both wore armour akin to the other warriors but much grander. There were touches of gold, and jewels glinted on their sword hilts and across their weapon belts and the foreheads of their helmets. Both wore metal breastplates that unlike the other warriors' scale armour were fashioned to look like bare, muscled torsos. The first one across wore a long blue cloak around his shoulders. Everything about their arms and armour spoke of rank and ostentation rather than practicality. It was clear these two were commanders.

With a pang of remorse, Einar remembered that he had worn a red cloak himself not that long ago. He had been in command of a company of men who wore armour as grand as these men did while he had been in the service of Aethelstan. Now he was back at sea, a landless, homeless viking who had lost everything and (he had little doubt) was at the very best about to become a prisoner for the second time in as many days. He felt anger spark within him. This was unfair. Life was supposed to get better, not worse. It was supposed to be a continual scaling of a ladder to wealth and fame, but he seemed to be stuck on the bottom rung and every time he managed to climb a few rungs it was never long before he somehow managed to end up back at the bottom. Had he made a terrible mistake by rejoining his friends?

One of the commanders in the blue cloaks was very tall and slender. He had a long narrow face and a hooked nose. His skin was tanned brown by the sun and sea. He walked behind the line of imperial warriors with a languid, measured step, his hands clasped behind his back as he surveyed the vikings with a cold gaze every bit as contemptuous as Ulrich's sneer. His nose wrinkled as if he had caught the scent of something unpleasant. When he had swept his gaze across all of the Wolf Coats, he turned to his companion and barked a few words in a tongue Einar did not understand.

The second man was squat, broad-chested and moved with a much more sprightly step. His nose was broken and a white scar sliced through the tanned skin on the right of his face, suggesting he was or had been more involved in the practicalities of warfare than his companion. Einar could not help notice the second commander also had the most piercing blue eyes he had seen for a long time and there was what looked like a slight, bemused smile on his face. He carried a large battleaxe, right hand on the handle, the head resting blade upwards on his right shoulder.

'Good morning,' the second commander said. To Einar's surprise he spoke in the Norse tongue. 'You men are all now prisoners of the imperial Roman navy.'

Twelve

Einar's jaw dropped further. He gaped at his companions but none of them seemed to share his astonishment.

What did this man mean by *the imperial Roman navy*? Affreca was right: Einar was fascinated by the Romans. He had gazed in wonder at the huge stone buildings they had erected in Jorvik and Wintanceaster, constructions that even today towered over the wooden and wattle modern houses they stood among. He had travelled the roads they had built across Britain, each one straight as an arrow's flight and even though centuries old still provided the quickest and most reliable way to move around that country. So skilled were these works that a lot of folk could not believe they were the work of men at all, but reckoned them the craft of jötnar, dwarves or even Odin himself. The Romans had conquered the whole world and everywhere they had gone they had left their mark.

That was centuries ago, however. The Romans were long gone, their empire torn apart by folk like the Norsemen's forefathers. Roman society and culture were now just heaps of ruins. All that remained of their mighty works was their tongue, which was still spoken by the Christian priests and monks.

Yet these men were claiming they were Romans. How

could this be? Had they been captured by revenants? *Draugr* or ghosts? Also he may be dressed in foreign clothes like the other Romans, but the commander with the axe was clearly a Norseman like Einar. What was he doing here? He had heard Norsemen sometimes travelled to Miklagard to serve the King of the Greeks, but not the Romans. Perhaps this man was one of those but had found an alternative master.

'What do want with us?' Ulrich said. 'We are simple traders. Merchants who came here in peace. Yet you murder our companions, burn their ship and board ours uninvited?'

The blue-eyed Roman who spoke the Norse tongue threw back his head and gave a hearty laugh. His superior officer shot a disapproving look at him down his long, thin nose.

'Simple merchants?' the Roman Norseman said, shaking his head. 'You must think we were born yesterday. You are vikings. Pirates. You meant to attack our ship. You would have killed every one of us and taken everything we had as plunder. But you chose the wrong victims this time my friend. You made a big mistake. A fatal one on the part of your companions on the other ship.'

As if in response to his words, Thord's ship gave a groaning, tearing noise and began to sink into the sea. As the blazing vessel sank below the surface, a loud hissing rose as the flames belched up clouds of steam. In moments the whole ship disappeared from sight, leaving a maelstrom of bubbles behind. After a few more moments this disappeared too and all that was left was scattered floating debris and several grisly, charred corpses.

'So are you going to kill us too?' Ulrich asked. He straightened his back.

'That depends on you,' the Norse-speaking Roman said. 'We have a proposition for you. We'd like you to do something for us: carry out a task on the island of Frumentaria. If you say yes then you will live. For a time anyway. I'll be honest and tell you that the task is dangerous and we cannot guarantee you will survive it.'

'We will do it!' Surt blurted out.

'You speak for all these men?' the Roman said.

'No he does not,' Ulrich said.

'My *daughter*...' Surt said, looking at Ulrich.

'And if we say no to this task?' Ulrich ignored the pleading look Surt was casting in his direction.

'We'll string you up from your own cross-beam and then sink your ship,' the Roman said with a grin.

'You're a Norseman, like us,' Ulrich said. 'You might choose to wear a dress now and that sissy Roman armour, but you can't fool men of your own blood. What sort of man kills his own folk for strangers?'

The other grunted. 'I kill whomever I'm paid to kill. And the emperor pays very well, believe me. And right now I am being paid to kill pirates. These waters are infested with them. There are enough Serks and Moor pirates without you lot from the north coming down here to add vikings as well. But if I was at home I would kill vikings too. You are nothing but a nuisance. Chancers and raiders.'

'You never went viking as a young man?' Ulrich said.

The Roman winked at Ulrich. 'We all do all sorts when we're young. They call me Araltes here, that's Harald in the Norse tongue and yes, I am a Norwayan from Kaupangr. This is a snekkja, isn't it?'

He ran an appraising eye over the sleek contours of the ship, his lips pursed in appreciation. 'A real work of art. It would be a shame to send her to the bottom. You are the leader of this company?'

'I am,' Ulrich said. 'My name is Ulrich Rognisson.'

'Rognisson?' Araltes said. 'My father knew a Rogni from Sogn. One of the Ulflings clan.'

'That was my father,' Ulrich said.

Araltes pursed his lips. His expression became more serious.

'Then if you are anything like your father you're a man to be reckoned with,' he said. 'These men are úlfhéðnar? Odin's wolf warriors? Correct?' He took a second glance at Surt and Wulfhelm. 'At least most of them, anyway. And is that a woman?'

His eyebrows shot up as he spied Affreca's face under her wolfskin hood.

'Every one of these folk have received the same level of training in the crafts of war,' Ulrich said. 'But only the wolfskin wearers have been initiated into the secret, sacred rites of Odin.'

'Well it's those crafts of war we need,' Araltes said. 'We can set religion aside for the time being. My commander, the strategos Theoktistos here—' he gestured to the man in the cloak '—was intent on incinerating both these ships, but I spotted your wolfskin cloaks. I told him you might have some special skills we could use to help us with a particular problem we face, so he has spared your lives. Now what do you say?'

Ulrich looked at the others. They returned nods. Skar shrugged.

'What choice do we have?' the prowman said.

'We accept your offer,' Ulrich said. 'Whatever it is.'

'Wise choice,' Araltes said.

Ulrich noticed Fisk lurking beside Einar for the first time.

'He's not one of mine,' Ulrich said, pointing at the lanky man from the Southern Isles. 'He's from the other ship. I don't know what he's doing here.'

'Then he's a lucky man if he's still alive,' Araltes said. 'Whether you keep him or not is up to you, but what have you to offer, stranger?'

'My name is Fisk,' Fisk said, pushing out his lower lip. 'I'm a poet.'

'We've already got one of those,' Ulrich said, pointing at Einar.

'I know runes and *galdr*,' Fisk said, twirling one of the bones in his hair with his forefinger. 'I can work magic.'

'*Seidr* more like,' Ulrich said, his upper lip curling, betraying his disdain for the unmanly magical practice.

Fisk straightened up and puffed out his chest. 'I'm the best fucking axeman in the Southern Isles,' he said.

'That's more like it,' Skar said. 'We always have use for someone good with an axe.'

'Very well,' Araltes said. 'We will take your ship in tow until we get to where we are headed. You will all hand your weapons and helmets to my men. Some of our *marines* – that's the name of ship warriors in the empire – will remain on board here to make sure you don't get any ideas about slipping off on your own. We'll tell you more when we are closer to the island where you will carry out your task. Right now the strategos and I will return to our ship for breakfast. I think we deserve it.'

Thirteen

'I'm glad I'm not one of their slaves,' Affreca said. 'We might be prisoners but at least we don't have to work like them.'

The snekkja was trailing behind the imperial galea, tethered to it by a long, stout rope that was strengthened by chains where it was lashed around the dragon-carved prow of the viking ship. The snekkja's square sail and both the triangular sails of the galea were filled with the warm wind, but with a ship in tow the slaves on the galea were straining at the oars to add propulsion. A drum sounded a steady beat to keep the slaves pulling in unison.

'That drum is driving me mad,' Ulrich said. 'Why can't they just sing like we do to keep a steady pace?'

Roan stayed at his post at the steering oar, even though there was little need as they were under tow from the imperial ship. The Roman warriors huddled around the prow, keeping a wary eye on the Norsemen.

There was little for the Wolf Coat crew to do. They raised the leather canopy that in the northern realms kept them dry from the sleet and driving rain, but here provided some relief from the blistering sun. Sigurd and Kari squatted around a game of tail. Affreca, her bow taken by her captors, nevertheless busied herself with examining the arrows from her arrow bag, checking their fletches and making sure they were straight. The rest lounged about. Surt, who of them all was most able to cope with the heat, lay on his back outside the shade of the canopy, eyes closed. Einar knew the man's heart must be a maelstrom of disappointment and worry at what had happened to his family, but Surt showed no sign of it as he lay, a slight smile on his lips, enjoying the hot sunshine in the same way Einar would have enjoyed a hot bath.

'Why are we here anyway, Ulrich?' Sigurd said.

'Because they captured us,' Ulrich said.

'I mean in this part of the world,' Sigurd said. 'What are we doing? We took enough silver from Aethelstan that we could have all lived the rest of our lives in comfort.'

'Comfort, yes,' Ulrich said. 'Luxury? No. We could all have bought ourselves a nice farm somewhere, with some slaves and cattle, and we'd not have had to worry about where our next meals were coming from for the rest of our lives.'

'Sounds all right to me,' Kari said.

'Does it?' Ulrich said, raising one eyebrow. 'You'd have been bored out of your minds after a year or two. And none of us would ever have been much more than a *bondi*, a freeborn farmer. Still at the mercy of the whims of kings and jarls. Still with the burden of their taxes and still having to fight in their armies.'

'There is no place on Middle Earth where you would not have to do that, Ulrich,' Sigurd said.

'If we were in our own realm we wouldn't have to,' Ulrich said. 'What if it was *us* who collected taxes, who decided what wars to fight, who kings and jarls came and asked us – *paid us* – to fight for them? Or even better, paid us to *not* fight for their rivals.'

'Eight of us will achieve that? We'll somehow find somewhere to set up our own kingdom?' Sigurd said with a sceptical grunt.

Ulrich made a face that suggested he thought Sigurd was being slow.

'I used Aethelstan's silver to buy those slaves,' he said. 'The silver we would have made from selling them I would have used to buy silk – Thord says it is plentiful here because of the Serk trade routes. That I'd have taken home. Wealthy people at home pay gold for silk. By the time I'd sold it I'd have tripled our wealth. Then I'd have looked for somewhere in a lawless, disputed realm: a land of war where kings or jarls have no power. You saw what it was like in north-west Francia. Or beyond Hedeby to the east. My plan was to buy or build a *borg*, a fortress, there and then we would have used the crafts in warfare we have honed over years to get *really* rich. We would recruit warriors from all over. We would train them so they are the best. Each one of you would be *hirdmen*, in command of your own company of warriors. Kings would come to us and pay us gold to add power to their armies. We would grow ever more wealthy and more powerful until we were as kings ourselves!'

The little man spoke through half-clenched teeth. His eyes had become glassy as if he stared at something very far away. There was silence for a few moments.

'So that was your plan,' Sigurd said at last. 'It's a pity it didn't work out.'

'It still could!' Ulrich said. 'We just need to find more silver. That's why I'm leader of this company. I have vision.'

'He's certainly having visions,' Kari said with a wink to the others. 'Are you sure you haven't been eating the holy mushrooms, Ulrich?'

'You can laugh,' Ulrich said. 'But I have no doubt this is inspiration sent to me by the All Father.'

Einar's heart was bursting with questions. When they were

underway and the imperial warriors at a safe enough distance that he was sure they could not overhear, he approached Surt, hoping he was not already asleep.

'You're from here, Surt,' Einar said. 'Maybe you can explain all this.'

'Firstly,' Surt said, opening one eye, 'I am not *from* here. I was born far to the south of here, beyond the great sand sea. But yes, I spent a lot of time in Al-Andalus. What is it you want to know?'

'Why do these people call themselves Romans?' Einar said. 'The Roman Empire fell hundreds of years ago. You said yourself Rome is just ruins now.'

Surt grunted, shaking his head a little.

'The ignorance of you barbarians never ceases to amaze me,' he said. 'But it is an incredible story. Let me enlighten you.'

Fourteen

Surt turned onto his side and raised himself up on one elbow. 'When the Romans had conquered the entire world,' he said, 'they realised such a realm was too big for one man to rule, even with the senate and their civil service organisation to help him. So they split the empire in two. There was an eastern part and a western part. There were two emperors, two armies, two capital cities: Rome in the west and in the east they founded a new city: Constantinopolis. It was created to be a new Rome, every bit as grand and impressive as the eternal city herself. And so it became. There is nowhere in the world like it. Your people call it Miklagard: the great city.'

'Miklagard?' Einar said. 'But that is home of the King of the Greeks.'

Surt shook his head again.

'That is what you barbarians call him, but he would not be too happy with that title if you called him that,' he said. 'The western Roman Empire fell. It collapsed under the weight of its own corruption and the waves of barbarian invasions that beset it. It is long gone and all it left behind was ruins. But the eastern empire continued and still exists today. They still rule half of the lands from here to the edge of the world. He may speak the Greek tongue, but the man who sits on the throne in Constantinopolis, Constantine the Seventh, calls himself the Emperor of the Roman Empire, the successor of the Caesars.'

'Really?' Einar said.

'He's every bit as rich and powerful as them,' Surt said. 'And if you think the ancient Caesars excelled in plotting, double dealing and treachery, their descendants in Constantinopolis outdo them in that. The place is a snake pit of plots, schemes and backstabbing. The old name for the city – Byzantium – has become a byword for double dealing, hidden murders and intrigue. Each emperor in turn lies, cheats and kills his way to the throne. He spends a few years murdering anyone who looks like they might betray him, then sooner or later someone he trusts kills him and takes his turn with the imperial crown.'

'How do you know all this lore?' Einar asked.

'I was in the army of the emir, remember?' Surt said. 'Our people crossed from Africa to what is now Al-Andalus. We took land by the sword but we are the descendants of the great caliphes of Egypt. The empire was our enemy. For centuries we have fought for who rules the lands around the sea. And the most important thing in any war is to know your enemy. Apart from that, my people preserve the wisdom of the past. We learn from it because it makes us better people today. The library in Cordoba is one of the finest in the world. Anyone can go there and find the wisdom of all the Romans and Greeks, as well as our own history.'

'I've heard of the library of Cordoba,' Ulrich said. He too had begun to listen in to the conversation. 'I heard it would make a good bonfire.'

He grinned. Surt scowled.

'And that is why you Norsemen will always live in benighted ignorance,' he said.

'We're not all as churlish as Ulrich, Surt,' Affreca, who had been listening to their conversation, said. 'Or as ignorant as Einar. Most of us know of Miklagard, Rome and Al-Andalus. Our forefathers and relatives have sailed there.'

'Mine went to all three,' Skar said. 'And burned and raided everywhere on the way.'

He and Ulrich chuckled.

'If these are the sworn enemies of your people and you're now their prisoner...' Einar said. 'If they are as dangerous a folk as you say, then this is risky for you.'

'Only as long as they don't know who I am,' Surt said. 'This is not the frozen north, lad. A black-skinned man is not that unusual a sight here. For all they know I am an imperial citizen.'

'Are we prisoners?' Affreca interjected. 'I thought we were now hired swords?'

'Why did they take our weapons away then?' Einar said.

He felt a chill at the memory of the liquid fire that had shot from the galea to consume Thord, his men and his ship.

'That fire weapon,' Einar said. 'What witchcraft was that?'

'That was Sea Fire, lad,' Surt said. 'Sometimes called Sticky Fire or Greek Fire. It's the secret weapon of the empire. It's why they still rule half the Great Middle Sea.'

'I can see why.' Einar said, remembering the jet of burning liquid that had set the very sea ablaze. 'How can you fight a weapon like that?'

'It's very hard to,' Surt said. 'The empire owes many victories to Sea Fire.'

'My great-grandfather was part of a viking fleet that raided the Great Middle Sea many years ago,' Kari said. 'They were beaten in the end by the Sticky Fire. Fifty ships left Norway. Only six returned.'

'How does it work?' Einar asked.

'If I knew that, lad, I would be sitting on the imperial throne myself,' Surt said. 'It's the most closely guarded secret in the world. No one knows how it's made or how they get it to squirt like that. If my people knew how it was made, we would rule all of the lands around the Great Middle Sea and the empire would be no more.'

'So despite all your libraries and wisdom you still have not worked it out?' Ulrich said with a sneer.

'My people know how to make devices that will explode into fire,' Surt said. 'I know how myself from my time in the army of the emir. However, the devices must be thrown, or launched from a catapult. Both ways are highly dangerous and the man casting the devices is as likely to end up on fire as the enemy he is casting it at. The trick is creating a wick for them that will burn itself just long enough before setting the rest of the device alight. If the wick burns too fast, the device will blow up in the hands of or too near the thrower. If it burns too long the enemy has time to catch it and throw it back. However if you are up against an imperial *siphōn* before you can get close enough to throw your device, the siphōnarioi will have hosed you down with their own Sea Fire.

'You see: the advantage the empire has is not just the secret of what makes their liquid fire burn, it's combined with the distance they can shoot it out of the siphōns without them blowing up into flames themselves.'

'You told us that your people know so much,' Einar said. 'You boast about how all the wisdom of the ancients are in the library of the emir. How come you haven't worked out how to build one of those siphōns?'

'We've tried many times,' Surt said. 'But all have blown up as soon as they try to pump the explosive liquid through it. We just cannot work out how it gets set on fire without setting the liquid still inside ablaze as well.'

'With such a powerful weapon I could take back Orkney,' Einar said. He turned to Affreca. 'Then you'd have to marry me.' He winked at her.

'What's all this?' Ulrich said, a bemused half-frown creasing his brow.

'Nothing, Ulrich,' Affreca said. 'Einar is just blethering about things that will never happen, as usual.'

'I am surprised that such a small vessel carried the fire, though,' Surt said. 'But then there is a strategos on it as well. Thord was indeed unlucky to try to attack that particular ship.'

'What is a strategos?' Einar said.

'That tall man in the blue cloak was one,' Surt said. 'It's one of the highest military ranks in the empire. A strategos is the commander of an army. Or a navy. He's a very powerful man.'

'What's he doing scurrying around the sea in a little ship?' Ulrich said. His eyes narrowed as he considered the question.

'I was wondering that too,' Surt said.

'Where is our new friend?' Skar looked around. 'How is the Fish doing?'

Fisk was lurking a little way off from everyone, awkward and unsure of himself.

'Fine,' he said.

'Don't get too comfortable,' Ulrich said. 'You're a lucky man to be here. Remember that. This company are the best of the best. Every single person in it has proven their right to be here by their prowess and being better than most at what they do. You have yet to do that.'

'If you lot are so great,' Fisk said, 'how come you've been prisoners twice in as many days?'

Recognising his cheek, most of the others glared warning looks in his direction. Fisk dropped his head.

'We're still alive though,' Ulrich said. 'And that's the difference between us and your own crew, who are now at the bottom of the ocean.'

'I thought you Odin fanatics were obsessed with gaining a glorious death?' Fisk said. His head was still down and his voice not much more than a petulant mumble, but Einar realised the man was one of those folk who could not take being put down and would always have his say.

'We're not afraid of death,' Ulrich said. 'We'd just prefer to keep on living. If death is the only option then we'll take it, and Odin will welcome us to his great feasting Hall of Valour, where we shall sit among heroes and drink the night away. But until then we'll go on staying alive and causing chaos. There's too much to be done here on Middle Earth. Odin needs heroes for the final battle at the end of the world, Ragnarök, yes, but in the meantime he has much work for us in the here and now.'

'Odin's work?' Fisk said with a grunt. 'Isn't one of his names *Bǫlverkr*: evil worker? Is that what you pride yourself in? Is that what you're so good at?'

It was a foolish taunt and unnecessary, but Einar knew already that the man could not help himself.

'Are you a Christian?' Ulrich narrowed his eyes.

'No.' Fisk pushed his lower lip out again and grasped the metal hammer pendant that hung around his neck by a leather strap. 'I'm Thor's man. My God is a decent, straightforward fellow. The sort you could have a drink and a laugh with without worrying what he's really up to behind your back.'

Ulrich's lip curled into its habitual sneer. He turned his head and Einar knew he would have spat had he not been in the middle of the deck.

'*Odin takes the noblemen who fall in death*,' Ulrich said, quoting the old lore. '*And Thor takes the slaves*.'

'I wonder what work this Roman Norseman Harald has lined up for us,' Skar said. 'I doubt he and his men are just taking us for a pleasant cruise of the Middle Sea.'

'We'll just have to wait to find out,' Ulrich said.

Fifteen

'There was a time when the Great Middle Sea was known as the Roman Lake,' Araltes – or Harald – said. 'Every country around it was part of the empire and the imperial navy kept it safe for traders and travellers. Anyone who tried to disrupt the peace was dealt with quickly. Julius Caesar himself spent time hunting pirates and crucified hundreds of them. That was a long time ago, however.'

He stood on the deck of the snekkja. The sun was sinking behind him, staining the sky and the sea blood red. The tall, thin strategos stood beside him, the look of disdain on his face betraying what his thoughts were on the wolfskin-clad barbarians who sat before them.

They had sailed east for two days and now, on the evening of the third, the galea had dropped anchor and come to a halt. Then the snekkja had been hauled close by the tow ropes and lashed tight to the bigger vessel. Warriors on the imperial ship set the *gangr* plank between the ships and a company of marine warriors, the strategos and Araltes tramped across onto the longship. They were accompanied by a third man who had curly black hair and a sleek beard. He was older than Einar, about the age when men start to get a few wrinkles around their eyes and some grey hairs appear in their beards. He was dressed in the same blue robes as the others from the imperial galea, but wore a leather apron like a blacksmith would wear. He had another leather garment folded under his right arm that may have been a hat of some kind.

Araltes requested the Norsemen gather round as he was ready to explain the task the strategos wanted them to do. To their delight he was accompanied by a couple of slaves laden with two large jars full of wine, which they used to fill glass drinking cups for the imperial commanders and the proffered drinking horns of Ulrich's men. The Norsemen sat down, cross-legged on the deck, while the strategos and the black-haired man remained standing.

'The Saracens – Serkir to we Northmen – first came from the south several centuries ago,' Araltes continued. 'They've steadily taken more and more territory away from the empire until now almost the entire north coast of Africa belongs to them.'

He glanced at Surt, looked like he was going to say something, but then Araltes went on.

'Then they crossed the Great Middle Sea,' he said. 'They conquered the Visigoths and took control of Hispania and most of Iberia. They've started to spread from island to island until today they are at the gates of Rome herself. Thankfully the heart of the empire is now further east, at Constantinopolis, but this situation cannot continue. The empire must begin to strike back. We are the vanguard of that.'

'One ship?' Ulrich said. 'Are you hoping to achieve much?'

'This is an imperial scout ship,' Araltes said. 'The fastest in the navy. But it does not normally have a siphōn for spraying fire. Nor would a strategos like Theoktistos here usually travel on one.'

He nodded to his superior officer, who acknowledged the gesture with a flick of his head.

'The Saracens have had many victories,' Araltes said. 'They

spread across the islands of the Middle Sea, their ships and warriors commanded by warlords of the Caliphate of Cordoba or the Fatimids of Ifriqiya in North Africa. Then they put into action a strategy of using piracy as a weapon. Trade is the lifeblood of the empire, and if its ships cannot travel the seas then trade cannot happen. The empire has less wealth and less to spend on its own navy and armies.'

'Clever,' Ulrich said. 'Perhaps Olaf the Red should have concentrated on going viking around the seas of Britain before he attacked Aethelstan.'

'Aethelstan has a strong navy too,' Einar said. 'He is one step ahead of everyone.'

Ulrich scowled.

'It was perhaps too clever a plan,' Araltes said. 'Or at least there was something the caliphes and emirs had not bargained on: human greed. Their plan came back to bite them. Their ships and warriors soon saw just how much wealth could be taken by preying on the empire's shipping, but it was all shipped back to the caliphe who was safe in Cordoba or Cairo while they took all the risks and did all the dying. It soon dawned on some of them that if they were doing all the work, they may as well keep the profits. Several of the islands began declaring caliphates of their own. Now the Great Middle Sea is dotted with these islands who are ruled by the Saracen faith but are independent pirate realms.'

'Why don't these caliphes in Cordoba and Cairo just take them back?' Skar said.

'They were hard enough to take in the first place,' Araltes said. 'And the pirate emirs have dug in and made the defences even stronger. However, we now plan to take advantage of this. Instead of facing one foe who can co-ordinate forces all across the sea and islands, there are multiple nests of pirates we can pick off one by one.'

'Wouldn't you be better starting nearer to home?' Ulrich said. 'By home I mean Miklagard – Constantinopolis – not Norway. We must be about as far as you can get from there – where we are now.'

'That was the plan, yes,' Araltes said. 'But we had to change it.'

'Few plans survive the first fight with the enemy,' Ulrich said.

'We sent out a fleet of ships, commanded by Strategos Theoktistos here,' Araltes said. 'It had many war galleys. *Dromons* they are called big three-masted vessels with two rows of oars and siphōns for shooting Sea Fire. They're much bigger than any longship you've ever seen.'

'I think we saw something like one of those ships in Mālaqah,' Einar said.

'We burned it,' Ulrich said with a smirk.

'The Saracens have dromons too,' Araltes said, nodding. 'But they don't have Sea Fire siphōns on them. We also had scout ships – fast galeas like the one alongside us now. The fleet made its way along the middle of the Great Middle Sea while the scout ships ranged all over, gathering knowledge about the islands where these pirates have made their bases. The idea was that we could then draw up a plan as to which islands could be attacked in what order. The ship sent to the island called Frumentaria, however, did not return. A second scout ship did not return either, so Strategos Theoktistos here decided to take a closer look himself. We took a larger force this time. Two dromons and three galeas to support it. Thank Christ the strategos decided to sail on one of the galeas and not the dromon.'

'Wanted to have a quick getaway if something went wrong,

did he?' Ulrich said. Einar could see the look of distaste that had crept onto Ulrich's face when Araltes spoke the name of Christ. It seemed that it was not only his name this Norseman had changed while in Miklagard.

'The island of Frumentaria is surrounded on all sides by rocks and cliffs,' Araltes continued. 'There is only one place to land ships or a force of any size and that is the main port, which is where a pirate emir has set up his fortress. We sailed into it at night, but they were ready for us. Worst of all, they had somehow got hold of Sea Fire and a siphōn to discharge it. They let us get close then incinerated our ships as they approached the harbour. The second galea and ours were lucky to be behind the others. We had time to turn and got away. They chased us but our ships were too fast for them.'

'Interesting,' Ulrich said, rubbing his chin with his forefinger and thumb. 'So the empire's secret weapon is no longer just in the hands of the empire?'

'This is a big problem,' Araltes said. 'Sea Fire is the one weapon above all that gives us an advantage over our enemies. It's saved Constantinopolis itself from being invaded at least twice. For that reason it's the empire's most closely guarded secret. If it's in the hands of our enemies, then we will no longer be able to command the Great Middle Sea.'

'One band of pirates, whether they have Sea Fire or not, cannot threaten an empire,' Ulrich said.

'Do you think if the Emir of Cordoba or Caliphe of Al-Andalus hears of this he won't want to get his hands on it?' Araltes said. 'We have news from our spies that the pirate emir is gathering a fleet for some purpose. He could already be on his way here. If the Saracens get hold of Sea Fire and discover its secret, then we will lose the advantage we have over them. Constantinopolis itself could fall!'

Ulrich looked indifferent. 'What's all this have to do with us?' he said, folding his arms.

'We are going to launch another attack,' Araltes said. 'The second galea that was with us has gone back to the main fleet and a new force should be on its way here, but if we try to take the harbour with that siphōn mounted, we will lose many ships and men. We might even fail again. And it's the only place on the island a large force can land. There are places, however, that a small band of men can go where an army can't. And if that small band are also highly trained warriors who are craftsmen in the arts of war in all types of country, then that small band could perhaps achieve what our fleet cannot. When you were foolish enough to attack us I spotted your wolf coats and the idea came to me that úlfhéðnar would be perfect for this task. I explained the unique skills you have to the strategos, and here we are. Your company could find a way onto the island and take out those siphōns, allowing our ships to get into the harbour.'

'So this isn't some grand strategy that is part of a bigger plan?' Ulrich said. 'It's something you thought up on the spur of the moment? That doesn't sound very reassuring.'

'You'll be well paid,' Araltes said. 'The wages will be sixteen pounds of gold. Each.'

Skar blew out his cheeks. Einar blinked. Sigurd and Kari looked excited.

'That's a lot of gold,' Ulrich said. 'Which means it's a very dangerous task.'

'Almost suicidal I'd say,' Araltes said, his face splitting in a broad grin.

'Wait, wait,' Fisk said. 'I'm not one of these heroes. I just happened to be on this ship because the alternatives were drowning or burning. If this is a one-way trip then I don't want to be part of it.'

'That's your choice,' Araltes said. 'All of your choice actually. Of course, the alternative is...'

He pointed to the cross-beam of the longship, set his head to one side and stuck his tongue out the side of his mouth while mimicking pulling a noose above his head with his right hand.

'Ah,' Fisk said. 'It seems I might have a bit of heroism in me after all.'

'Good man,' Araltes said. 'I will go with you, as well as Diogenes here.'

He laid a hand on the black-haired Roman's shoulder.

'Wait, we don't take passengers,' Ulrich said. 'It's bad enough having the Fish with us. Why do we need you two as well?'

'The siphōn is our most secret weapon,' Araltes said. 'How it works is a very closely guarded secret. Only an elite number of men in the imperial navy are trained in how they work. They are called siphōnarioi. Diogenes here is one of them. We will need him if we get to the harbour so we can ensure when we leave they are not working and not repairable.'

'And you?' Ulrich said.

'I am there to make sure you don't decide to just run away and join the pirates,' Araltes said.

'On your own?' Ulrich scoffed. 'You might be a big man here with the Roman army round you, but even you must know that on that island and alone with us you won't stand a chance. Come on. What's your real reason for coming along?'

'You're more clever than you look, Ulrich,' Araltes said, pursing his lips.

'It's a look I work hard at,' Ulrich quipped.

'Well I said that Sea Fire is our most secret weapon,' Araltes said. 'That goes for how it is made and where it is stored. Only those involved in the process, the emperor and a few very senior state officials know about it. Diogenes here knows how to shoot it from a siphōn but has no idea how it's manufactured. My job will be to try to find out how these pirates got their hands on the most closely guarded secret in the empire.'

'So when do we get started?' Ulrich asked.

'We should be near the island by morning,' Araltes said. 'Until then, everyone should get a good night's sleep. It could be our last.'

Sixteen

The rising sun did indeed reveal an island on the horizon. It sat alone in the midst of the sea, rising from the waters in sheer, rocky cliffs with little or no beach at their feet. As the bleeding-red light of dawn faded into glaring sunshine Einar could see that the cliffs were of a white rock that reflected the light, giving the island a strange, otherworldly look as if it were glowing amid the sapphire blue of the sea.

'If ever there was a place such as *Ljósálfheimr*,' Einar said, staring ahead at the island, 'then this must be it.'

'The home of the light elves?' Skar asked. He stood beside Einar and had overheard his awed remark. 'Let's hope so, lad. They say Álfheimr is the highest of the three heavens. If that is where we are heading, then this should be a real treat.'

From the mild sarcasm of his tone, it was clear the big prowman thought the exact opposite.

Their captors had returned the Wolf Coats' weapons and arms and allowed them to take their pick of any other equipment they might need that was available on the galea. Now each member of the company had good weapons, armour and a leather pack they could strap across their back, which carried their gear as well as dried food – fish and meat – to keep them going until they could forage or steal other sustenance. They each had a skin bag filled with water, but in the heat of the day it would not last long. The main imperative when they found a way onshore would be to find a source of fresh water.

Fisk, who had lost everything with Thord's ship, had availed of the armoury on the imperial ship and now had two short francesca throwing axes tucked into his belt, as well as a long-handled, bearded battleaxe he rested across his shoulder.

'Good choice of weapon,' Araltes commented, patting the handle of his own axe.

The galea cut the snekkja free and the ships parted company. As the imperial ship turned south to sail away, the strategos stood on the stern, his right arm raised in a salute that Araltes returned. Then the snekkja set a course west and sailed into the night. The next morning they awoke and Frumentaria was on the horizon.

'The main town where the pirate emir has his fortress is on the north-east of the island,' Araltes said. 'We should sail south-west to avoid it and see if we can find anywhere to get ashore, well away from watching eyes.'

'All the same, I'd like a look at where those fire spouts are,' Ulrich said. Araltes shot a dubious look in Ulrich's direction.

'Are you sure about that?' he asked. 'What if they see us?'

'We won't get too close,' Ulrich said. 'We'll stay far enough out that if anyone comes after us, we'll have too much of a head start for them to catch us. I'd at least like to get an idea of where the place is.'

Roan turned the ship and they began to sail around the island, keeping well away from the shore. After a while the cliffs got lower until they merged with a jumble of buildings, all looking like they were built from the same white stone as the island was made from.

'You've got the sharpest eyes of all of us,' Ulrich said to Kari. 'Get up the mast and see if you can get a better look.'

The viking with the runes tattooed on his face shinned up the mast to the cross-beam. He stayed there, peering at the town for a time, then wrapped his arms and legs round the mast and slid back down to the deck.

'I could see there is a tower that looks like some sort of fort maybe,' Kari said. 'And what looks like two stone-built piers that meet in a harbour entrance, just like at Mālaqah. Behind that there are the masts of ships. Many ships, by the look of it.'

There was no movement from the harbour and Ulrich directed Roan to sail on to the north, to give the impression to anyone who might be watching that they just happened to be passing on their way to southern Francia or Al-Andalus. Then, as the island was beginning to slide towards the horizon again, they turned west and began tracking the coast.

When they were well out of sight of the town, Roan turned the steering oar and the snekkja headed closer in to the island. The coast was once again rocks and cliffs, but now they could see that the land at the top of the steep sides of the island was covered with low green trees that were a contrast to the white of the rocks. Beyond, in the interior of the island, some gentle hills rose, which were likewise covered in green trees.

Ulrich went to the prow and began scanning the shoreline as it passed. Here and there were small strips of sandy beach, but nowhere big enough to land the snekkja. The sun was now past the middle of the sky and starting its descent. After sailing some more, Ulrich raised his arm. The others gathered around him at the prow.

'Over there,' Ulrich said, pointing towards what looked like a crack in the cliff face. 'We'll see if Roan can get closer. Get the sail down. Someone keep a watch here: Einar. Everyone else to the oars.'

Einar took Ulrich's place as he went to the stern to explain to the skipper where he wanted him to go. Einar could see the sceptical look on the Fleming's wizened face, but nevertheless the steersman guided the ship further shoreward. The rest of the crew furled the sail then took their places on the oar benches and began propelling the ship towards the land.

As they got closer, Einar saw that the crack in the cliff was actually a narrow gully or ravine. The sea gushed in and out of it and it was just about wide enough for the snekkja to slide into, but once in there, there would be no room to turn. If they went in, he had no idea how they would get back out.

Ulrich bade Roan to sail straight towards the gap. The sea was mostly clear and an incredible blue, but around the base of the cliffs it churned to foam. Amidst it Einar could see rocks poking up from beneath the surface, any one of which could tear a hole in the hull of the longship if they rowed over it. He pointed his arms left and right in the directions of any he saw, hoping that Roan would be able to ensure the ship missed them.

To Einar's astonishment it appeared that Ulrich did indeed intend to take the ship right into the gap in the cliff. 'Oars in!' Ulrich shouted as they neared the entrance.

Those rowing pulled their oars in and fell silent. Einar held his breath.

Then a wave caught them and propelled them forwards and through the entrance of the ravine. The cross-beam banged off the left wall of the canyon and swung round to hang parallel to the deck. There was a grinding of wood and the right side of the ship scraped against the opposite wall, sending shivers down Einar's spine. The bright sunshine disappeared as the high sides of the ravine cast the ship into the cool shadow that filled it along with the water.

Einar looked ahead and saw the ravine was short and narrowed to a point where it came to a dead end. There was a spit of bright white sand, however, that came from the end a little way out into the water. Roan had no choice but to guide the ship onto that and with a soft grinding sound it came to rest, the point of the prow a few strides from the point at which the two canyon walls met.

'It's almost like she was made for this ravine,' Ulrich said. 'She fits it like a hand in a glove.'

'But how do we get back out?' Araltes said. The surrounding rock echoed his voice, as did the sloshing of the sea as it flowed in and out around the ship.

'We can push her,' Ulrich said. 'What's wrong? Worried about getting your fancy uniform wet?'

They looked around. The walls towered above them, sheer cliffs of white stone that went up, higher than the mast of the ship, to eventually open into bright blue sky.

'Let's not just stand here all day,' Ulrich said. 'Skar: get the ropes.'

The big man went to one of the storage chests on the snekkja and hauled out a thick rope, one of the pieces of extra gear they had taken from the galea the night before.

'We're going up the wall aren't we?' Einar said, his heart sinking a little at the prospect.

'We could try that trick Abd al-Malik used to get us out of prison in Mālaqah,' Sigurd suggested. 'Get Affreca to shoot an arrow up to the top with the rope attached to it.'

'To work, that would require us to have someone at the top,' Skar said. He sounded a little disappointed that one of his crew would suggest something so stupid. 'No. Someone will have to climb up and take the rope with them. Then haul everyone else up behind him.'

'That's a hard climb,' Araltes said, looking up at the towering rock walls. 'It won't be easy.'

'Yes,' Skar said. 'But we're lucky enough to have one of the best climbers in Iceland among us. A lad who has scaled much higher cliffs just to collect birds' eggs.'

He clapped Einar on the shoulder.

Seventeen

Einar groaned inwardly. He had expected this task to come his way from the moment he realised there would be no other way out of the canyon.

Skar was right: he was good at climbing. It was one of the three essential crafts for all Icelandic lads: how to play *knattleikr* on the ice, how to wrestle and how to climb. In a land where every scrap of food needs to be wrestled from nature just to survive, birds' eggs were an essential source of nourishment and the cliffs that swarmed with nesting seabirds were a rich supply. The only way to get them was to climb, and Einar had been one of the best.

Looking up at the ravine, Einar judged that he had climbed harder walls. The cliffs at Drangey were much higher and had overhangs so frightening the lads who climbed them sometimes felt that their balls had crawled up inside their bodies. However, these white rocks were cracked and flaking in places and looked like they might be prone to crumble if too much weight was put on them.

'Remember how you got us out of that stone prison tower in Scotland, Einar?' Skar said. 'Well, if you could show us some of those skills again it would be great. We're all behind you, lad.'

'I had all my fingers then,' Einar said, holding up his maimed right hand. As he did so, however, the thought came to him that this could be an advantage.

Einar pulled on his fighting glove, fastening the straps tight around his wrist. He slung the coiled rope over his right shoulder then looked upwards, assessing the rock walls for finger and footholds. He spotted a protruding stone an arm's length above his head and knew this would be the start of his route up. There was little point in delaying things further, so Einar took a deep breath in and out through his nose, reached up and started to climb.

The metal hooks of his glove, designed to replace the grip of his missing finger on a sword hilt, acted like a metal claw, which he anchored into the rock face then hauled himself up after it. At first the going was easy enough, certainly in comparison to some of the more difficult cliffs at home in Iceland. The white rock was weathered by the heat and sea. It was chipped and cracked, offering plenty of nooks, crannies and cracks to place toes or grasp with fingers. The glove's hooks allowed him to dig hand holes into the cliff that were not there without it.

It was not long before he was several times his own height up the wall and above the deck of the ship. It was then that his nerves began to make his stomach churn. He had the rope over his shoulder but there was nothing to stop his fall if he slipped. If he lost his grip or foothold, he would go hurtling down towards the deck and painful, serious injury would be the inevitable result.

The higher he went, the more the possibility of injury turned into the risk of death. As he pulled himself up the rock face, he tried to put that thought to the back of his mind. As he began to move above the shadow of the cavern, the heat of the sun started to beat down on him and the sweat already provoked by his efforts and nerves flowed freely. The rock was indeed crumbling, and while that gave lots of purchase, it also left pointed edges that dug into his knees or forearms, adding to the discomfort of his muscles that were already screaming from the effort. The straps of his fighting glove, pulled extra tight to stop it slipping off, dug into the flesh of his right forearm and he started to feel the prickly sensation in his hand that told him it was short of blood.

He pushed himself on. His shoulders and arms burned, but the ends of his fingers that clung to the rock like iron pincers had become numb, as were his toes. This concerned him. If he could not feel properly, he might make a mistake and grab something that could not hold his weight.

When he was about two-thirds of the way to the top he stopped for a moment both to rest his burning shoulders and thighs and to wipe his left hand on his tunic to make sure it did not become slick with sweat and cause his downfall.

He stared at the rock, only a hand's breadth from his face. It was his entire world now. He was alone on the rock face. He took deep breaths, wondering for the first time if he really could make it to the top.

The memory surfaced in his mind of Helgi Asbjornsson, the wiry lad from back home with an uncanny ability for climbing. He was so good some thought a spider had crept into his mother's mouth as she slept on the night he was conceived. He had always collected more eggs than everyone else, which he did because he was able to climb higher and reach more difficult parts of the cliffs than all the other lads.

Helgi's luck had run out, however. Climbing near Hafnarberg, his foot had slipped on a wet rock and he went plummeting towards the rocky shore below. He should have died but by some cruel whim of the Norns he survived, but for the rest of his life he was a bent, lame cripple who huddled beside the fire in his father's farmhouse, unable to look after himself. No woman would ever marry him.

Einar knew if he fell off the cliff now, he would drop to the deck of the ship and – if he was lucky – spend the rest of his life like Helgi. If you could call that lucky. The thought made his heart thump faster and he realised it was getting hard to breathe. Sweat was now running free down his back and face, stinging his eyes and soaking his shirt. He closed his eyes and breathed in and out through his nose in the way he had in the prison, forcing his heart to calm from a frantic pounding to something at least closer to normal.

'Get a move on, lad.' Ulrich's voice drifted up from below. 'We haven't got all day.'

Einar opened his eyes. Anger flared in his heart.

'I'd like to see you up here, Ulrich,' he said through gritted teeth. He added *you bastard* under his breath.

Spurred on by the taunt, Einar began moving again. In a few moments he was into a rhythm, reaching with one hand, pushing with the opposite leg, moving up a bit, grabbing a higher hold with the opposite hand and pushing from his other foot. It was not long before he got to the top.

'I knew that would get him moving,' he heard Ulrich saying to Skar.

Einar flopped to the ground. The cost of the effort, made even greater under the hot sun, had taken its toll. He lay on his back, chest heaving, as he tried to regain control of his breathing.

As he lay, his ears filled with the rhythmic rasping noise that he had heard several times when they had come ashore on these southern realms. Surt had told him it was the sound of countless insects rubbing their legs together. Einar wondered how they all knew how to do it at the same time and suspected it might actually be down to elves or other tricksters.

After a short while of staring up at the hot blue sky, Einar saw a bird. It was a large predator, a hawk or similar. Its long wings were outstretched as it sailed on the warm air, watching the ground below for prey. The sight of it reminded Einar that he was now on enemy land, and he could not just lie around all day. This was added to by the shouts that now echoed out of the cavern from the others still on the ship.

He got back up, his breathing now nearly back to normal, though his heart still pounded more than usual.

Taking the heavy rope from his shoulder he looked around. He had no intention of wrapping his end of the rope round himself and trying to hold the weight of the others climbing it. He needed something to tie it to. The top of the cliff was bare scrubland – dust, gravel and bare rock – but it was surrounded by low woods made up of short, prickly-looking green trees. They looked a little like the pine trees of the north except, instead of growing tall and pointed these seemed to be squat, as if wizened and stunted by growing up in the blazing sun. He looped the end of the rope around the trunk of one of them then jogged back to the top of the ravine.

With a shout of warning to those below, he dropped the rope down the cliff, watching it uncoil all the way to the deck of the grounded longship below. Kari grabbed it, wrapped it around his middle and prepared to start hauling himself up the rock face.

Something caught Einar's eye and he glanced out to sea.

A ship was coming around the end of the island. It had two triangular sails like the imperial galea and was about the same size, with a high, pointed prow. There were people on the deck.

'Wait,' Einar shouted down to Kari. 'There's a ship coming. Keep quiet.'

He dropped to the ground, lying flat on his stomach, hoping that he was hidden from view by the angle of the cliff.

He raised his head as much as he dared so he could watch what was going on without exposing too much of himself. He saw the new ship, its prow crashing through the waves, as it tracked the coastline. The people on the deck were all gathered on the landward side. He could see several of them were shading their eyes with their hands. They were looking for something.

Einar wondered if they knew about the ravine the longship had sailed into. The snekkja was completely inside it and hidden from view, but if the newcomers were aware of it and they decided to sail in, Ulrich and the others would be trapped like rats at the far end. Perhaps he should try to get them up? Then again, the noise and movement was bound to attract attention. He decided instead to stay still and watch.

The ship slid by, perhaps eight or nine lengths away from the shore. Einar could see the men on the deck. Their skin was dark like most in this realm and they had swords sheathed at their sides. Some were dressed like the warriors he had seen in Mālaqah and some wore different clothing. Some had helmets and some did not. The most obvious thing about them was that unlike the imperial warriors who were all dressed in the same uniforms, each person on the ship looked different.

They scanned the cliffs with intent gazes and, as the ship drew level with where he was, Einar ducked his head back down just in case he was spotted. They were some distance away but some sharp-eyed individual might just have noticed Einar's sweat-clogged hair sticking up above the rocks. Ulrich had taught him that the best way to ensure someone could not see you was if you could not see them. He kept his head down.

There followed long, agonising moments as he lay in the hot

dust, ears straining for cries of surprise or excitement from the ship that would indicate they had seen something. Would they, like Ulrich, notice the narrow ravine the Wolf Coats had sailed into? Ulrich had, but then again this new ship was further out than where the snekkja had been when Ulrich spotted it.

When no sounds came that would suggest they had been seen, Einar raised his head once more to see the ship had passed on and was sailing on down the coast.

He went back to the rope and peered down the rock face to where Kari still stood, ready to climb, looking up with an expectant expression on his face.

'Come on,' Einar said. 'Hurry.'

One by one the rest of the company wrapped the rope around themselves and either hauled or walked their way up the cliff until they all stood at the top.

Einar told them about the ship.

'I would swear they were looking for us,' he said.

'But how would they know we were here?' Affreca said.

'They might have spotted us when we sailed past the town,' Araltes said. 'I told you that was foolish.'

'We were too far away and heading north anyway,' Ulrich said with a scowl. 'And that lot didn't spot us anyway thanks to that ravine. It's the perfect hiding place.'

'We were lucky to find it,' Einar said.

'It's not luck,' Ulrich said. 'Odin led us here. Now let's see if he can't find us some water, then get us across this island and into that pirate fort.'

Eighteen

The company scouted through the woods of stunted pine trees for a time until they came across some animal tracks.

Knowing these often led to water, they followed them for a bit. From the coast the land flowed up towards a low hill that appeared to cover most of the centre of the island, at least this end of it anyway. The hillside was also covered in trees and scrub, and these provided welcome relief from the baking sun. It was still hot though, and the warmth brought a heady aroma from the carpet of pine needles that coated the forest floor. The insects kept up their constant racket, but apart from them the woods held the eerie quietness that all pine forests – even this strange, foreign one – guarded.

After a while of trekking they came to a stream that bubbled over a rocky bed. Its water tumbled down from the hill towards the sea, and the Wolf Coat crew fell down beside it and slurped greedy mouthfuls of the running water. It was far from the cool, clear waters of a Norwegian or Icelandic mountain stream, but compared to the warm, brackish water they had been drinking on the ship it was delightful.

When they had sated their thirst they filled their water skins and prepared to set off again.

'We will climb that hill,' Ulrich said, pointing upwards. 'We should get a better view of the island from up there.'

The others sighed. They all had guessed that Ulrich would want to go up the hill but had been quietly hoping the thought of trekking uphill in the heat would put even their wiry little leader off. That was not the case.

'I am not one for sneaking around the undergrowth – you know that, Ulrich,' Roan said. 'I'm a skipper and that's what I'm good at. If you don't mind, I'll go back and watch the ship.'

'It could be dangerous, Roan,' Ulrich said, pursing his lips. 'What if those fellows in that other ship come back for a closer look? We won't be around to help you.'

'Don't worry,' Roan said. 'If that happens I'll find somewhere to hide. But you will need to find another ship.'

Ulrich nodded. Einar was jealous that the skipper would get to stay behind and laze around in the sun, but it made sense. He was an excellent steersman but he was most at home on a ship and knew none of the sly crafts the Wolf Coats had perfected in stealing across enemy lands without being detected.

He wondered about Araltes and the Greek, Diogenes, as well. Would they be as big a liability as Roan would?

As Roan headed back towards the coast, the rest of the company began climbing up the hillside. It was not exactly a mountain, but in the crushing heat it was not long before their breathing was laboured and sweat was once more dripping from their foreheads.

As they climbed, Einar spotted glimpses of something white through the trees ahead. After a while they came to a clearing in the woods, and they all saw that on top of the hill, rising above the treetops, was a tower made of the same white stones as the cliffs that surrounded the island. There were two narrow windows in the wall, the sort designed for defenders inside to shoot arrows from without exposing themselves to danger. The top of the tower was crenellated, which enforced the impression that it was some sort of fortress, albeit a small one.

'Forts mean warriors.' Ulrich said. 'Kari, you go up ahead and take a closer look at that tower, will you? Check if it's safe for us all to go up there. We will wait here. Surt, you go with him.'

'Why me?' Surt said. 'I'm not one of your Wolf Coats, remember. If things had been different in Mālaqah I would not even be here.'

'If things had been different in Mālaqah none of us would be here,' Ulrich said. 'We'd all be rich and enjoying the taverns as we counted our silver. But they weren't and we're not. So you're still a member of this crew and while you are you'll do what I say.'

Surt shrugged.

'Apart from all that you understand the Serk tongue,' Ulrich said. 'If anyone is up there maybe you can learn something useful.'

Kari and Surt set off towards the hilltop while the others found shelter and rested on the forest floor.

'So he *is* a Moor,' Araltes said, as he watched Surt disappear into the undergrowth. 'I thought as much. You realise these people are enemies of the empire?'

'He's spent most of the last thirty winters a slave of Harald of Norway,' Ulrich said. 'And from the way his people treated him in Mālaqah, I would not say he is exactly on their side.'

'All the same,' Araltes said. 'I'll be keeping an eye on him.'

'You can keep as many eyes as you want on whoever you want,' Skar said. 'But if you lift one finger towards any of our crew, I'll deal with you. Got that?'

Araltes made a face and sat down on the pine needles.

It struck Einar how the heat was making everyone tetchy, even the usually mild-mannered Surt who was supposed to be used to it. As if the tension of being on a strange island with potential danger all around was not enough, they would have to be careful they did not end up at each other's throats as well. He realised the others must have sensed this too, for everyone sat waiting in silence, as if wary of provoking one of the others through a careless word.

After a while Einar began to get bored, however.

'How long have you served the Romans?' he asked Araltes.

'Seven years, lad,' the Greek Norseman said. 'I was a youngster like yourself when I came south looking for fame and gold. And I found it. Miklagard is the greatest city in the world. There is nothing like it in the north. There is much opportunity there for a man with sharp wits and the heart to work hard. I've gone from a foot soldier to second in command to the strategos and assigned to the *Scrinium Barbarorum*, the Office of Barbarians. The strategos is a trusted adviser of the emperor himself.'

'What's the Office of Barbarians?' Einar said.

Araltes tapped the side of his nose. 'It's a secret arm of the empire that, shall we say, *keeps an eye* on our enemies,' he said with a wink. 'And if I told you more than that I'd have to kill you.'

'Keep your voices down,' Ulrich said. 'If there are warriors up in that tower, there might be more in the woods around us.'

As if in response to his words the sound of a scuffled footstep came from the trees nearby. The company tensed, hands dropping to weapon hilts. They relaxed when they realised that the sound came from Surt and Kari returning.

Their relaxation did not last long, however. Both men were out of breath and their expressions serious.

'Well?' Ulrich demanded.

'There are warriors up there all right,' Kari said. 'The trees go right up to nearly the top of the hill, so we were able to get quite close. There were four men at the bottom of the tower and I spotted one on the top.'

'Five?' Araltes said. 'Men like you could take that many easily.'

'And what if someone is sent to relieve them?' Ulrich said. 'And finds their dead bodies? We may as well walk right into the town and announce that we have arrived.'

'I think they may already know that,' Surt said. 'While we were watching another group of warriors arrived. They looked like scouts or skirmishers. I could not hear everything they said, but the men in the fort were definitely directing them, giving them areas to search and asking for reports. I heard them say there were many hunting parties out across the island.'

'Looking for us?' Ulrich said.

'I didn't hear specific mention of a crew of Norsemen,' Surt said. 'But they are definitely looking for someone. Who else could it be?'

There were several moments of silence. Then Ulrich broke it with a sharp intake of breath. 'Well we can forget about going to the top of the hill for now anyway,' he said. 'If there are men out searching for us, there's no point in us wandering around in broad daylight making it easier for them to find us. We'll go back to the ship and hide there until nightfall.'

Nineteen

Once back at the ship, Einar expressed his desire not to have to climb back up the cliff with the rope so they left it in place and settled down in the shade of the trees. Ulrich divided them into pairs, sending Affreca and Kari a little way south along the cliff, Wulfhelm and Sigurd northwards along the cliff, and Einar and Araltes a little inland to the east. That way they could spot anyone approaching before they landed right on the rest of them and the ship. He, Skar, Surt, Starkad, the other Roman and Roan relaxed in the heat, promising to begin rotating those on watch as the day wore on.

Einar and Araltes found a hollow in the pine-carpeted forest floor and settled down on their stomachs in it. That way they could peer up and keep an eye out for anyone coming.

The heat was oppressive but they could not sleep, knowing that the rest of the crew depended on them keeping watch. As the day wore on, however, with the hot air and the constant, endless drone of the insects, Einar caught himself nodding off twice.

He needed to do something to keep himself awake. Ulrich had ordered those on watch to stay silent, so as not to alert anyone approaching to their presence, but all the same Einar judged if he kept his voice to a low whisper it would probably be fine.

'Tell me more about Miklagard,' he said to Araltes. 'How did it come to be so great? How vast is its empire? Is it really as great as the Roman Empire was?'

'Lad,' Araltes said with a bemused frown. 'Miklagard – Constantinopolis rather – and its empire *is* the Roman Empire. When the western part fell to the barbarians, this half continued on. It's not a new empire. It's the same one as before, though now thoroughly Christian. And we are the centre of the Christian world. Constantinopolis stands as a fortress of the faith, holding back the tides of the heathens.'

'Aethelstan would approve of it, then,' Einar said.

'King Aethelstan of the Aenglisc?' Araltes said. 'What do you know of him?'

'I was once a trusted warrior of his,' Einar said with a sigh, and told him about the events of the previous two years, realising as he did so what a central role Aethelstan had played in it all. Ulrich had likened the king to a giant spider who sat in the middle of his web, a tangled weave of alliances, marriages and plots. Until now Einar had thought Aethelstan's influence stretched across the whole world. Now he realised they were all just backwards little players on the smaller game pitch, the frozen northern edges of a world that was much, much bigger, more complicated, more amazing and more dangerous than he had even imagined it to be.

'Aethelstan and his kingdom stand like a beacon amid the benighted northern heathens,' Araltes said. 'A bright flame of civilisation amid the darkness of the barbarians. You look at me askance, I see. No doubt you're wondering why I should talk so about my own homelands?'

'That did cross my mind,' Einar said. 'Don't you miss home?'

'Einar, in Constantinopolis there are race tracks, arenas, theatres,' Araltes said, his eyes taking on a faraway look. 'There are hot baths, people from all nations and from none. The knowledge of all the world is in its libraries. To say nothing of the great weather, the superb wine and the women!'

He patted Einar on the shoulder.

'By Christ, lad,' he continued. 'You've never seen women so beautiful. And I am someone there. In Norway I was just a bondi – the lowly son of a farmer. I'd never have risen further than what my father was. But in Constantinopolis I am the right-hand man of a strategos who answers to the emperor himself! I could never have done that at home.'

'And it's that sticky fire that gives the emperor his power,' Einar said. 'How is it made? Is it by witchcraft? Christian witchcraft, obviously.'

'There is no such thing as Christian witchcraft, Einar,' Araltes said, his smile fading a bit. '*Suffer not a witch to live*, the scriptures say. But as to your question I don't know. No one in the army does. It is said only the emperor knows the secret and it is passed from one on to the next.'

'What about that fellow, the siphōnarioi?' Einar said. 'I thought he was coming along because he knows how it works?'

'He knows how the siphōn works,' Araltes said. 'That is the weapon that shoots the fire. There are three parts to this secret, all closely guarded: the substance that creates the fire, the weapon that shoots it, and the man who knows how the siphōn works. Diogenes is part of a select band of men, a guild of artificers, highly skilled and sworn to secrecy, who understand how to make the fire jet from the siphōn. He is not allowed by his guild and forbidden by the emperor to reveal to anyone how it works.'

At that moment Skar and Starkad loped out of the undergrowth. Araltes started. Neither of them had even heard the others coming.

'Our turn on watch,' Skar said. 'You two can go and relax for a bit.'

Araltes and Einar strolled back to the clifftop above the cavern that hid the longship. Einar was hoping there was some sort of food on the go, as he had not eaten since that morning.

The others were indeed munching away when they got back. Ulrich had forbidden any fire. With the possibility that there were people looking for them, drifting smoke or the smell of burning wood would be as good as a banner proclaiming where they were. There were ways to conceal smoke while on the run but everything on the island was so dry a stray spark could end up setting the whole place ablaze. So it was dried fish that the others from the crew were munching on when Einar and Araltes returned.

All the same, the effect of the food seemed to have improved everyone's mood. Those back at the makeshift camp were chatting away, albeit in low voices so as not to send too much noise through the woods.

Einar saw Araltes stiffen at the sight of Surt and Diogenes, the siphōnarioi, sitting beside each other, talking and smiling. At the sight of Araltes approaching and the stern look on his face, the siphōnarioi shot to his feet, his own expression changing to a mixture of guilt and worry.

'You two understand each other?' Araltes said in a demanding tone.

'At first, no,' Surt said. 'I speak a little Greek but not much. We both, however, know the Latin tongue and found we could understand each other well in that.'

Araltes spoke some sharp words to Diogenes. It was in the Greek tongue, but it was clear he was admonishing him for talking to someone who was one of the enemy.

'Don't worry,' Surt said. 'He did not reveal any imperial secrets. We were just comparing how our lives have been similar.'

'This man is a highly paid artificer in the imperial navy,' Araltes said, looking down his nose at Surt. 'You are a Moor. A former soldier of the caliphate of the Saracen faith and a former slave. What have you in common?'

Surt stood up so he was eye to eye with Araltes.

'A slave is a slave in whatever part of the world he lives,' he said.

He went off into the woods to take his turn on watch.

Twenty

The sun melted into the sea, setting the horizon ablaze with blood-red fire. This soon died away and stars began to blink into view in the blue-black sky above.

Einar was amazed at how quickly night fell in these southern realms. At home in Iceland in the summer, the days were long and the evenings dragged on towards midnight as the sun seemed reluctant to leave. Even when it finally sank from view it left an afterglow that lingered on for a long time. In midsummer the sun did not set at all. Here in the lands around the Great Middle Sea the sun dipped towards the horizon early and then was gone in a moment.

When darkness fell, the Wolf Coat company prepared to leave their camp. Roan was to stay behind, as was Diogenes. Neither were trained in stealth crafts. Araltes announced he was coming too, which Ulrich was not happy with but he insisted, threatening that their deal was off if he was left behind, and so Ulrich relented. They left armour and anything that might clink or make noises that could give them away behind. Then they smeared their faces and any exposed flesh with dirt, took their weapons and skins full of water and slunk off through the trees.

They headed westward, skirting around the hillside to avoid the fort on top. A bright crescent moon arose, which cast some light, but beneath the trees was deep in shadow. All the same, they had trained to move quickly through dark uncertain terrain using a style of step where they swept their feet close to the ground ahead rather than plonking them down and blundering into some unseen hazard. Araltes did not have the same knowledge of the craft. He did his best to keep up but fell a few times. Even though he did not cry out, he still made an audible crashing sound as he hit the ground, which provoked disapproving glances from the Wolf Coats.

Twice they came upon companies of men. Both were easy enough to spot by a company that travelled swiftly and silently. The first was on the hillside. They had lit a fire and were gathered around it, chatting and cooking something. The Wolf Coats hung in the darkness for a time, listening to their conversation, then they slunk on into the night.

'What did they say?' Ulrich hissed to Surt when they were well enough away.

'Nothing of interest,' Surt said. 'They were grumbling about having to be out in the woods searching when everyone else was back in town enjoying themselves.'

The next company they came across announced themselves by the noise they made as they rode along a path that wound through the trees on the other side of the hill. The Wolf Coats crouched in the shadows as the cohort – eight horsemen carrying spears and with shields on their backs – rode past and on down the track.

When they had gone, Ulrich decided they should follow the track. It was the first sign of human habitation they had come across – apart from the fort it headed uphill towards – and Ulrich reasoned that it could run all the way back to the town. They did not walk straight down it but tracked alongside it, about twenty paces to the right in the undergrowth.

It had not been visible from the sea as they sailed around the north coast, but now they were on it they could see that the island was in fact formed from two islands joined by a narrow ridge. They had landed on the main part, which was roughly circular with the hill with the fort on top at its centre. To the west of this was what looked like a smaller island, a knob of land at the end of which the town lay. Between the two ran a peninsula formed from a high, narrow ridge with steep cliffs on each side that fell away into the sea.

As they neared the peninsula, the ground to the south sloped towards the sea, forming a small bay with a beach before the cliffs rose again. Ulrich signalled they should stop and they all fell to a crouch. Einar, his eyes now well used to the dark, could see Ulrich was rubbing his chin, a sure sign he was thinking about something.

It was clear what. The path continued onto the ridge but the trees became sparse and the ground rugged and bare. There would be nowhere to hide on that track and if anyone came along it they were sure to be seen. They could either chance it and run across as fast as they could, hoping they would make it, or they needed to find another way across.

He signalled towards the beach and they trekked down the slope towards the sea. It was there the Wolf Coats came across a second sign of human habitation. It looked like there had been a small settlement on the beach: a few huts and wooden fences for animal pens. There were a couple of boats: long, wide skiffs for offshore fishing that sat near the houses. They were worse for wear, with holes in the bottom. Their wood was very pale in the moonlight, and Einar saw it was dry and bleached by the sun.

The whole place was dark and silent. There was no sign of life. Holes showed where parts of the house roofs had fallen in.

The fences had collapsed in places. Lying on the ground near the door of the biggest house were jumbles of bones that had most likely once been its inhabitants.

'This must have been a fishing village,' Ulrich said, looking around. He pointed at the bones. 'It seems the locals have not thrived under the new regime of the caliphate.'

'We don't know that,' Surt said. 'These people could have died from a disease.'

'Yes, or perhaps they ate bad fish?' Ulrich said. His voice was heavy with sarcasm.

They went to the beach that ran in a crescent along the bottom of the cliffs of the ridge. In the middle, the sand petered out and the waves crashed directly against the base of the cliffs.

'There's no way across to the other side without getting our feet wet,' Sigurd said.

'I wonder how deep it is,' Skar said.

'If it gets too deep we can swim,' Einar suggested.

Ulrich nodded. 'Of course we can.'

'That could be dangerous,' Kari said. 'If a wave catches you, you could be battered against the rocks. You'll be ground to chopped meat in moments.'

'And who knows what creatures lurk under the sea?' Wulfhelm said.

'There must be another way over,' Affreca said.

'I would never have thought you would be scared.' Ulrich cocked his head.

'I'm not.' Affreca's voice betrayed her irritation. 'But I'd rather not get my bowstring wet. A bow never shoots as far or as hard after that.'

Ulrich rubbed his chin again. 'There's no point in all of us going over. We don't know if the tide is coming in or out. We could get stuck over there if it comes in further and we'd have to hoof it over the ridge instead. If that happens and we are leaving in a hurry due to being spotted, I want someone on this side covering us.'

He laid a hand on Affreca's shoulder.

'And I don't want her to have a soggy bow when she's doing it,' he said. 'Kari, Einar and Surt will come with me and we'll try to get a better look at the town. The rest of you wait on this end of the ridge path. Keep yourselves hidden but if you see us come running, get ready to give us a hand. Understand?'

'I am going with you,' Araltes said.

'No you're not,' Ulrich said. 'The way you were crashing about in the undergrowth we were lucky you didn't get us all captured. Closer to the town there will be even more of the enemy about, so you will stay with the others.'

'I will remind you that I—' Araltes began.

'Don't worry, when we work out a way into the place you will come along,' Ulrich said. 'But until then I want only my most stealthy warriors with me.'

Araltes nodded but did not look pleased. Einar, on the other hand, was thrilled at the thought Ulrich had picked him to go. Perhaps the little man was finally starting to forgive him for leaving the company the year before.

'Right,' Ulrich said. 'Let's get on with it.'

Twenty-One

Einar, Ulrich, Kari and Surt handed any long weapons – spears and swords – that could weigh them down if they were in the water to the others. They stripped to the waist and created bundles of their clothes and boots, which they tied around their waists. Then they jogged off along the small beach while the rest of the company faded back into the undergrowth. It did not take long before the party of four were running out of sand as the strip of beach narrowed to where the tide crashed directly against the rocks of the cliff.

Sigurd had been right and there was indeed no way across that was not now under water. They dove in. Einar felt an initial frisson as he entered the sea, but it was nothing compared to the paralysing shock of jumping into the icy waters of the north. Here the water was comparatively warm, even downright pleasant. It still had the same hazards, however, of currents, rip tides, sea creatures and hidden snags, all dangers that could catch a swimmer and hold him under until his breath ran out. Added to that it was dark, which made it impossible to make out anything that might be lurking under the surface.

To avoid the waves smashing them into the cliff base, they swam outwards at first, directly away from the beach. The going was hard as they were striving against the tide. Soon Einar felt himself out of breath, but he knew he had to keep going until he found his second wind. When they were far enough out from the cliff base they turned and headed for the opposite shore where the beach was still not covered by the tide.

That the tide was incoming was soon confirmed. As he struck across the waves Einar felt each one push him sideways back towards the cliffs. He knew he would have to get across fast or he would end up driven against the rocks. To compensate he began to swim diagonally away from them instead of straight across.

As Einar ploughed through the waves, an old fear surfaced in his heart. When he was a child his nurse – the old Norsewoman his mother had paid to look after him while she saw to the farm – had told him tales of the old giant called Aegir who lived in a hall at the bottom of the sea. Aegir would get lonely, and when he did he prepared his hall for a feast. He brewed ale, and the froth from the ale was the froth on the surface of the sea. There was plenty of that around Einar from the waves churning against the rocks.

Aegir's wife, Rán, went up from the sea bottom with a net and snared sailors or swimmers above, dragging them down into the depths so they could share in the feast. Of course, once down there in the deep, it was all over for them, and their fate was to sit in that endless, joyless feast in the cold, unseen depths forever.

Beneath him the water was pitch-black and in his mind he wondered if deep below Rán was looking up, her net grasped in her cold, clammy hands, ready to cast it upwards to catch him.

The thought made him swim all the faster but it was hard going. His wolfskin and clothes, light as they were, were now sodden and their weight began to feel like a stone tied around his waist, pulling him down towards Rán. His arms and legs felt heavy too, but that was from exertion. His breath went and came in underwater explosions of bubbles, followed by a deep gasp on the surface.

Then he felt sand beneath his knees and realised he was across. He swam a few stokes more and then planted his knees on the bottom. First he struggled up to a crouch, then up to his feet. The water streamed from his body and soaking breeches as he caught his breath, his heart pounding in his chest, his limbs feeling like Rán had indeed caught him and was trying to pull him back into the water.

After a few moments his breathing began to return to normal and he waded through the surf on the beach.

The other three were there too. All the mud they had smeared on their faces was gone and he could see from their gaunt expressions that they had found the short swim as hard as he had.

They struggled back into their wet clothes, which was only a slight discomfort in the hot night. The warm wind that fanned the beach meant everything would dry fast too. Then Ulrich signalled towards the top of the beach.

After a short search they found a little path that wound upwards. Keeping low they jogged up it until they came to level ground that marked the opposite end of the narrow ridge. They had achieved their aim of getting across to the other side without crossing the ridge. Now they needed to find how to get to the town.

Ulrich decided to once again steer clear of the path that led across the ridge and instead the Wolf Coats went directly west, moving in what should be parallel to it. The ground on this part of the island was rocky with a few scrub bushes here and there. It was bare of the trees that had provided cover for them in the other part of the island, and Einar felt very exposed knowing the only thing that hid him was the darkness.

It was not long before they came upon another impediment. The ground they were crossing sloped ever downwards, and Einar knew it would culminate in the cliff walls of the town. He knew therefore the town should be out of sight and was not expecting to see a glow of lights that would show where it was. What he did not expect was some sort of dark mass rising from the ground in front of them about twice the height of a man, blotting out the way ahead and the view of the sea and stars that were low in the sky.

He judged they had gone about halfway towards the western tip of the island. At the sight of the obstacle ahead the Wolf Coats halted, eyes straining in the dark to try to make out what it was.

'It's a wall,' Kari, who had the sharpest eyes of the four, said in a whisper. 'Some sort of rampart with a palisade fence on top. And look—'

He pointed and Einar just about managed to see the outline of a man standing behind the palisade, no doubt on some sort of fighting platform behind it, his top half outlined against the stars in the blue-black sky. He had a spear in one hand.

Now he recognised the outline, Einar spotted the outline of another warrior about twenty paces along the rampart to the north of the first man Kari had seen. There was another twenty paces along the rampart to the south.

At the sight of the warriors the Wolf Coats froze. Then Ulrich hooked his thumb back the way they had come. They resumed their crouching run and retreated back towards the path up from the beach.

'What now?' Surt asked when they got back to the top of

the slope and they were well out of view of whoever stood on the rampart.

'We look for another way in,' Ulrich said.

This time they set off across the island, heading north towards the main trail that crossed the narrow ridge. As they got closer they slowed to a cautious creep. This seemed to be the main route across the island and if they were going to run into anyone, it was more likely here.

When they got to it, they started to follow it westwards, though still moving along to the side of it rather than on it. As they did, Einar's eyes constantly hunted for rocks, gulleys, bushes – anything that could provide a hiding place if the need arose all of a sudden.

The trail, like the ground, sloped downwards in the direction of the town. As they moved forwards the ramparts came into view again, and Einar saw that they led from the south side of the island up to the trail then continued north on the other side. It seemed there was a wall built right across this part of the island, protecting the town from anyone who wanted to attack it from the landward side on the east, just the way the sea protected it from anyone coming from the west.

Where the walls met the trail, it dipped dramatically into a narrow rock gulley in the ground – about wide enough for two men to ride side by side. The glow of firelight came from within it.

The Wolf Coats got down on all fours and loped forwards towards the gulley, getting as close as they could for a better view. With their wolfskin hoods up, there was a chance anyone who saw them in the dark might think they were a pack of wolves or wild dogs and ignore them. When they got to the edge of the gulley, Ulrich dropped to his belly and the others followed suit.

Looking ahead, Einar saw the walls ended at the sides of the gulley, which dropped between them. The trail went into the gulley where it was blocked by a gate. Firelight glowed from braziers behind the gate and on platforms that allowed more armed warriors to stand on the top behind it. The gate was three times the height of a man but it only reached halfway up the sheer walls of the narrow ravine. On the far side of the gate, Einar could see what looked like some sort of cave high up on the southern side of the gulley wall. It was not a natural cave – or at least it had perhaps started that way but had been amended by human hands so the opening was now rectangular. There was some sort of waist-high wall across the front. The flickering firelight from behind the gate played across several figures moving around inside the cave.

After a short while Ulrich motioned to the others that they should retreat and once more they went back the way they had come. They began to descend back towards the beach, but it soon became obvious that while they had been examining the rest of the island the tide had come all the way in. The crescent of beach was now gone, covered with churning waves that battered against the rocks at the base of the cliffs. Einar felt his heart drop at the thought of how difficult it would be trying to swim back. It had been hard enough going getting here and that swim had been a lot shorter.

'It's too far to swim,' Ulrich said, to Einar's relief. 'We're going to have to chance the ridge after all.'

'It will be risky,' Kari said.

'There won't be anywhere to hide,' Ulrich agreed, nodding. 'So run as fast as you can. The less time we're on that ridge the less chance there is of being spotted.'

They changed course and headed back towards the trail. When they reached it they followed it east, as before tracking along beside it rather than following the path itself. When they got to where the trail began to cross the narrow ridge, they had no choice anymore. There was no room on the top of the ridge for anything but the trail itself, with cliffs falling away to the sea on either side. It was not far at least, but while they were on it they would be completely exposed. There would be nowhere to hide.

'Right,' Ulrich said. 'Every man for himself. If anyone falls or gets in trouble the rest keep going. That includes me. If one of us gets caught, there's no reason they should get all of us.'

They began to run. Einar was out of breath in no time, but he knew he had to keep going. It was uphill, which made the going harder, but the track was quite level and it was clear it was well used. Einar kept his legs pumping, trying to concentrate on sticking as close to the middle as possible. To the left and right there was nothing but air all the way down to the sea below. A slip or stumble could send him over the edge and tumbling down the cliffs.

They ran in silence. The only sounds were the thump of their feet on the track, the buffeting of the warm wind and the roar and crash of the waves at the bottom of the cliffs. As Einar ran, he felt a prickly sensation down the back of his neck, reaction to the knowledge that they would be in full view of those on the ramparts.

They made it to the other side without incident. It was only when they reached the far end of the ridge that Ulrich slowed and looked back.

'We got away with it,' he said. 'There's no one following us.'

The others came to a halt as well. For a few moments they stood, breathing heavily. Then movement from the edge of the pine woods made them all tense. Einar's hand dropped to the seax knife at his waist, but he relaxed when he saw that it was Affreca, Wulfhelm, Skar and the others who had, as ordered, been waiting for them in case they got into difficulty.

They handed back the long weapons they had been holding for them. Einar took his fighting glove, sword and spear from Skar, nodding his gratitude. He felt much less naked once they were in his hands again. The others gathered around, keen to hear the news from the search party.

'Things might be a bit more difficult than I hoped they would be,' Ulrich said. 'They've built a rampart right across the island and have a man stationed about every twenty paces on top of it, which means they know what they are doing. These "pirates" aren't just a rabble.'

'Most of them would have been soldiers of the caliphate before,' Surt said. 'Like I was. Now they use the skills they gained in the army to make themselves rich through piracy.'

'It looks like the only way into the town is down a narrow ravine, which is guarded by a gate,' Ulrich continued. 'If an attacker got through the gate, there is a cave up on the ravine wall with warriors in it who can pour spears, arrows, rocks, whatever down on anyone below.'

'And if we try to sail in, they have that fire-spurting weapon guarding the harbour,' Skar said.

'It sounds like it's impossible to get in,' Affreca noted.

'Nothing is impossible,' Ulrich said. 'But it will be difficult for sure. And dangerous.'

'We *have* to get in there,' Aralorn said. Einar could see his gritted teeth in the moonlight.

'Do we?' Ulrich said. 'I think that's up to us to decide.'

'What are you saying?' Aralorn asked.

'I'm saying that I'm wondering whether this job is worth losing any of my company over,' Ulrich said. 'Maybe it's best if we get back to the ship and head for home.'

'What?!' Araltes said. 'If you break our agreement I'll have you all hanged!'

'You seem to not have thought this through,' Ulrich said. 'There's just you and your fire-weapon friend here with all of us. There's very little to stop us killing you right here and sailing off into the sunset.'

Araltes mouth worked soundlessly for a moment. Then he said: 'What about honour?'

'We're vikings, remember?' Ulrich said.

'Ulrich, what about the silver?' Sigurd reminded him. 'If we don't fulfil this task we return home with nothing. Aethelstan's silver is gone. The slaves were taken. We're poorer than ever.'

'We still have our lives,' Ulrich said.

'We're vikings, yes,' Kari said. 'But the point of being a viking is to win fame and gold. No one will compose poems about the deeds we never did on this island no one has heard of. We'll have nothing to show for all this.'

'My daughter is in that town somewhere,' Surt said. 'You can sail away if you want, but I'm staying.'

'There's the Sea Fire as well, Ulrich,' Einar said. 'If we could get our hands on some of that, just think of the battles we could win. I could take back Orkney!'

'Don't get carried away, lad,' Ulrich said.

He looked around at the semicircle of expectant eyes that surrounded him for a moment. Einar could tell he was thinking, trying to decide if he would face them all down or accede to the prevailing sentiment of the company. If they left, they would live to fight another day but go away empty-handed. While they were all loyal to Ulrich, he could only hold the company together if he brought success to those in it, and there had been precious little of that over the last few winters. It was a difficult decision, and Einar was glad he was not the one making it.

'Very well,' Ulrich said. 'I can see which way the wind is blowing. We will stay and try to find a way into that town.'

At that moment a blast of horns startled everyone. Someone, somewhere was signalling. It was not close by. As Einar looked around he realised it was coming from the tower on the top of the hill.

'Those bastards up there must have seen us coming over the ridge,' Ulrich said. 'Come on: Let's get back to the ship before whoever they're signalling comes along.'

Twenty-Two

The sun was starting to crawl upwards, again, sending a haunting pink glow into the sky above the trees when they got back to the far side of the island where the ship was.

They had taken a similar, though not the same, route they had come by, steering clear of any obvious pathways and moving through the pine forest. Einar knew they were almost back at the ship when he spotted glimpses of the sea through the trees.

It was then that Skar stopped. He raised his left arm in signal that the others should too, and be silent. The big man was standing stock-still, and his eyes were fixed as if staring straight ahead, but Einar knew he was straining his other senses – smell, hearing – for something.

After a few moments he turned to the others, cupped a hand behind his right ear, then pointed ahead. They all listened. At first all Einar could hear was the ever-present rasp of the insects, which seemed to be getting quieter as the sun rose. Then he heard a soft thump, followed by another: the unmistakable sound of a horse hoof falling on soft earth. A moment after came the murmur of men's voices. They were somewhere up ahead, in the direction of the ship.

Ulrich pointed at Kari, pointed to his eyes then pointed ahead;

then he made a deliberate glance around the others to make sure they knew he was issuing an order and hooked his thumb back the way they had come. Kari slunk forwards while the others retreated, all now moving at a much more careful pace. A little way back through the trees they found a hollow in the ground and slid into it, lying flat as they waited. Ulrich peeked his head up, keeping watch in the direction of the ship while the others kept their heads down to stay out of sight.

After a tense wait, Einar heard a crack of a dry twig and then Kari arrived, sliding into the hollow in a shower of dead pine needles.

'There's at least ten of them,' Kari said in a hushed voice. 'I couldn't get close enough to count. But they are milling around the top of the ravine where the ship is. They're Serks. They have spears and weapons. Horses too.'

'Do you think they found the ship?' Ulrich said.

Kari shrugged.

'What about Roan?' Skar asked.

'And Diogenes?' Araltes added.

'No sign of them,' Kari said.

Araltes cursed.

'Let's get out of here,' Ulrich said. 'Then we can make a plan.'

They crawled out of the hollow and began loping back through the forest the way they had come. They had not gone far when the harsh cry of a raven made Einar prick up his ears. The others stopped as well. It sounded exactly like a raven or crow but it was also the sound the Wolf Coats used to signal to each other in the dark of night. It was not dark now, however.

Ulrich cupped his hands before his lips and called through them, creating a similar sound. A moment later the other crow responded.

A little uphill the scrawny figure of Roan appeared from

behind a pine tree. The Greek, Diogenes was beside him. They both jogged down to join them.

'What happened?' Ulrich said.

'They've taken the ship,' Roan said. 'I was lucky enough to hear them coming. There was a whole company of them and their horses made a racket loud enough to wake me up. I woke him and we ran up there and hid. They rode straight to the ravine. They knew where the ship was. I could see the water from where we were hiding and some of them sailed off in the snekkja. The rest stayed around.'

'They were probably thinking we would return to the ship sooner or later,' Skar said. 'And they were right.'

'Thank the Lord Diogenes is all right,' Araltes said. 'Skilled siphōnarioi are very hard to find and we can't disable that siphōn without him.'

'How did they know?' Einar said. 'I don't think the ship that sailed past yesterday saw me. I was well hidden.'

Ulrich sighed and pointed up the hill.

'That fucking tower,' he said. 'They can probably see everything from up there.'

Soft thumps made Einar's ears prick up.

'There's something I should have told you all before now,' Surt said. 'They don't have crows on these islands.'

The random thumps Einar heard coalesced into the unmistakable sound of the hooves of several horses pounding in the direction of where the Wolf Coats stood. If the skin of Roan's coloured face had not been tanned to walnut colour by years on the sea it would have blanched.

'I'm sorry,' he said. 'I've gone and given us away, haven't I?'

'How many? Ten did you say?' Ulrich turned to Kari.

'At least,' Kari said. 'With horses.'

Ulrich made a face.

The horse hoofs pointed closer. It was too late to run.

'We could hide?' Fisk said. The note of futile hope in his voice betrayed the fact he really knew his suggestion was pointless.

'Too late,' Ulrich said. 'They'll kill us one by one. We have to fight.'

Einar was already pulling on his fighting glove. He drew his sword and fastened it to the hooks at the bottom of his hand.

'Skjaldborg?' Sigurd asked.

'Not against horsemen,' Skar said. 'They can ride round it. Fisk, you said you were an axeman. Did you really mean it?'

'Aye,' the vikingr-scotti said.

'We will form a hedgehog as a *kið blót* for the horsemen,' Skar, who always took charge in battle, said. 'You and Affreca will spring the trap.'

They all ran about twenty paces further into the pine forest where the tree trunks opened up into a small clearing. Fisk ran downhill to the edge of the forest and hid behind a tree. Affreca did the same uphill. The remaining eleven formed a rough square in the middle of the clearing. Ulrich directed Araltes, Diogenes and Wulfhelm to face back towards the way they had come. He, Skar and Starkad formed a line behind them with their backs to them. Einar and Kari faced downhill, Starkad and Surt up. Roan, who was not a warrior, stood in the middle of them all. They all faced outwards, weapons ready.

The pounding hooves drew ever closer. Einar tried to still his heart, which felt like it was drumming every bit as fast and loud. He tried not to think about the meaning of the *kið blót* formation, the Sacrificial Goat.

There were no wolves in Iceland, but he had learned that in Norway when hunters wanted to ensnare wolves they would stake out a young goat in a forest or field. When the wolves went for the goat, the hunters shot them with their bows while they were eating. The goat usually died as well but that was the price of getting rid of the wolves. Today he and the others in the *kið blót* formation would be the goat. He hoped they would not pay too dear a price.

Diogenes said something to Araltes. Einar did not understand what he said, but his tone of voice said he was very nervous. He could see Diogenes was not a trained warrior. His stance was all wrong and the way he held the sword in his hand meant it could be easily batted aside.

'It's a good question,' Araltes said, turning his head to speak over his shoulder to Ulrich. 'They'll hit us first. Why are we at the front? Aren't you the trained fighters? Diogenes is a skilled artificer, not a hack-and-slash foot soldier.'

'He managed to burn all of Thord's crew to death with his *siphōn*,' Ulrich said. 'I'm sure he will manage all right.'

At that moment the horsemen burst into the clearing.

Twenty-Three

Einar braced himself. To his left he heard Diogenes give a little whimper. Glancing round he saw the first horsemen coming.

There were ten of them. They rode two abreast in a disciplined formation, which showed they had at least some war training. They were clad in long white and blue robes of linen. Each man had a shirt of mail over his clothes and they had round, iron caps on top of their heads, which had visors that covered the top half of their faces. Their heads beneath the helmets were swathed in what looked like lengths of long white cloth wrapped many times around their heads. The same cloth was wrapped around the bottom half of their face beneath their helmet, hiding their mouths from view. Between the helmets and the scarves their faces were totally hidden, which made them even more intimidating. Each rider had a big, triangular shield protecting his left side and a drawn sword in his right. Their shields were painted green and bore some sort of squiggled design in black. The sword blades were curved, almost like a sickle blade, and their metal gleamed like oil on water. It was a pattern Einar had seen before in the Ingolf swords made by the same master craftsman who had created his fighting glove. It meant they were made of the finest of steel.

The riders let out a high battle cry and charged straight at the square of Norsemen. Einar felt the ground shake beneath the pounding hooves and knew if Araltes and the others did not deter them they would plough straight into the formation, smashing them all to the ground to pulverise them beneath the thrashing hooves.

The first two were only a horse length away when Affreca swung from behind her tree, bow drawn and arrow notched. She took an instant to aim then shot. She had lost her powerful Finnish bow in Mālaqah but at such close range her arrow ploughed right through the lead horseman's chest, shattering the rings of his mail shirt like they were made of ice instead of iron.

The impact carried him right out of the saddle to land with a sickening crunch head first on the ground. His horse, finding it no longer had anyone on its back to drive it, instinctively veered sideways to avoid the prickly weapons the square of armed men presented before it.

A moment after Affreca emerged from hiding Fisk did the same from the opposite side. He had his arm cocked to throw and grasped one of the francescas in his hand. He hurled it at the second rider.

The throwing axe tumbled end over end through the air before its blade struck the horseman on the side of the head, shattering his helmet and burying itself deep into his skull. The rider tumbled out of his saddle, already dead before he hit the forest floor. Like the first horse, his mount also saw no point in impaling itself on the blades of the men in formation and turned aside.

Affreca already had another arrow notched and shot the third rider before he even reached his fallen comrades. Fisk came running forwards, roaring a war cry, now with his long-handled battleaxe gripped in both hands. Seeing him, the fourth rider changed course and began to ride straight at him, intending to ride him down and crush him under the hooves.

Einar expected Fisk to try to dodge out of the way but to his surprise the lanky vikingr-scotti stood his ground. Just as the horse was about to reach him he struck it a huge blow with his axe, swinging it two-handed over his head. The long-bearded blade sliced into the horse's neck just behind its ears. The blow almost severed the beast's head. Einar grimaced as the creature collapsed in a heap of tangled, twitching and thrashing legs, great gouts of hot blood spouting from the massive wound Fisk had dealt it. As it fell it rolled, crushing its rider under its weight, just as the horseman had moments before intended to do to Fisk.

'Go!' Ulrich shouted.

The Wolf Coats turned and swarmed around Araltes, Diogenes and Roan who remained rooted to the spot.

'I give you to Odin!' Sigurd screamed as he hurled his spear with all his might. It took a fifth horseman from his saddle. Another rider slashed his sword down at Einar. Einar stepped aside and countered, shoving his own sword upwards. It slid into the horseman's armpit and into his chest. His body stiffened. Einar pulled his sword back, unleashing a torrent of blood as the rider fell backwards out of his saddle.

Skar confronted the seventh horseman, brandishing his sword at the man as he galloped towards him. The rider chopped down with his curved blade. Skar, with surprising dexterity for such a large man, sidestepped the blow then struck the horseman across the back as he rode past. His blade severed the man's backbone and he too was out of the fight. Ulrich hurled his spear at the next rider, who batted it away with his shield. The movement opened up his defences, however, and Affreca shot him in the chest with an arrow.

The last two horsemen realised the battle was lost and wheeled their steeds around to flee back the way they had come. They were still turning when Kari hauled one of them out of the saddle and impaled him through the chest with his sword. Surt speared the last man through the back.

It was all over in a few moments of shocking violence. Without their riders, the horses milled around aimlessly, apart from two, which decided to make the most of their new-found freedom and galloped off into the forest. For a few moments there was only the rasping of the insects and the heavy breathing of the Norsemen as they recovered their wind. The metallic stink of blood mingled with the smell of pine in the hot air.

'Everyone all right?' Skar said.

'I'm not,' Kari said.

All eyes swivelled towards him but he was clearly unharmed.

'I was joking!' he said, holding up his arms.

'You're not funny,' Ulrich said as he rolled his eyes.

'I see that you were not just bragging,' Skar said to Fisk. 'You really are useful with an axe. Of any kind.'

'I'm the best axeman in the Southern Isles,' Fisk said. He was grinning, and Einar realised this was probably the first time he had ever seen the man look really happy.

'I'm glad you're good at something,' Kari said. 'Because you're a dour enough bastard to have for company.'

Affreca came down the hill to rejoin them. Ulrich crouched beside one of the fallen horsemen. He pulled down the material that was wrapped around his face like a scarf, revealing olive-coloured skin and a dark black beard.

'They're Serks,' he said. He looked up at Araltes. 'This place seems very well organised for a den of pirates.'

'True,' Araltes agreed. 'But they make their living from

raiding shipping, that is for sure. They're still Saracens from the caliphate.'

'Which means they're not barbarians,' Surt said.

'And they know we're here for definite now,' Araltes said.

'The fact that they found our ship already give that away,' Ulrich said.

'Where do you think they took it?' Einar asked.

'The only place they could have is the harbour in the town,' Ulrich said.

'This is bad.' Araltes looked at the butchered corpses on the ground around him. 'When they don't return to the town, they'll send out more – larger – companies to hunt us down. Without a ship we'll be stuck on the island, chased around these woods until there is finally nowhere left to run. It's just a matter of time until they get us.'

'Last night you were the one who *didn't* want to leave,' Ulrich said. He too looked at the dead bodies. Then his face lightened in a sly smile that Einar knew meant the little Wolf Coat leader had got an idea.

'This lot won't be missed if they *do* ride back into town,' he said.

'They're a bit dead for that,' Skar said. 'I know you have many talents, Ulrich, but in all the years I've known you, raising the dead is not one I've seen you show before.'

'I don't mean actually them,' Ulrich said. He lifted the scarf-like material from the face of one of the corpses and held it over his mouth, covering the bottom half of his face. 'I mean someone who might be mistaken for them. Get these corpses undressed. Let's see if we can wash the blood out of their clothes.'

Twenty-Four

Later in the day, six horsemen trotted down the trail towards the ridge that led to the town. They wore the robes and armour of Saracens and the curved swords of the caliphate were sheathed at their sides, but a closer look would have revealed holes in their clothing made by the spear and sword blades that had ended their previous occupants' lives.

Ulrich had again been very deliberate in who he picked for this task. This time Araltes did come along and he was accompanied by Diogenes as, if they did manage to bluff their way through the gates and into the town, this could be the only chance they got to get a good look at the fire siphōns. Surt came along too because he spoke the Serk tongue and, because he was one, could pass better than all of them as an ex-warrior from the caliphate. Ulrich went along himself but he excluded the bigger men of the company because the Serks were by and large of smaller build. Affreca was coming along too, despite the misgivings of Surt, who had told them that in some places ruled by his faith women might not even be allowed outside their homes, never mind be a warrior. Ulrich wanted to be able to call on her archery skills though, if they got into trouble, so she now rode along the track, heavily swathed in mail and the clothes of the largest of the dead Serks so as to hide any hint of the lithe woman's body beneath. Both Affreca and Ulrich, the two of the company who had no beards, were careful to wrap their lower faces in the long, scarf-like garments in the manner of the horsemen who had attacked them.

The last horse was ridden by Einar who, though nervous about the danger that lay ahead, was delighted when Ulrich had picked him again as one of the company who would go into town. Ulrich, it seemed, had come to the conclusion that Einar was lucky, so wanted him to come along in case things went wrong and they needed a bit of luck. Einar took this as another sign that perhaps Ulrich was getting round to forgiving him at last.

After they had arranged several choices for meeting later, the others had been left behind to find somewhere to hide while the company of six rode to the town.

They all wore the clothes of the horse warriors they had killed, which were still, despite the heat and warm wind, damp from being thoroughly washed in the sea to get the bloodstains out. Einar was surprised that despite the amount of material they were made of they were cool and did not hold the baking heat of the sun. He guessed that the Serks, through centuries of living in hot conditions, must have perfected a style of making clothes that kept them cool in the heat, the way his own folk in the north had created many types of clothing to keep out the cold and wet.

Their disguise had passed its first test already. On their way along the track, they met another band of Serks coming in the opposite direction. Surt had greeted them in their own tongue and the others had waved back. One had even smiled in friendly greeting. They had asked Surt a question and when he replied they nodded and rode on past.

'What did they say?' Ulrich asked Surt when they were far enough away not to be heard.

'They asked if we had seen any sign of the *kufaar*,' Surt said with a smile. 'That's you lot. I said no, we saw no sign of them.'

'What does that name mean?' Einar said.

'It means people not of our faith,' Surt said.

They rode on along the track until they reached the narrow ridge they had crossed the night before, when they'd been running as fast as they could. They dismounted and led the horses across. A carelessly placed hoof that led to a horse slipping or rearing up could send one of them tumbling over the edge of the cliff and hurtling to their death below.

Once across they remounted and walked the horses down the narrow ravine at the middle of the two ramparts. The trail went into a steep slant and soon the gulley walls towered above them. The clicks of the horses' hooves on the stones echoed off the rocks.

As they had noticed the night before, in line with the ramparts that crossed the peninsula, there was a wooden fence across the ravine with double gates in it. The fence was perhaps twice the height of a man with a walkway behind it at the top. There were four Serk warriors with spears on the walkway, visible above the top of the fence from the waist up. They leaned on their spear shafts and looked casual but were watching who came and went through the gates below. The gates themselves were now open. There were more armed men on the far side, and one stood to one side in front of the gates.

As they approached, riding as casually as they could manage, Surt raised his hand and greeted the warrior at the gate. The guard shot a question at Surt that Einar did not understand but he guessed that, like any guard on a gate, the man was asking what their business was.

As previously instructed by Ulrich, speaking in the Serk tongue, Surt said they were part of the party that had captured the ship. They had been left behind to capture the kufaar but they still had not returned. Surt explained that he and the others with him had been sent back to town to get water and provisions for their comrades still out searching the woods.

The guard on the gate seemed to believe the tale and cocked his head towards the gates, signalling that they could go in. Surt and the others rode forwards again, entering the gates and heading on down the path beyond.

Inside, the ravine continued. Einar noticed there were many warriors behind the gate, perhaps twenty or more. They milled around, sat on the ground or on stools, their weapons near at hand. On the wall of the ravine to the left he saw the cave he had spotted the night before. It was about half the length of a ship and cut to be rectangular. There were more warriors inside. He could see the top halves of their bodies beyond the wall built waist high across the front of the entrance. Some looked down on the riders as they went past. No torches burned inside, so they could not tell how far the cave went back into the rock.

To his surprise he saw what looked very like two sleds on the ground beneath the cave. They were flat on top, with runners along the bottom, just like ones used to move heavy loads across the snow-bound lands of Iceland. What they would be used for, here in the baking sun, he had no idea.

Attacking the gates would be difficult, Einar mused as he looked up into the darkness of the cave. Not only were there the warriors behind it to deal with but, when through, those in the cave would rain all sorts of havoc down on whoever was below. Ulrich had surmised this was the only way into the town apart from the harbour and it looked like he was right. Otherwise it would not have been so well guarded.

Beyond the cave the ravine opened up into steep cliff walls on either side. These stood above the town and its harbour, which lay below. The path sloped at an even more pronounced angle that was too steep to ride down. They were forced to dismount and lead their horses down it for a short distance until the angle of the path became less acute as it continued into a street of white stone houses. This street led to the harbour. It was merely steep as opposed to precipitous and they were able to get back on their horses again and walk them the rest of the way into the town.

'You know, Ulrich,' Einar said in a quiet voice in case he was overheard beyond his immediate company. 'One day your ploy of just walking into an enemy stronghold will fail and you'll have to come up with another one. I am glad that day is not today, however.'

'Like I always say, lad,' Ulrich said. 'There are places a small company can walk into where an army cannot storm. Kings and jarls want vast armies but give me a small band of battle-hardened fighters – masters of warcraft – and I will do great damage.'

They rode on into the town. In truth it was not much of a town. A collection of stone buildings with a quay gathered around a harbour. It was busy, however, with many people, mostly men, hurrying to and fro in the manner folk seemed to do in towns and cities. Einar wondered what it was they were all hurrying to or from, and why those who grew up in the countryside like him did not have such needs.

Down the hill and into the town they came to a small square before the harbour. Here they dismounted as it was too crowded to ride. The harbour was full of ships, all triangular-sailed, two- and three-masted vessels like the ones Einar had seen in Mālaqah.

Like in Mālaqah, the harbour was a horseshoe shape, with

two stone quays that met in a narrow entrance that would allow one ship to sail through it at a time. At the end of the left-hand quay a tower guarded the harbour entrance. It was made of stone to the height of two men, then a wooden turret sat on top of it.

'The siphōn is there,' Araltes said in a low voice.

Einar peered and saw the sun gleam off the brass of the fire-spitting tube that protruded from a rectangular opening at the front of the tower. Any ship that passed in or out of the harbour would have to pass before it.

'There's our ship,' Affreca said.

Sure enough, the Wolf Coats' snekkja was one of the vessels tied up on the right-hand quay. The sleek ship with its high, dragon-carved prow and single mast looked foreign amid all the ships of the Serks, a strange reversal of fate that rammed home to Einar the fact that here they were the foreigners, the outsiders who did not belong in this realm.

'We'll have to do something about that fire-spewing device if we're going to get the ship out of the harbour,' Ulrich said.

There were lots of people milling around the square, which seemed to double both as a quay and a marketplace. Little urchin-like children ran around, playing chase and getting up to no good. A merchant with a barrowload of fish stood on one corner, swatting the flies off his goods as he proclaimed their quality. There were other hawkers too, some with barrels of fruit and others with bread, all shouting to inform passers-by of the merits of their own goods while trying to drown out their competitors' claims.

A line of buildings ran along one side of the square. One was big and had no windows and had the look of some sort of warehouse. There were other buildings with striped, coloured awnings at the front. About the middle of the row was a smaller, two-storey building. It had double doors in the front that were open. The sound of raucous laughter came from inside.

'If I'm not mistaken that's a tavern,' Ulrich said. 'There's a hitching post outside. We can leave the horses there and go and take a closer look at that fire siphōn.'

'If this is really a den of pirates,' Affreca said, 'are we wise leaving the horses unattended? What if someone steals them? We might need them to get away quickly later.'

'Good point,' Ulrich agreed. 'You stay here and watch them. Diogenes will stay with you.'

'Don't you need him to see the siphōn?' Einar asked.

'I'm sure he's seen plenty before,' Ulrich said. 'He doesn't need to look at another one today. We do though. It's us who will have to work out how to get him into that tower so he can stop that one working.'

'No,' Araltes said. 'I won't be parted from Diogenes. At all costs he must not fall into the hands of the enemy. If he does and they find out he is a siphōnarioi, they will torture him horribly to learn his secrets.'

'And worse, right?' Surt looked Araltes in the eye. The Norseman who served the Greeks did not reply. Einar wondered what could be worse than torture.

Ulrich shrugged. 'Very well. He comes with us. Affreca, I'm sure you can look after the horses on your own?'

Affreca nodded.

'Good,' Ulrich said. 'Now let's go and see what we can find out about that siphōn.'

Twenty-Five

They pushed their way through the crowd in the market that filled the square outside. Einar noticed there were many men who wore scars, had broken noses or displayed other signs of a life of violence. These were fighters, not fishermen. There were few women too. He saw some old grandames swathed in black clothing who were haggling with merchants over the price of their wares but not many young women. This was another sign that this town was more of an army camp than a fishing port.

The type of goods for sale and the men haggling to buy them reminded Einar very much of the viking market they had been to on the island of Mikla Fjall in Francia. Some of the merchant stalls sold fish and fruit, but many sold what could best be described as loot. Christian statues and pictures – many showing the cuts where they had been hacked away from the place they had been secured, in whatever church they had been taken from – nestled on stalls among heaps of fishing tools, glass cups, silver plates, fine clothing and much jewellery. They were stacked together as if a flood or great wind had picked them up, mixed them together and dumped them on the stall. There were a lot of weapons and armour for sale. Many were damaged and some, Einar was sure, still bore the bloodstains of their late owners. There were several stalls selling odd bundles of what looked like hay or dried grass and gave off a strong herbal scent as Einar and the others passed.

The men selling all this looked like they did not bear much haggling and would sooner cut your throat than drop their prices. Their customers were a mix of folk. They did not look like the pirates and most were not dressed like them. Looking at the many boats in the harbour Einar surmised that this was the sort of place people might sail to in order to buy things that would not usually be available in local markets run by a king, a nobleman or indeed anyone who had any sort of regard for the law.

If people sailed here, they would no doubt be thoroughly checked on entry to the harbour, and like at Mikla Fjall, they would all be expected to leave before sunset. Every one of them would also have to sail in and out of the harbour under the terrible, one-eyed gaze of the brass tube that protruded from the tower that housed the siphōn. Even so, it was worth noting. Perhaps here was an alternate way to get into the town in the future.

There were many slaves. They appeared to be of all peoples, though there was a large group who were pale-skinned northerners, like the ones Ulrich and Thord had brought from Hedeby. They all bore the empty, soulless expressions of the enslaved, complying with meek acquiescence to the prods, grabs and pokes of the men checking their worth in the way of a merchant buying cattle. Einar knew they would have been beaten into accepting this submissive state. He wondered if, were he ever in the same situation, would he be able to keep his own dignity? Could he remain defiant even in the most hopeless of situations? Ragnar Loðbrók may have sung in the face of death, but would he have done the same if instead the prospect was to spend endless years enthralled in misery?

Having crossed the market, they began to make their way along the stone quay towards the end where the tower with the siphōn was. Along the quay were eight stout wooden posts about twice the height of a man, erected every ten paces or so.

With a thrill of horror, Einar realised each post had a human corpse nailed to it. Their arms were up above their heads, laid one on top of the other and nailed to the post by a big iron spike driven through both wrists. Their bodies dangled down below, their legs crossed at the ankles, another pin driven through both ankles and into the wood beyond. The first five were little more than skeletons, their bones bleached by the sun and picked clean by seabirds except for a few stubborn pieces of blackened flesh.

The rest had not been on the posts as long. Their eyes were all gone, gobbled up by greedy birds, but their flesh was still intact, their skin was dark red and blistered from the sun, except in the places where it was turning green with rot. The stench of corruption was horrible and the warm sea wind, incessant and strong as always, did little to dispel it.

'Crucifixion,' Surt said in a low voice. 'It is the execution method of the empire, but my people use it now too.'

With a thrill of revulsion, Einar realised that these corpses had not been placed there on display, perhaps as a warning to others; the people had been nailed to those posts while still alive. This was how the Christians' God had been killed. Cynewulf, the monk Aethelstan had assigned to teach Einar their religion, had stressed the slow and agonising nature of such a death.

The thought of it sent a shiver down Einar's spine as he walked on, doing his best not to gape at the grisly sight or otherwise pay too much attention lest he betray the fact that he did not pass by this shocking scene of cruel execution every day like the rest of the locals.

Halfway down the quay the number of armed warriors increased. Einar saw them all around, sitting on trunks or leaning on their spears. They were watchful, but Ulrich led the company on towards the siphōn tower unperturbed.

Einar knew, through Ulrich and Skar's teaching, that looking as nonchalant as possible was the key to not appearing out of place and consequently getting caught. So despite his racing heart and every nerve in his body screaming with tension, he kept his breathing regular, the pace he walked at casual and never let his eyes linger too long on anything, particularly the warriors who guarded the tower. This was especially hard to do, as all his other training in war crafts had drilled into him to never take your eyes off the enemy.

He was perhaps too good at this, as he never saw the Serk warrior who motioned for him to stop. When he was not obeyed, the pirate grabbed a handful of Einar's robe and shouted something at him.

Einar stopped, shock running down his spine like cold water. He assessed the situation. The warrior who had grabbed him was about the same size as him. He had a spear in one hand and a handful of Einar's robe in the other. He shouted at Einar again. Einar could tell the warrior was too close to use his spear. He could draw his own knife and take the man down, but there were already other Serk warriors starting to prick their ears up and pay attention to the confrontation. Ulrich and the others stopped too and turned to see what was happening. They could fight but they were outnumbered by many and the crowd was thick, which meant a getaway could be hard.

The Serk shouted something else. His eyes and tone were now angry. Then Surt stepped in front of Einar and said some words to the pirate. He grabbed Einar's maimed right hand and pulled it up. Einar let him do it and Surt pointed at his missing finger and lower palm. He said something else and the Serk warrior's anger dissolved into a broad grin. He let go of Einar's robe and said something else to him he did not understand, then clapped him on the shoulder and they walked on.

'What did you say?' Einar said from the corner of his mouth.

'I told him you had been punished by the Caliphe of Cordoba for being a pirate,' Surt said. 'I said the caliphe had sliced off your finger and cut out your tongue, which was why you could not reply to him.'

'He seemed almost pleased with me?' Einar said.

'Yes,' Surt said. 'The way he reacted worries me a little. But hush now. Enough talk in your barbarian tongue.'

They sauntered on down the quay until they reached about halfway along. Here there was a line of warriors who were alert. It was obvious any attempt to go further would be stopped and result in awkward questions.

Alert to this, Ulrich nodded to the warriors and stopped. He pretended to be looking at the ships as he and Surt talked rubbish. Einar and the others pretended to be engaged by the conversation while they glanced around and tried to take in as much as they could about the tower and how it was guarded.

They had been there for a short time when Einar noticed movement at the door in the back of the tower. It was a little off the ground and reached by a short flight of four wooden steps. A man poked his head out and looked around. He was olive-skinned and dark-haired and wore a strange headdress that looked like it was made of leather. It had long pieces that hung down each side of the man's face. He also wore a long leather apron not unlike what a blacksmith would wear and was identical to the one Diogenes had worn when they had first seen him. The man peeked out, looked up and down the quay, then went back inside again.

Einar looked at his companions to see if they had spotted the same thing. Diogenes looked like he had seen a ghost. He did his best to get a hold of himself and looked out to sea again, but Einar could tell from the way he kept glancing back at the tower that he was agitated.

Whether Ulrich had seen this too or not he could not tell, but the wiry leader nodded as if satisfied with whatever he had been looking at in the boats in the harbour and began to walk back down the quay towards the square.

They all followed suit. Affreca still stood with the horses at the post. As they rejoined her a blast of raucous laughter came from the open doors of the building nearby.

'That's a tavern all right,' Ulrich said. 'Let's go inside.'

'What about me?' Affreca asked.

'You too. We'll be just inside,' Ulrich said. 'I'm sure we can keep an eye on the horses through the door.'

'Are you mad?!' Araltes looked incredulous. 'We're here to find out about the Sea Fire, remember? We're in the heart of an enemy town. What are you going to do in a tavern?'

'Have a drink?' Ulrich said. 'Come on. You learn all sorts of things in taverns.'

Twenty-Six

Inside the tavern was gloomy but cool, the stone walls soaking up the heat of the glaring sun, so little made it inside. The men who sat at the tables inside – they were all men – were to Einar a dangerous-looking lot. They were of all skin colours and wore foreign clothes of many different types. Their faces and arms bore scars, some had missing hands or ears, a few wore patches over one of their eyes. Engaged in their own lively debates, they ignored the group of six newcomers who entered and found a table near the door with enough seats for all of them.

There were a couple of musicians in the corner who played strange, slow music on foreign-looking instruments – one stringed and played with a bow, the other some sort of horn – which Einar found disconcerting and a little sinister.

On the right-hand side of the room was an area covered with pillows and rugs. Einar was fascinated to see three men reclining on the pillows as if asleep; however, their eyes were open and they stared up at the ceiling above. Another two Serk pirates sat cross-legged beside them, staring down at the rug between their thighs as if captivated by it. The pattern woven into it was indeed fascinating, but Einar doubted it was so engrossing it could hold the attention of grown men for long. None of them spoke or even looked up when the newcomers entered the room. There was a plate in the middle of them all with lumps of some sort of moss or dried grass on it. Were these men so drunk they were in a stupor and had been moved to that corner of the room to sober up?

Einar forced himself to look away, aware as he was that looking at anyone too long or seeming overly interested or surprised while in a strange place would alert locals to the fact he did not belong here.

A long counter ran across the far end of the room, behind which shelves groaned under a variety of canisters, urns and the big clay pots wine was transported in. A man perhaps ten winters older than Einar with long, curling black hair stood behind the counter, leaning on his elbows and watching all that went on around him with a hawklike gaze. From his position and commanding stare, Einar surmised this was the tavern keeper.

A couple of grubby-faced children, a boy and a girl, dressed in little more than rags, ran up to the table as soon as Einar and the others sat down. Surt spoke to them and they hurried off to the counter to deliver his order to the long-haired man there.

Four young women sat at a table close to the counter. They were reasonably dressed and pretty, but their eyes bore the haunted, empty expressions common to slaves. Einar had no doubt the women were as much for sale as the drinks behind the counter.

The urchins brought clay cups to the table and two jugs, one of rich red wine and one of water. Surt threw some metal coins to them. They all had some, taken from the purses of the Serks they had killed in the woods, but Einar had no idea of their worth. Surt, however, seemed to. The children scurried back to the counter where the tavern keeper waited, hand extended, for the money.

Einar caught the rueful glance Surt cast in the direction of the children and the slave girls.

'You're worried about your daughter, aren't you?' he asked.

The black-skinned man sighed and nodded.

'This place is not good. It is not a righteous place,' he said. 'I don't mean just this tavern. The whole island. It is full of scum. I know them. We dealt with their sort when I was in the army of the emir. They say they are of our faith but they care more about gold than God.'

'So that's why that man was so pleased when you told him I'd been punished by the emir?' Einar said.

'Indeed,' Surt said. 'He sees you as a kindred spirit. These men are pirates, not warriors of God. They've broken from the caliphate and now form their own godless country where immoral places like this flourish.'

He shot another disparaging glance around the room.

'I was going to ask about that,' Ulrich said. 'I thought your folk did not allow drinks like wine, yet here is a tavern.'

'There are places like this even in the caliphate,' Surt said. 'We call them *meyhane*. They're usually run by Jews. I'd say this place is too.'

He cocked his head towards the man behind the counter.

'Christians and other *ahl-al-kitab*, those of other faiths but people of the book, who are allowed to live in the caliphate, visit them,' Surt continued. 'They are heavily watched, however. Tolerated rather than encouraged. But here I'd say they are not just encouraged but nurtured as dung feeds mushrooms. All are corrupted by it. If my daughter is on this island, she will be in a dire situation.'

Einar glanced at the slave children, thinking how Surt must be wondering if his daughter was in a similar situation nearby in the town. Then he frowned.

'Wait,' Einar said. 'What age are you anyway, Surt? How long were you a slave in Norway?'

'Many winters,' Surt said. 'At least twenty.'

'So your daughter must be a fully grown woman,' Einar said. 'I've been thinking of her as a child.'

Surt looked at him as if the same realisation was just dawning on him too.

'When I last saw her she was just a child,' he said, his voice cracking a little. 'I think of her that way.'

Ulrich sloshed wine from the jug into the cups and handed them round. Surt poured himself a cup of water.

'What's wrong with that lot?' Einar said to Surt, sliding his eyes towards the five men slumped on the floor at the right-hand side of the room. 'Can they not hold their drink?'

'That lot are the worst of all,' Surt said with a derisive grunt. 'They are a degenerate crowd of religious fanatics. They eat the *ḥašiš*, a dried herb that captures your mind and turns it to shit. You think they are staring at the floor but they will tell you they are seeing visions inside their heads. They think God speaks to them.'

'Like a *völva* or other witch back home?' Einar said. 'They eat mushrooms and herbs that allow them to talk to spirits.'

'Very like that,' Surt said. 'Though it is *djinn* and other devils who talk to these men, not God. They can be like your *berserkers* too. This amount leaves them helpless but a large amount can send them into a violent rage. They'll charge into battle, heedless of pain, brave to the point of suicide.'

'It will be difficult to get to that fire spout,' Einar said to Ulrich. 'It's well guarded.'

'Aye,' Ulrich agreed. 'I'll need to come up with some sort of plan for that. We need to put that thing out of working order if we're to get the ship out of the harbour. What does your siphōnarioi say, Araltes? Can he give us any advice on how to put one of those things out of use? It looks like it's made of brass, which is hard to break.'

Araltes looked unhappy, and Einar felt that it was not just because they were in a tavern. He said something to Diogenes in the Greek tongue. The man nodded and replied, speaking in a low, earnest tone, while fixing the Norseman with a steady, serious gaze.

'There are ways to destroy them, yes,' he said. 'In fact every one is built with a mechanism in it for doing just that. They are so vital to the survival of the empire we cannot risk one falling into enemy hands. Each siphōnarioi like Diogenes here swears that they will never allow that. If the ship they are on is overrun, they set that mechanism to work and the siphōn is destroyed. More often than not it destroys the ship with it, and these brave men sacrifice themselves to keep the emperor's secret. Such is the strength of their adherence to their oath that not one has fallen into the hands of the Saracens or any other enemy of the empire in the last hundred years.'

'It's not just an oath though that drives the men to destroy the fire spouts and with them their own lives, is it?' Surt said.

Araltes glared at him across the table. For a few moments there was a prickly silence.

'It seems you had quite the conversation with Diogenes then?' Araltes said at last. There was some bitterness in his tone. 'I'll have you know that the emperor's siphōnarici are very well treated and very well paid, highly trained and highly skilled craftsmen.'

'I had no doubts they are,' Surt said. 'But there is something else, Diogenes told me, an extra piece of surety the emperor holds over these men, that ensures they never leave his service and always fulfil their oath to never let one of the fire spouts fall into the hands of your enemies.'

'What's that?' Einar said.

'Each siphōnarioi is told that if a fire ship is captured by an enemy, their family will be killed,' Surt explained. He was looking at Araltes as he spoke. 'If they are married, then their wife and children will pay the price. If they are not married, it will be their parents or brothers and sisters. Such is the price of keeping the emperor's secrets.'

'They are very well paid,' Araltes said in a low, even tone. 'Better paid than any other soldiers or artificers in the army or navy.'

'They are not free though,' Surt said. 'A well-paid slave is still a slave.'

Diogenes said something to Araltes in the Greek tongue. The Norseman nodded, a grim expression on his face.

'However, it appears these pirates have managed to find a siphōnarioi who values something else – gold or gods probably – above his faith to the emperor or his family's safety,' Araltes then said to the others. 'And who now works the siphōn for them.'

'Did it ever occur to you that your enemies may have worked out how to use it?' Surt said. 'We are a learned people. The library in Cordoba has books by Euclides, Pythagoras and many other works of the ancients. How can you be so sure we have got our hands on one of these siphōnarioi?'

'Oh I'm sure of it,' Araltes said. 'We all just saw him with our own eyes.'

Twenty-Seven

'Did you see the man who poked his head out of the tower door?' Araltes said.

'The one with the strange headgear on?' Einar said. 'With leather straps hanging down at the sides that made him look a bit like a hound?'

Araltes nodded. 'That's the headgear of an imperial siphōnarioi. It's part of their uniform that they can wrap around their lower faces to protect them from the heat. This means these pirates have a siphōnarioi as well as a siphōn. It makes sense, I suppose. Otherwise they couldn't have used the weapon with such effect the last time we attacked. I just find it so hard to believe one of them would betray the empire and their family. Diogenes is as shocked as I am. More so, being a siphōnarioi himself.'

'So they've managed to get a siphōnarioi to betray not just his emperor but his own family,' Affreca said, shaking her head. 'Surt is right. Miklagard really is the home of treachery, plots and deceit.'

'Too right,' Ulrich said. 'As soon as we get off this island I'm taking us all back home.'

'Home?' Affreca said. 'Where is that for us now, Ulrich?'

For a few moments there was silence around the table.

'You're a Norseman, like us,' Einar said. 'Don't you ever long for home?'

'Home?' Araltes snorted. 'A frozen wilderness of mountain and forest, where the largest building is a jarl's hall? Let me tell you, lad, compared to the villa of the lowliest nobleman in Constantinopolis, a king in Norway's house is little more than a hut made of mud and straw. If you ever go there, you will see what I mean. We don't call it Miklagard – the Great City – for nothing.'

'I've been to cities,' Einar said. 'Jorvik, Dublin.'

Araltes made a face. 'Those are not cities. Beside Constantinopolis they are mere villages, hamlets whose peasants still keep their animals inside the house with them to keep warm in winter.'

Einar frowned. Growing up in Iceland that was exactly what he and his mother had done during the months of darkness and ice.

'In Constantinopolis they have floors that are heated,' Araltes went on, his eyes taking on a faraway look. 'Water runs in channels to the door of your home; you don't have to trek to a river or draw it from a well. You can buy whatever you want without having to walk more than two streets from home.'

'I've been to Wintanceaster,' Einar said, aware that his lower lip was starting to pout a little. 'King Aethelstan's City. It was like that.'

'Perhaps now you are starting to get close, lad,' Araltes said. 'Aethelstan is an interesting man. He recognises how benighted and ignorant the lands of the north are, and he is doing his best to bring the civilisations of the Romans back there. But even he has a long way – a very long way – to go. He lives amid half-repaired Roman ruins in Wintanceaster but Constantinopolis goes all the way back to the days of the great Caesars. There was no break.'

'Constantinopolis is bigger than Wintanceaster?' Einar said.

Araltes chuckled. 'Its walls alone stretch so far they could encompass the whole of the isle of Meginland in Orkney. They rise in two tiers above a moat to many times the height of a man and have roads between them big enough to drive wagons along. City gates and the buildings associated to them are as large as the village I grew up in. There is one entirely made of gold! It shines like the rising sun and can be seen from many miles away by those approaching the city. There is a horse-racing track inside the city that can seat one hundred thousand people. You're an Icelander, right? That's probably more than the entire population of your country.'

Einar blinked, trying to imagine what a crowd of so many people would look like. The only thing he could imagine was the stars that dotted the night sky.

'Then there are the churches, fountains, palaces, the arches, the theatres, the baths!' Araltes went on. 'Have you ever been in a Roman bathhouse, Einar?'

Einar thought of the decrepit, moss-clogged tunnels he and the others had used to break into the city of Rúðu in north-west Francia. They had said that was the remains of a Roman bathhouse.

'They have pools of hot water you can swim in,' Araltes said.

'We have the likes of that in Iceland,' Einar said. 'There are ponds where hot water bubbles up out of the ground and we wash in them. Every sixth day, whether we need it or not, is *Laugardagr*, wash day.'

'I don't mean bog ponds, Einar!' Araltes said. 'These are great buildings with marbled walls and tiled floors showing pictures of great heroes and sagas. The water is heated in furnaces and that flows into the pools. And there are rooms where it is so hot you sweat all the impurities from your body. These places are open to the people of the city to come and bathe there. Everyone is clean and they don't smell of piss and sweat all the time.'

Einar felt Araltes' words having an ever greater effect on him. They wove the same spell that the Roman ruins in Jorvik, the remains of their roads and all the other glimpses of what Aethelstan and others had called 'civilisation' had on him. The old fascination of what wisdom and lore they possessed and the possibilities of what life could be achieved somewhere beyond the violent, filthy and short one most men in the north endured, awoke once more in his heart. It was this very fascination that had led him to break with Ulrich and the others the year before and take up Aethelstan's cause.

'I'm telling you, a capable lad like you could go far in the imperial service,' Araltes said. 'Look at me. Look how far I've gone.'

'I saw what Aethelstan was trying to build,' Einar said. 'I understood that it meant something.'

'You're a smart lad, Einar,' Araltes said. 'I meant what I said before: A fellow like you could go far in Constantinopolis. You should go there. If you do, look for me and I will get you started. My brother is there too.'

'But what about your gods?' Ulrich asked. His voice bore an edge of accusation. 'The Aesir? You have forsaken them for the Christ God. Don't you want to enter Odin's Valour Hall when you are dead?'

'Odin is a god for kings, jarls and wolf warriors like you,' Araltes said. 'I told you before I'm the son of a low-born farmer. Our kind has as much chance of getting into Valhǫll as we do of getting into the king's mead hall. But let me tell you this. When I was a boy my father took me to the great *þing* at the home of the kings, the place where their ancestral burial mounds watch over everything. There is a great *hof* there, a temple whose walls are covered with gold, and there are statues of the gods: Thor, Frey and Odin. Outside it is the great ash tree they call the world tree. Every nine years folk gather there and there is a sacrifice to the gods: nine males of every species are hung from that tree. I saw it with my own eyes as a boy and when I did I thought I would never see such a thing again. The power of our gods was so horrifying and awe-inspiring. Odin was all powerful.

'But now I've seen the churches built in honour of Christ and can see that squalid tree and that dingy hut for what they are. There's a cathedral in Constantinopolis. It's the largest building in the world and it's built of stone! I cannot even describe what it's like standing inside and looking up at its vast, vaulting roof above. And sacrifices? The day after I arrived in the city a hundred and seventy criminals were executed in the Forum, and that was just like any other day. I can assure you, the works on this earth done in the name of Jesus Christ far outstrip anything Odin has done or ever will. Christ is the king of this world. His power is greater than any other god. So who would not want to be on the side of the most powerful?'

Einar felt like his head was spinning. He found it difficult to even imagine some of the things Aral[??]es was telling him. Part of him wondered if they were really true, but then he had seen glimpses of similar glory with his own eyes.

'I think the lad has heard enough,' Ulrich said. 'I'll thank you to leave him alone. Talk of Romans, libraries and what you call "civilisation" will turn his head.'

'You don't appreciate civilisation?' Araltes said, raising his chin.

'I am not a friend of the Scots,' Ulrich said. 'In fact I hate the bastards. But they had a king once who the Romans came to conquer. They gave him the choice to surrender and become part of the empire by choice. He told them to piss off. *These plunderers of the world*, he said, *where they ravage, slaughter, usurp with lies – they call that civilisation. They make a desert and they call it peace.* My God may be a bloodthirsty one, but at least he is honest about it.'

For a moment Ulrich and Araltes locked eyes.

At that moment the sound of a ringing bell came from outside. It was constant and insistent. It was followed by the sound of trumpets blowing.

'What do you think that's about?' Affreca said to Ulrich.

'I don't know,' he said. 'But it sounds to me like an alarm.'

Twenty-Eight

The others in the tavern all got to their feet at the sound of the alarm. Their previous laughter disappeared, replaced by an air of serious intent as they grabbed weapons and hurried out the doors.

'This is not a disorganised rabble,' Ulrich noted. 'They have discipline and training.'

'As I explained, many of them will be former warriors and sailors of the caliphate,' Surt said. 'Just because I said they were not good Muslims does not mean they are not skilled in war crafts. Apart from those fanatics, that is. They are useless.'

The men who had eaten the ḥašiš remained in their holy stupor on the rugs.

'Do you think this is because of us?' Affreca said, cocking her head towards the blaring of trumpets that were coming through the doors.

'I don't see how it could be,' Ulrich said. 'We haven't done anything to give ourselves away. Maybe they found the other bodies but whatever this is, it's big. A lot bigger than eight Norsemen running about their island. Come on. Let's go and take a look. Maybe we can see what's going on.'

Einar took a swig from his wine cup then with some regret placed it back on the table. As the fiery liquid poured down his throat, he welcomed the momentary feeling of wellbeing it induced in his taut nerves and agitated heart. Then he stood up with the rest and they filed back out into the sunlight.

The little square before the harbour was already a swarm of activity. Merchants were packing up their barrows and starting to leave, encouraged by shouts and prods of warriors eager for them to clear out of the way. Their customers were hurrying off too and it was clear that anyone not a warrior was no longer welcome in the harbour. While they left, more armed and armoured men were filling the harbour from the surrounding streets and buildings.

A bell was making an incessant, metallic clanging from the tower where the siphōn was. Across the town, other horns echoed the alarm from different places. A constant, ringing, metallic clatter seemed to be coming from multiple places. Einar looked around, trying to discern where it came from. He spotted several big iron triangles hanging from walls at different points around the market square. Pirates were beating these with their swords or spear heads. It was a simple, yet effective, warning system that was probably set up all over the town.

As Ulrich, Einar and the others wore the outfits of warriors they were not directed to leave. Their main dilemma then was what they actually should do. If they left they would look conspicuous at a time when it was clear all the warriors of the town were filling the harbour. If they stayed they had no company to follow or leader to give orders as to what positions they should take.

'Don't worry,' Ulrich said. 'In these sort of situations there's always some jumped-up little commander who'll take it upon himself to tell us to do something sooner or later.'

Sure enough, a man in black robes with a curve-bladed sword at his waist came striding towards them, his boots clicking on the flagstones of the square. He began shouting at them and pointing to the landward end of the quay with the siphōn tower on it. There was no need for Surt to translate that he was telling them they should be joining another band of fighters who were forming up there.

As they fell in with the others, another commander in black directed groups of them to different defensive points along the bottom of the quay. Einar saw pre-prepared barricades made from wood being thrown up to form short walls that six to eight men could use to defend against attackers coming from a ship if it made it into the harbour. It was clear the pirates were preparing to be attacked.

Ulrich did not wait for them to be directed to one of these and hustled the others to fall to a crouch behind one. The six of them took up most of the length of it, which discouraged any of the other pirates from joining them.

'Perhaps the caliphe is coming to end this den of snakes,' Surt said in a low voice. 'I can see a ship approaching.'

They all popped their heads up above the barricade and peered out to sea. Through the harbour entrance Einar could see that indeed a ship was approaching, its sails full of the warm wind and two rows of oars undulating up and down from either side like the wings of a dragon.

'That's not a Saracen ship,' Araltes said, squinting to see against the bright sun. 'If I'm not mistaken... no, it can't be!'

Einar narrowed his eyes to look, shading his vision with his palm.

'It looks a bit like your ship,' Einar said to Araltes. 'The galea. Only bigger.'

'Do you think your strategos is coming?' Ulrich said. 'If it is, you'd think he would have given us more time to put that fire spout out of action. Oh well. It looks like he will just have to pay the price for his impatience. I still want to be paid by the way. Keeping him alive was not part of the bargain.'

'It's not the strategos,' Araltes said through gritted teeth. 'Unless he's changed ships. That's a dromon. An imperial warship.'

'If there's fighting, Ulrich,' Affreca said, 'who do we fight for?'

'Ourselves,' Ulrich said. '*If* the ship makes it past that fire spout, when they all start killing each other, we will slope away in the chaos.'

'If that's an imperial ship,' Araltes said, 'I will not stand by and do nothing while they are slaughtered!'

'Don't be stupid,' Ulrich said. 'There's six of us and hundreds of them. What do you hope to achieve, beyond your own death?'

Araltes and Ulrich glared at each other once more for a long moment.

'You do what you want,' Ulrich said at last. 'But I won't have any of my folk die for your emperor.'

Then there was little to do but wait. The ship kept coming for the harbour entrance. The Serk pirates around them crouched, lay or stood behind their defences, clutching their weapons and waiting for what was to come. Around the tower at the end of the quay a company of Serk warriors formed up into defensive ranks around the building. Men ran in and out of the door. They were too far away for Einar to see what they were doing, but he surmised it was all part of the preparations for battle. He could feel his own heart beating faster and his nerves starting to strain. Even if they did not take part in whatever coming battle might occur, they might have to fight to escape. At the very least they would have to run as fast as they could at some point, which in the blazing sunshine would be difficult enough.

The sound of horse hoofs on the flagstones made him turn to look back at the square. A company of riders emerged from the street that led up to the ravine and the gates that guarded the way into the town. They surrounded a horse-drawn wagon that rattled its way across the square to the end of the quay.

The men on the barricades around Einar and the others began to pull theirs aside and Ulrich signalled that they should do the same. The horsemen dismounted but the wagon trundled on along the quay. It was drawn by four horses and a driver sat at the front, holding the long reins. As it passed by Einar, he saw a long black box was on the back. At first he thought it was painted, then he realised it was made of lead. It looked like the coffin for a very tall man and from inside, above the rumble of the wagon wheels on the flagstones, came the unmistakable sound of liquid sloshing around. There was a sort of round spout on the top of one end of it that was stopped with a large blob of yellow wax. A strong smell filled the warm air. It was like intense pine resin mixed with something else completely alien that Einar had never smelled before.

When the wagon passed by all those on the quay, including Einar and the rest of the company, moved their barricades back into position again.

'That's the liquid Sea Fire that gets loaded into the siphōn,' Araltes said in a low voice. 'The siphōn will be charged with one of those canisters already but each one does not last long. That extra lot will allow them to keep spraying fire after the first lot runs out. This means they have a supply of Sea Fire liquid somewhere as well as the siphōns.'

'Would it not be easier to keep it at the siphōn?' Einar said.

'It can explode into fire at any moment,' Araltes said. 'If it gets too warm. If a spark is brought near to it. Sometimes even when the sun shines on it. If it ignites by accident it could destroy the siphōn as well, so it has to be kept somewhere safe. Somewhere cool, dark and where there is no chance of accidental flames.

Even on ships we keep it at the stern and only charge the siphōns with it when we go into battle.'

Einar watched as the wagon reached the tower at the end of the quay. Ten of the pirates manhandled the big case from the back of it and brought it inside the tower, staggering under its weight.

'This gets worse and worse,' Araltes said with a sigh. 'We had hoped the pirates had been lucky and somehow captured a ship with a siphōn and worked out how to use it. But they would only have the Sea Fire liquid carried on that ship and if we continued to attack that would run out. We would lose some ships but eventually we'd overrun them. Now it looks like they have got their hands on a siphōn, a trained siphōnarioi and a supply of more Sea Fire liquid. If we attack this harbour it will be a massacre.'

'Well, we'll soon see,' Ulrich said. 'That imperial ship is nearly here.'

Twenty-Nine

Einar watched the approaching ship as it headed towards the harbour mouth. He could see the eagle flag, the emblem he knew to be the standard of the empire, fluttering in the wind from the first of the vessel's two masts. There were men on the deck too, warriors in armour that glinted in the strong sunlight.

From the tower Einar heard the same strange clanking and hissing he had heard just before Araltes' galea had attacked Thord's ship, which he now knew was the noise of the siphōn being readied for action.

'They won't stand a chance,' Araltes said, glaring at the ship, his voice laden with despair.

'They're taking their flag down,' Kari said.

The others looked and saw that the eagle standard was descending from the mast of the approaching vessel. Another flag, this one bright green, was run up the mast in its stead.

'That's a flag of peace to my people,' Surt said.

'What is going on?!' Araltes said, frowning.

At the sight of the flag, the warriors around them relaxed. Tense expressions were replaced by smiles. Men stood up from behind the cover of their barricades and the sucking and hissing of the siphōn in the tower began to wind down again.

Commanders began barking orders and the pirates began pushing the barricades to the side. When they were moved they started forming lines that spoke more of an honour guard than defence. Signal trumpets blasted again but they were less urgent and played a different tune than before.

'Stand up,' Ulrich said. 'We don't want to look out of place.'

The large imperial ship hove into the harbour entrance. As it did so the mariners on board furled the sails and it was the oarsmen who brought the ship into a berth that waited for it on the quay before the siphōn tower.

The pirate warrior dressed in black who had earlier shouted at Einar and the others strode along the quayside to the imperial dromon. There he stopped and stood, feet apart, fists on hips, waiting.

'He must be a major commander,' Ulrich said out of the corner of his mouth. 'See how the other pirates are so deferential to him? If there's any trouble kill him first. The rest will be thrown into confusion and we might be able to escape.'

Einar swallowed, looking around at the swarms of enemy who thronged the quay around them. If there was any trouble he doubted killing one man, no matter how great a commander, would be enough to save their skins.

Warriors on the quay threw a gangr plank across the short gap from the edge to the dromon. Men on the ship lashed their end to the strakes while pirates did the same on the quay.

A man came out of the door of the siphōn tower. Einar realised he was the same person they had seen earlier with the odd leather headdress on. He too strode over to stand beside the pirate commander before the dromon. Einar saw he was swathed in leather, including breeches and a jacket, as well as the long leather blacksmith's apron he had seen before. Einar surmised that the leather must be to protect the man from any spillage of the liquid fire that spewed from the siphōn. In the baking sunshine the heat of his uniform must be overpowering, and he could see the man's face was slick and shining with sweat.

Warriors in the uniform of the empire began tramping off the ship, making the gangr plank rattle and bounce. After ten men with spears had come over, more men followed in pairs, each pair carrying a wooden chest between them. From the strain on their faces and the way they struggled it was clear the chests were heavy. When they arrived on the quayside they set their burdens down, relief evident on their faces. Einar counted there were six chests in all.

Slaves brought horses and the chests were strapped to their backs. The imperial warriors formed a guard around them as a broad-chested man dressed in the same garb as the strategos strolled up the gangr plank off the ship. He looked around him with a cool, commanding gaze that somehow, mostly from the angle he held his head, made it seem like he was looking down his nose at everyone around him. When he spotted the siphōnarioi he nodded. The man raised his arm in salute.

'By Christ!' Einar heard Araltes gasp. 'I don't believe it!'

'Who is that?' Ulrich said.

'It's Aleksander, strategos of the Macedonian *Theme*,' Araltes said. 'He's one of the emperor's other right-hand men and a favourite of the imperial mother too. What is he doing here?'

'I think that's becoming obvious,' Ulrich said.

Araltes stared at him, his face a mask of incomprehension.

'You really can't see it?' Ulrich said.

Araltes shook his head.

'This lot were all prepared to fight off an imperial ship,' Ulrich said, indicating with his right arm to the pirates on the quay. 'Then it changes its flag and everyone relaxes. Welcomes them with open arms. The flag was some sort of signal. This was all pre-arranged. They were expecting an imperial ship to come and the flag told them this was not the one they should burn.'

Araltes looked at Ulrich, frowning.

'Do you really not see it?' Ulrich pressed. 'Or do you just not *want* to? Your beloved strategos Theoktistos is the victim of one of these infamous Byzantine plots.'

At that moment the commander in black spoke to Strategos Aleksander, who nodded and then began to walk down the quay. The horses with the chests on their backs and their guard of imperial warriors went along too.

'Someone else is coming,' Affreca said. She was looking back towards the square at the top of the harbour. Another entourage of people had arrived from another street that led into the town.

'Let's go along and see what else we can learn,' Ulrich said. 'I don't like standing around here now there's nothing to distract people. Sooner or later someone will start paying too much attention to us.'

He began to saunter off down the quay towards the square. The others followed. As they joined the throng of warriors, both Roman and pirate, who now thronged the square, Einar briefly considered just how much danger they were in. They were surrounded by enemies in the heart of the enemy town. One wrong word, one wrong glance even, and they were all dead. He had always respected Ulrich and followed whatever orders he gave, but right then the thought occurred to him that perhaps this was one risk too far. Their wiry leader's courage had strayed beyond brave to reckless.

They reached the end of the quay. Pirate warriors lined up around the square and Einar noticed that some of the merchants and other civilians had returned from wherever they had been hiding.

The entourage Affreca had spotted arriving were

important-looking. There was a man who looked like a Serk in a magnificent red headdress that had a huge red jewel pinned to it above his forehead. He was tall, broad-chested and dressed in flowing black robes that from the way they shimmered Einar could tell were made of pure silk. The cost of his shirt alone would have been enough to buy a decent mail brynja in Hedeby or Dublin. So much of the material had been used in his garments – an ostentatious display of his wealth – that they flopped and flowed around him. His breeches were of the same material and ballooned out around his thighs as if his legs were encased in two silk balls. He had a magnificent black beard that spilled over his chest and was decorated with gold and silver toggles.

A magnificent sword, curve-bladed in the manner the Serks fashioned their weapons, was sheathed at his waist. The scabbard was studded by many jewels – red, green and blue – which glinted and glittered in the sun. Einar noticed that instead of a hilt the sword had a metal hand fashioned out of what looked like copper in the shape of a grasping fist. The hand had a short piece leading away from it like a gauntlet.

A little behind the man walked a woman. She was black-skinned like Surt, with fine features that held a captivating beauty unlike any Einar had seen before. Its power was checked somewhat, though, by the hard look in her eyes, and the pinched expression on her face as she surveyed everyone in the square suggested a heart filled with anger and judgement. She too was swathed in blue silks that flowed around her lithe figure like the waters of the turquoise sea.

The couple walked under a square canopy held above their heads by four slaves who bore it on poles, one at each corner, so it shaded them from the baking sun.

Surt let out a small gasp. Einar looked around and saw he

was staring at the woman, his bottom jaw hanging open a little. Ulrich noticed this too and gave him a casual tap on the shin with his foot. This broke whatever spell the man was under before his ogling drew unwelcome attention.

The horses with the chests were led into the square and unloaded from the beasts. Slaves set them before the couple who stood beneath the canopy as the imperial warriors formed a line behind them. The strategos, Aleksander, then produced a key and went to the first chest. Squatting before it he used the key to unlock it, then threw back the lid.

An audible gasp went around the courtyard and the sunlight fell on the gold, silver and gemstones piled within. Strategos Aleksander then repeated this for the other five chests until they all lay open, their similar contents gleaming in the sunshine. Einar blinked at the sight, trying to work out how much wealth was set there. One chest alone held more than all the silver the Wolf Coats had taken from Aethelstan.

The imperial strategos said something in a tongue Einar did not understand to the man in black, sweeping his hand over the chests as he did so. The pirate's beard split in a wide grin. He nodded, lifted his left hand and gestured towards a street that led away from the square to the north. As he did so Einar noticed the man's right hand was missing. He had not noticed until now as the man had kept it tucked away inside his voluminous silk robes. Like Einar's own fighting glove, the copper hand fastened to the sword at the pirate's waist must be a device to allow the man to wield a sword despite being maimed.

The strategos kicked the chests shut again. The slaves loaded them back on the horses. Aleksander joined the couple beneath the shade of the canopy and they all began to move off in the direction of the street to the north. The horses and chests followed them, along with a contingent of pirates and the company of imperial warriors.

The rest of the throng in the square began to break up.

Einar's company turned to each other. They looked at Ulrich to see what to do next. Einar noticed that the faces of both Araltes and Surt bore looks of concerned astonishment like men who had just seen a ghost.

'What did your Greek friend say about those chests of gold and jewels?' Ulrich said in a quiet voice.

'He said he had brought them as a gift for Abu Hassan,' Araltes said. 'I believe that is who that one-handed man in black is. He is the leader of this nest of pirates. I know Abu Hassan lost his hand fighting the imperial navy so that has to be him.'

'*Timeō Danaōs et dōna ferentēs*,' Surt said. He blew out his cheeks.

'What does that mean?' Einar said.

'Beware of Greeks bearing gifts,' Surt said.

Thirty

'What now?' Affreca asked.

At that moment the sound of wheels rattling on the flagstones made them turn to see that the wagon they had seen carrying the Sea Fire liquid to the siphōn was returning. The big chest was loaded back on it.

'Now there is no danger they won't want too much fire liquid out in the heat,' Araltes said. 'In case of accidents. It's standard imperial procedure, no doubt taught to these pirates by that bastard traitor siphōnarioi. They must be taking it back to wherever it is stored.'

'That would be a useful thing to know,' Ulrich said.

'It can't be too far away,' Affreca said. 'It got here in very little time when those alarms sounded.'

'Let's follow it now and see,' Ulrich said.

'I'm going after Abu Hassan and Aleksander,' Surt said. Einar could see the balls of muscle tight at the top of his jaw.

'What are you talking about?' Ulrich said. 'We need you with us if we run into anyone who starts asking questions. You speak the Serk tongue.'

'I think that was Rahanna,' Surt said.

'Who?' Ulrich asked, twisting his face in incomprehension.

'That woman with Abu Hassan,' Surt said. His eyes flicked

from right to left and Einar was surprised by how rattled the big man looked. He had never seen him so discomfited in all the years he had known him. 'She is the image of my late wife. It is like looking at her from the past.'

'You think she's a ghost?' Ulrich said.

'I think she's Rahanna, my daughter,' Surt said. 'There can be no other explanation. But I don't understand. I was told she was a slave. She looked like Abu Hassan's wife.'

'I need to know what Aleksander is doing here,' Araltes said. 'I am going with Surt.'

Ulrich flicked his eyes around the company. 'Einar, what do you think?'

Einar was startled. Ulrich was actually asking for his opinion.

'We can split up,' he said. 'I can go with Affreca and the rest can go after Surt's daughter.'

'And the treasure,' Ulrich said. 'Let's not forget about that.'

'You think that is why I want to go that way?' Surt looked both offended and angry. 'I care nothing for jewels. I care about my daughter!'

'And I need to know what is going on for the sake of the empire,' Araltes said.

'And I'd like to keep an eye on where that treasure goes,' Ulrich said. 'Even if you two insist on having more noble intentions.'

Diogenes said something to Araltes.

'Diogenes says he wants to go with you,' Araltes said to Einar. 'He might be able to say a few words if there is trouble. And the siphōn is his area of knowledge anyway.'

'Very well,' Ulrich said. 'We can't do both so we'll test our luck and divide our forces. You three go and find out where the Sea Fire liquid is kept. I will go with the others to see where the pirate king and the treasure end up. If all goes well, we meet back at the tavern, or if all else fails, head to the abandoned fishing huts. If not, it's every man for himself.' He glanced at Affreca. 'And woman,' he added.

The company divided. Ulrich, Araltes and Surt strode off down the street the pirate leader, his consort and the imperial company from the ship had taken. Einar, Affreca and Diogenes followed the wagon, which was going up the hill towards the ravine where the gate out of the town was.

As Affreca had predicted, they did not go far. The wagon halted at the point where the street became too steep to ride. Einar saw one of the sleds he had noticed on the way in was waiting at the bottom of the steep part. It dawned on him that these were used to haul heavy goods – like the Sea Fire canister – up the part of the slope too steep to drive a wagon.

Warriors from the gates above swarmed around the wagon to unload the heavy lead canister from the back of it. They lashed it to the sled then went to the top of the slope beside the gate and hauled the sled and canister up to them, using stout ropes. Once there the canister was taken off the sled while from the rectangular cave entrance above, others threw down more ropes, which their comrades on the ravine floor began lashing around the Sea Fire container.

Einar and the others halted a little way away down the path. Affreca sat on a nearby rock, pretending to be trying to get a stone out of her shoe while the rest did their best to watch what was going on.

'So they keep it in that cave,' Einar said. 'It makes sense if that stuff is as likely to catch fire as they say. It will be cool and dark in there.'

'And it explains why there were no torches burning in there last night,' Affreca said.

Einar looked with longing at the lead box as the Serk pirates struggled to haul it up to the cave. If he could get his hands on even some of what was inside he could cause such havoc to Eirik Bloody Axe's fleet of ships.

Getting it would be hard though. The same issues would present themselves as for anyone trying to storm the gate: once through, the defenders in the cave could rain down all sorts of trouble on them. They could wait until the defenders ran out of missiles but by then help would have come for them from the town. If you did manage to storm your way in, then there would be the problem of how to get the Sea Fire away again. There was no doubt the canisters were heavy. Too heavy to carry, unless you had a lot of men.

'I think we've seen enough,' Einar said. 'Let's go before someone starts asking why we're here.'

At that moment shouting broke out from the other side of the gates: voices raised in excited demand using words Einar could not understand. Through the open gates rode a company of warriors, dressed in the same white flowing robes Einar and the others now wore. There were fifteen of them and ten had the bloodied corpses of men draped across their saddles as they rode. Six of the dead bodies were naked. The riders halted once inside the gate. A thin man dressed in black who had the air of a commander clambered down from the cave and for a few moments he exchanged excited chatter with the horsemen.

'They've found the bodies of the men we killed,' Affreca said. 'Do you think the others are safe?'

'There's no sign of the rest of our crew,' Einar said. 'Which is good. But we really are running out of time now. Come on. Let's get back and find the others.'

The gate commander shouted something to the horsemen and pointed towards the town. They nodded and spurred their horses into motion once more, heading on down the path through the ravine that led to the settlement. Einar, Affreca and Diogenes took advantage of this distraction to turn around. Acting as nonchalantly as possible, they began trekking back to the town as if it were the most normal thing in the world to walk up to the gate, swing round and walk away again. As they tramped back down the ravine Einar felt the familiar itching sensation down his spine as with each step he anticipated a shout of challenge from behind them or to feel the sudden impact of a hurled spear.

Neither came, and before long they were back at the tavern. To their surprise and delight their horses were still tied up outside. There was no sign of the others, however.

'What now?' Affreca asked.

'We can't go in,' Einar said. 'They'll expect us to order something and neither of us know what to say. I know Diogenes said he knows a few words of the Serk tongue but I know no Greek, so can't explain to him what we need.'

'I don't know it either,' Affreca said. 'We'll be safer out on the streets among crowds. No one has time to talk in a town.'

'If the alarm is raised by the arrival of the riders, then we will be in real trouble,' Einar said. 'But yes, let's stay outside until the others arrive. We can't just stand here though. Sooner or later someone *will* come along and ask us questions. We'll go for a little wander. At the very least we might find another way out of this place.'

He signalled to Diogenes that he should follow and they set off. It soon became apparent that there was not very far to go. After walking down a few streets to the south of the square, they soon found all of them ended in either the sea or a rock wall.

'So it looks indeed like the only way in or out of the town

is by the gate in the ravine,' Einar said when they had returned once more to the tavern. 'Or by ship through the harbour.'

'Where can Ulrich and the others be?' Affreca said, looking around the square. 'They should be back by now.'

'There's Surt,' Einar said, spotting the black-skinned man entering the square on the far side. The initial flood of relief in his guts dissolved and was replaced by an unpleasant sensation of unease when he saw Surt was alone. He was also walking a little too fast and even at a distance it was possible to tell from the way he kept glancing around that Surt was agitated about something. Einar was aware that he was oversensitive to these cues himself due to the situation they were in, but if he could spot them, then there was always a possibility that an alert enemy could as well.

Surt saw them and hurried over to join them by the horses. Einar gestured that they should go inside and they all entered the dingy gloom of the tavern. The same table they had left earlier was still free and they gathered around it. The same urchins scurried over to take an order and Surt sent them for another jug of wine.

'Where's Ulrich?' Einar said. 'And Araltes?'

Surt glanced around, then leaned forwards onto the table on his crossed elbows.

'They're inside the palace of the pirate emir,' he said. 'They've been captured.'

Thirty-One

'There is a large building at the far end of the town,' Surt said. He spoke in a low, urgent voice. 'It looks like an ancient temple or palace of the old Romans or Greeks. It's got stone columns across the front and stone carvings there is no way this bunch of pirates built themselves, but I gathered from the chat in the crowd that Abu Hassan has turned it into his home. It looks like he has put a roof on it and patched up cracks and breaks in the walls. There's an impressive flight of stone steps leading up to the front doors, and they unloaded the treasure at the bottom of them. We were standing among a herd of people – pirates and a few townsfolk – at the far side of the street who had followed the procession from the harbour.'

The children returned with the jug of wine and Surt tossed them a few coins. When they had left again he poured out a cup for everyone. To Einar's surprise Surt included one for himself. Surt looked down at the ruby-coloured liquid in the cup for a moment, then took a swig of it. He swallowed hard then let out a little gasp. With a shake of his head Surt managed to regain some of his usual composure.

'Abu Hassan has his own special warriors who guard him,' he said. 'They all wear black like him and carry Lion's Fang swords.

Those are the curved bladed weapons only great warriors bear. As Abu Hassan, Strategos Aleksander and Rahanna my daughter went up the steps, the bodyguards came down and formed a line across them.'

'You are sure that's your daughter?' Affreca said. 'It's a long time since you saw her.'

'Now I've seen more of her I've never been more sure,' Surt said. 'She has her mother's mannerisms and looks.'

Affreca exchanged a glance with Einar, a dubious expression on her face, and he realised she too must have notice the woman's arrogant, sour glare earlier.

'What happened?' Einar said.

Surt squeezed his eyes shut, shook his head and took another swig of the wine.

'It was bad luck,' he said. 'But partly my fault. Abu Hassan and the others were about to go through the main doors when a company of horsemen came down the street. They had the bodies of the men we killed in the forest.'

'We know,' Affreca said. 'We saw them arrive at the gate.'

'The commotion made Abu Hassan and Aleksander turn around,' Surt said. 'At that moment Ulrich said something to me. He was probably saying we should get out of there but I didn't hear him and asked him to repeat it. He pulled down the long part of his turban that was wrapped around his face. I think so I could hear him better, but as he did so one of the pirate bodyguards spotted he had no beard and pointed at him. A grown man without a beard is unheard of in people of our faith. The bodyguard started shouting, demanding he come over.'

Affreca, aware that she had pulled the scarf-like part of her headdress away from her own face to drink from the wine cup, glanced around to see if anyone was watching. When she saw they had not noticed she pulled the scarf back up over her lower jaw.

'The ruckus drew Aleksander and Abu Hassan's attention,' Surt went on. 'The strategos looked down and recognised Araltes standing beside Ulrich.'

'Did he not have his face covered?' Einar said.

Surt shook his head.

'He has no need,' he said. 'His skin is dark from time spent at sea and he has a full beard. You saw him walking around this town earlier. No one gave him a second look.'

'What happened then?' Affreca said.

'The strategos started shouting too,' Surt said. 'He was pointing at Araltes and demanding Abu Hassan seize him. There were warriors all around us. We couldn't run. Araltes shouted that we can't escape. Ulrich turned to me—'

Surt gasped and took another glug of wine.

'He turned to me and said, "*You can get away*",' he continued after swallowing hard once more. 'He told me to grab him, pretending I was capturing them. I did what he said. I grabbed both of them by the shoulders. As Abu Hassan's warriors came across the street, Ulrich told me to get away, find you and get help. He was shouting it like he was protesting about me grabbing him but the pirates did not understand the Norse tongue. In moments we were surrounded by Abu Hassan's bodyguards. They started beating Ulrich and Araltes. Then they hauled them up the steps and in through the front doors.'

Surt's voice caught and he shook his head again, as if he was unable to believe his own memory.

'The captain of the bodyguards actually slapped me on the back,' he said. 'He congratulated me. Thanked me for grabbing the wanted men!'

Affreca looked at Einar. Neither knew what to say. Einar felt like the bottom had dropped from his stomach.

Surt opened his fist to reveal a large ruby.

'Abu Hassan even gave me this as a reward for my loyalty.' His voice was laden with shock. He stared at the gem in disbelief. 'I've never felt such shame.'

Aware Diogenes was looking on, wide-eyed and uncomprehending, Surt cobbled together the story as best he could in the Latin tongue for the benefit of the siphōnarioi. His eyes widened at the realisation that Araltes was now a prisoner.

'As they were dragging him up the steps Ulrich shouted one more thing,' Surt said. He locked eyes with Einar. 'He said you were to take leadership of the company.'

'*Me?*' Einar started back on his stool. He felt like he was going to throw up.

Outside, across the town, a bell and other trumpets and iron triangle began sounding alarms once more.

'That's not good,' Affreca said. 'They must be starting to hunt for us.'

In a bizarre way Einar felt his astonishment, misgivings and confusion drain away at the sound of the alarms. It was like they calmed his frayed nerves rather than tightening them. He could work things out in his own mind later but right now it was time for action.

'I don't know how we save Ulrich yet,' Einar said, standing up. 'But if we don't get out of here right now we won't be able to. Let's go.'

Thirty-Two

They hurried outside. There was general alarm all around like when the imperial ship was arriving, except this time the bell in the siphōn tower was not ringing. Instead there was a clanging coming from the direction of the town gate, which other trumpets and alarms around the town echoed. Pirate warriors were forming up into parties and heading towards the gates of the town. No one was running to guard the harbour.

'They're going to search the island again,' Affreca said. 'He's got Ulrich and Aralts; now Abu Hassan must be trying to round up the rest of us.'

Einar spotted a group of black-clad pirates pulling apart one of the merchant stalls at the far end of the market square. Two of them held the owner by the collar of his shirt while a third was shouting questions at him.

'They're searching the town too,' Einar said. 'Which makes sense, given they caught two of us here. We need to get out of here and find the others – if they haven't already been caught as well, that is.'

They unleashed four of the horses and mounted, then headed up the steep street that led to the ravine and the gate. As they rode they fell into a two-by-two formation. At the steep part at the top of the street they dismounted and led the horses up.

There were other companies of horsemen heading in the same direction, and at this point Einar and the others found themselves mingled among a larger band of around twenty riders.

Einar felt a surge of excitement that dispelled the anxiety hovering on the edge of his consciousness, threatening at any time to rush back in and swamp his judgement. This, at last, was a real piece of good luck. They were just more pirate warriors in a bigger band of them. None of the guards at the gate would pay too much attention to the individual members of it if the leaders looked genuine. If Ulrich really had believed Einar was lucky then this was evidence he might be right.

Once at the top of the steepest part, they all got back on their horses and reformed into columns. A pirate warrior in black stood at the gate shouting orders to the riders as they passed by, flinging his arms in various directions as he did so. When it was their turn to pass by, Surt nodded to the man and said a few words, acknowledging the orders.

Then they rode out through the gate. Einar felt a degree of relief but they were not free yet. They were still at the tail of a larger body of enemy horsemen. As they approached the narrow ridge, the formation moved into single file but kept going. The pirates were either well used to riding the narrow dangerous path or it was a point of bravado for them that they did not dismount and ride across.

Einar and the others had no choice but to do the same. As they clipped across the ridge, buffeted by the warm wind from the sea, Einar did his best not to look down, trying to ignore the cliffs that dropped away to the left and right. One badly placed hoof would send him tumbling down them.

After a short, nerve-shredding time, they reached the far side and onto the main island. There four riders split from the company and set off towards the north shore. The rest kept going along the track that led into the stunted pine forest and up towards the tower on the hill. Einar kicked his heels into his horse's side and turned to the south. Seeing him do this the other three followed his lead. They parted from the rest and rode down towards the shore. They kept on riding until they came to the abandoned fishing hamlet beside the sea.

Riding onto the sand they dismounted. If the little collection of buildings had been in disrepair the day before, they were now wrecked. What was left of the roofs had been torn off completely and lay in bits on the ground. Pieces of old furniture – a table, some bed cots and a bench – had been pulled out and likewise discarded. Here and there patches of the dirt floors had even been dug up. The two broken boats had been turned upright and now sat as if waiting for the tide to come in so they could – had they not had large holes in their hulls – float off.

'Is it wise to be here?' Affreca said. 'It looks like they've been searching the place.'

'Which means they won't be back for some time,' Einar said. 'They won't think anyone is hiding here. Ulrich knew what he was doing when he arranged this place as the point to meet up again. It's also about the only place on the island apart from when you're off the tracks and under the trees that you can't be seen from that cursed tower on the hill.'

Affreca glanced up. Due to the way the settlement was tucked into the edge of the forest at the shore, the tower was indeed out of sight, and if they could not see it, then those in the tower could not see them.

'What do we do about Ulrich?' Affreca said.

Einar sighed. 'I don't know yet. There's not a lot we can do right now.'

'We can't just leave him at the mercy of the pirates, Einar!' Affreca said. 'We don't have much time to do something.'

'Do you think I don't know that?' Einar said. 'Let me remind you, though, of the problem we face. Ulrich is imprisoned in a very well-guarded palace or fort at the heart of a town full of our enemies. The island is covered with search parties hunting for us. If we remain on this island then it's only a matter of time before they find us. Even if we get Ulrich out, they have our ship too. If we manage to get it back, that cursed imperial fire spout will incinerate us if we try to sail out of the harbour. There is no way I'll leave Ulrich behind, but getting him out of that place is going to be hard.'

'Einar, my daughter is in that building too,' Surt said. 'I won't leave without her either.'

'Surt, I'm sorry to say this,' Einar said, 'but she did not exactly look like she was there against her will.'

'Even so,' Surt said, 'if the imperial navy comes and they destroy this place she will perish with the others and I cannot let that happen.'

'That's another thing that is questionable,' Einar said. 'It looks like these modern-day Romans are working with the pirates in some way Araltes was not aware of. Will the imperial navy attack here? I'm not so sure anymore.'

'I don't care.' Surt shook his head. 'This is a place of dishonour and faithlessness. I won't leave my daughter in it.'

'She's not a prisoner,' Einar said. 'So I doubt she'll be in the same place inside Abu Hassan's palace where Ulrich and Araltes are being held.'

'No,' Surt said. 'Unless the pirate wants to—' he swallowed hard '—to spend the night with her,' Surt continued. 'She will be in the harem.'

'The what?'

'The harem,' Surt said. 'It's a secluded place in the house of a man of my faith reserved only for women. No men are allowed to enter. In the house of a rich man like the emir, all his wives and concubines live there.'

'All his wives?' Einar raised his eyebrows.

'A man can have many wives,' Surt said, 'if he can afford to keep them. Mistresses and slave girls too.'

'Men can have more than one wife where I grew up too,' Einar said. 'And they certainly have mistresses and bed slaves, but it's usually not a good idea to put them all in one place together where the head of the house cannot keep an eye on them. Some women can't bear to have rivals, never mind live in the same place as them. Don't they fight?'

'There are eunuchs who are allowed to live among them,' Surt said. 'Their job is to keep order among the women.'

Einar sighed. 'Well, that complicates things even more,' he said. 'And we need to solve all this with – even when the others arrive, if they have not been caught too – a band of *nine* warriors plus Diogenes, who I doubt will be much use in a hand-to-hand fight. And Roan, who won't be much help either.'

Affreca was quiet for a moment. Then she said: 'Nine is a holy number.'

Einar looked at her. There was a faint smile on her lips. She arched one eyebrow.

'It is Odin's holy number,' she said. 'Perhaps this is a sign?'

Einar rolled his eyes. 'A sign we're all mad maybe,' he said. 'What we need is a plan for how we fix all this. Maybe that and an army of warriors. If Odin is watching us then let him send that.'

Thirty-Three

They tethered the horses under the shade of the trees then settled down to wait for the rest of the company. If any other search parties arrived, the plan was to look like they were searching the ruins themselves and so hopefully encourage them to move on and look somewhere else.

Time passed with the sluggish slowness of a lazy snail with nothing to do. Each crack of a branch made them jump, ready to pretend to be mid-search. Nothing happened, however, and no one came. There were noises from birds or animals moving among the trees and the continual rasping of insects. The only other sounds were the rush of the waves on the shore, the blustering of the warm sea wind and the odd cry of seabirds.

They were under the shade of some trees near the water, though ready at all times to spring to their feet and pretend to be searching. For a time they talked about possible ways to get Ulrich out. After a while Diogenes, who could take little part in the conversation, fell asleep in the heat. Surt cast some branches over him to hide him in case a search party arrived. After that they lapsed into silence, each one lost in their own thoughts.

The sun was well beyond the middle of the sky when Einar felt a prickly sensation in his neck. He could not tell what it was, perhaps the incessant scratch of the insects had changed tone, or his ears had picked up a faint rustle of dead pine needles. Maybe there was a slight change in smell in the air, but somehow his senses were alerting him to a change. He had been in danger for days now, and knew from experience that this heightened all senses. It was best not to ignore these pokes that meant something within him, perhaps his heart, had detected something different in the surroundings and was warning his mind about it.

Someone was watching him; he would almost bet silver on that.

He was about to cup his hands over his mouth to make the raven call when he remembered how that had gone when Roan tried that. Instead he tried an owl hoot, the Wolf Coats' other signal, hoping that if there were no crows on this island there would perhaps at least be owls. The sound of one hooting during the day would be unusual but with any luck not totally out of the question.

Another owl hoot came back to him from not far away in the trees at the edge of the beach.

With a sigh of relief Einar stood up and waved at the tree line.

'It's us,' he said in the Norse tongue. 'You can come out.'

'There was a time I could have sneaked right up on you, lad,' Skar's voice came from the trees. 'I'm pleased to say that time is gone. All due to my great teaching, of course.'

Like ghosts, the shapes of the rest of the Wolf Coats – Skar, Kari, Sigurd and Starkad and Wulfhelm the Saxon – came into view amid the trees. They rose from hollows in the ground, from behind tree trunks or out of clumps of undergrowth.

One moment they were not there, the next they were. After a short moment Roan and Fisk appeared from further back among the trees.

'It was him gave us away again, right?' Kari said, glancing at Fisk who traipsed through the fallen pine needles to catch up with them, creating noisy whooshes and crackles as his feet moved through the debris. 'He has none of our stealth craft. It's a wonder he hasn't got us caught already.'

'It was probably the smell of you gave us away,' Fisk said, poking out his bottom lip. 'It must be washday soon. You need a bath.'

Einar grinned at the banter, aware of the sudden rush of happiness and security he felt at seeing the rest of the crew once more.

Diogenes was woken by the voices and sat up. Affreca, Einar and Surt went to join the others at the edge of the trees, making sure they were well out of sight of anyone watching from the tower on the hill.

'We came here earlier but the pirates were searching it,' Sigurd said. 'So we decided to leave and come back later.'

'Where's Ulrich?' Skar said.

Einar, Affreca and Surt told them what had happened. When they finished, there was silence for a moment. The other Wolf Coats looked at them, aghast.

'You left Ulrich *behind*?' Starkad said after a moment. His tone was disbelieving and with an edge of accusation.

'It was my decision,' Einar said. 'It seemed like the only choice at the time.'

'What else could we do?' Surt said.

'You could have tried to save him!' Kari said. 'But you deserted him twice!'

'I did what he told me to do!' Surt said. 'He told me to get away. If I'd stayed with him I'd be a prisoner too.'

'If he's not already dead,' Sigurd said.

'And I'd be dead too,' Surt said. 'What is it Ulrich was always saying your god says? *A corpse is no use to anyone?*'

'Don't you quote Odin to me,' Sigurd said through clenched teeth. 'If you had died there at least you'd have died with some honour.'

Surt's nostrils flared with anger. He and Sigurd locked eyes, glaring at each other.

All fellow feeling at being reunited had gone. Anger, disappointment and fear, both for what might happen to Ulrich and what the future now held for the rest of them, had taken its place. There was something else too, Einar realised. He could tell the others were feeling the same sensation he had when first hearing Ulrich had been captured: Ulrich was their leader. He decided their plans. Without him, what should they do?

'Then you decide everyone runs away?' Kari turned to Einar with a sneer.

'Fuck off,' Einar said, anger setting his heart ablaze. 'You weren't there.'

'And since when did you make the decisions?' Starkad said. 'Who made you king?'

'Ulrich,' Affreca said.

Silence fell. The only sounds for moments were the waves crashing on the shore and the insects rasping in the trees. The impact of her words stunned everyone as much as the news of Ulrich's capture. It dispersed the growing conflict like opening a door and letting fresh air into a smoky room.

All eyes turned to Affreca.

'Ulrich said Einar was to lead us until we got him back,' Affreca said. She glanced at Surt, looking for confirmation.

'That is true,' Surt said. 'It was one of the last things he said to me.'

'*You?*' Sigurd glowered at Einar. 'You betrayed Ulrich – you betrayed all of us – when you left the company last year. You stole that book and gave it to Aethelstan! You helped the Christians by doing that. Ulrich wanted you dead for all that. You know that? It was us who persuaded him to let you come back. And you're telling me now he chose *you* to lead us?'

'I'm as shocked as you are,' Einar said. 'If you don't want me to—'

Surt gave a gravelled cough and laid a hand on Einar's chest, the gesture stopping Einar from saying anything more. Einar turned to him, realising the big prowman, Ulrich's right-hand man, his oldest companion and second in command of the company, had not yet said a word.

Skar was staring at the ground, his eyelids heavy. He took a deep breath, as if trying to quell the emotions swirling within his heart. Then he looked up, taking a moment to look everyone around him in the eyes until he was sure he had everyone's attention.

'Ulrich has told me this as well in the past,' he said. His voice was serious. 'I always thought he would be here to tell you all himself, but that has not turned out to be the case. What Einar did was right. He got the rest of the crew out of danger. They saved themselves and by doing that we now have a chance of saving Ulrich, as opposed to no chance if they'd all got themselves captured or killed. It's what Ulrich would have done and what Ulrich and I have taught you all what to do if you're ever in that situation.'

'But it should be you who leads us, Skar!' Kari said. 'You're the most experienced viking. You're the stafn-búi. You lead us in battle.'

'I can lead a charge,' Skar said. 'That is why Ulrich deferred to me in the fighting. But I cannot direct an army. The leader of the company needs to be able to think like a great *tafl* player: always two, three moves ahead of his opponents. Ulrich sees this quality in the lad here.'

He laid a hand on Einar's shoulder. Einar felt his back straighten and his chest swell, as if the touch had somehow conveyed power into him.

'And Ulrich believes that Einar is gifted by Odin himself,' Skar said. 'He can compose poems for the mead hall and go berserk in a fight. There are few so doubly blessed by Old One-Eye. Lately Ulrich began to think the Norns had also blessed Einar with good luck. For all those reasons Ulrich made the right choice. I support him in that and will follow Einar the way I followed Ulrich.'

'He's right, Skar,' Einar said, nodding to Kari. 'It really should be you who leads us. You say Ulrich has all these beliefs in me but—'

'Enough!' Skar said in a stern voice. 'The decision is made. The fact that you don't want this position is all the more reason you should have it. Now we have a task to do, so let's get on with it. How do we get Ulrich out of there and get off this cursed island?'

All eyes now turned on Einar. He looked back at them, realising that though some were still reserving their judgement, the decision had been made whether he, or anyone else, liked it or not.

'I think we'd all agree that if we're going to attack it will be in the dark,' Einar said. 'It's what Ulrich would have done and as there are so few of us it will bring our best chance of success.'

The others nodded, some enthusiastic in their agreement, some reluctant.

'So get some rest until sunset,' Einar said. 'We have a busy night ahead.'

Thirty-Four

Huddled around the fire on the long winter nights in Iceland, Einar had heard tales of the draugr. These were bad folk who after an inglorious, malicious or otherwise evil life had died, only to return as walking corpses who harassed and harmed their relatives and neighbours as they had done in life, except now with more sinister and murderous intent.

These *aptrgangrs* – "after walkers" – came in the night to do their evil work. During the day they lurked in their burial mounds or in caves or under cover in other places, hiding away from the sun.

As they waited for darkness, the úlfhéðnar lay like draugr in hollows under the trees, buried under branches and heaps of fallen pine needles, away from the sun and the prying eyes of any casual passer-by. They took turns on watch in case any search parties returned while the others grabbed what rest they could. Most slept, not knowing when the next opportunity to do so would come along. The air was thick with heat and the constant, rhythmical rasp of the insects acted almost like a lullaby, so sleep was not hard to fend off.

Except for Einar. He lay under a mound of pine needles, his nostrils filled with their heady scent. His ears were filled by the rasp of the insects as he stared up at the patches of blue sky that were visible through the branches above. He found sleep impossible. His mind churned with thoughts of what he should do. What made it harder to think about was the fact that whatever they did next, and ultimately the success or failure of the whole venture, were now down to him.

Could he really take this burden? Was he really capable of leading this company to victory? Or even survival? And where should he lead them anyway? Where did his, and now, if he took this responsibility on his shoulders, their path really lie?

He thought of Araltes and how he had talked in such glowing terms about this thing called 'civilisation'. It sounded like what might wait for him in Miklagard was a vision like that offered by Aethelstan except one hundred times greater.

Aethelstan's dream had fascinated Einar. It had led him to forsake the very companions he was now supposed to lead into battle. And he had done well with Aethelstan, he considered. He had been given his own war band and entrusted with tasks vital to the survival of Aethelstan's kingdom. He had not just played tafl with the king but been a real player in Aethelstan's greater game, his vision of building a new Roman civilisation in the north of the world. Of bringing peace and order across the realms. Could he do the same in Miklagard, perhaps on an even bigger scale?

But where had the adventure with Aethelstan led him anyway? Aethelstan's plots had just provoked wars. The Saxons had never fully accepted Einar. He had led a war band, yes, but had no real friends. He had been a foreigner, a stranger who spoke with an odd accent. Never fully trusted. He had been an odd creature, a fish out of water. A man who walked alone. An eingangr maðr.

An eingangr maðr was not a lucky man.

Not for the first time he wondered about Ulrich's belief that he had become blessed with luck by the Norns. This supposition had taken him by surprise. He had never thought of himself as being particularly lucky, in fact mostly the opposite. Recently this belief had been reinforced by Affreca and Ulrich's comments about him being an eingangr maðr. Such men were usually shunned by others – not because of any fault of their own, but because they were deemed to be unlucky, and no one wanted someone like that on board if you were heading on a dangerous voyage or embarking on a hazardous quest.

If Ulrich was in fact right and Einar had been blessed with luck, the trick would be to ride this luck without becoming overconfident, which would without doubt bring about his downfall.

Not just his downfall. The downfall of all the company he would now lead. If it were true, and Ulrich was right, then the Norns, those three all-powerful women who wove the fates – the *wyrds* – of men, must have decided this for him. If so, was there a reason they had done this, or was it just some whim? Some kind of cruel joke of the powers who govern the worlds whose humour is beyond the minds of any mortal to understand the funny side of.

If they got away, perhaps this path should lead him to Miklagard where he would rise through the ranks of its army and one day return home and take Orkney at the head of a fleet of fire-spouting imperial warships. He would be the one who brought 'civilisation' to the north. Aethelstan would beg for his alliance.

Yet this was everything Ulrich despised. To him what people called 'civilisation' was just an illusion. A false vision used to enthral folk without them realising it. To Ulrich, Aethelstan's peace was subjugation. Order that was really just slavery.

A bird crossed his vision moving between a gap in the tree

branches above. It was a hunter, a brown hawk or similar, sailing, wings spread on the hot air as it looked for prey below, just as the men in the tower at the top of the hill were no doubt scouring the island below for Einar and the others. He had seen several birds that day. Apart from this hawk the rest had been white seabirds. No crows or ravens.

Every morning, Odin sent his ravens, Huginn and Muninn, out to fly around the world and observe what was happening. In the evening they returned to him and whispered all the news into his ears. That way he knew the deeds of men. They saw every brave deed and every cowardly act. You never knew if the crow watching you from a branch was really one of Odin's ravens or not, so it was best to assume it was either Huginn or Muninn and act as best you could.

There are no crows or ravens on this island, Surt had said. It was something that was beginning to gnaw at Einar's already frayed nerves. It meant whatever deeds they did that night, whether good or bad, right or wrong, could not reach the ears of Odin, and if that was the case, was there any point in doing them? If they died that night, there would be no reward waiting for them beyond.

That, he chided himself, *was an excuse*. A reason dreamed up by his reluctant heart for shirking the responsibility that had been thrust upon him. They had to save Ulrich; there was no question about that. They *had* to get the ship – or any ship – back or they would never get off this island. There really was no choice in the matter. They could not leave Ulrich behind.

He sat up, the blanket of pine needles falling off him like the grave dirt falling off one of the rising undead.

'So be it,' he said to no one in particular. If Odin's ravens could not watch them then maybe the Valkyries could. And if no one was watching then they would send enough men to Hel before them that they would tell everyone there the úlfhéðnar were coming.

There was movement not far away. Affreca too rose from a bed of pine needles. She saw Einar scrambling to his feet, brushing dead needles off his clothes.

'What's happening?' she asked.

'We're going to get Ulrich out of that town,' Einar said. 'Then we're getting off this island.'

Thirty-Five

'You have a plan?' she said, her eyes lighting up.

'I have,' Einar said. He locked eyes with her. For a moment it felt like she was looking straight into his heart. 'It depends on you. But it will be very dangerous. Are you all right with that?'

Affreca made a face like he had just asked the most irritating and stupid question she had ever heard.

'I'll get the others up,' she said.

Before long the company was roused. They all gathered in a semicircle around Einar, squatting on their haunches and looking at him with expectant gazes. Sigurd and Kari still bore sceptical expressions but they did not give voice to any of their misgivings.

'Well?' Skar said. 'Let's hear it, lad. How are we going to do this?'

'We need to repair those boats for a start,' Einar said. 'We should be able to get enough wood from the forest around us and our weapons are all the tools we should need.'

'What about nails?' Starkad said.

'There was a chest of iron nails on the ship,' Roan said, his voice miserable.

'That's not much use,' Sigurd said.

'We can make glue,' Einar said. 'That should be enough to hold any repairs for long enough for what we need to do. We need ropes too. Roan, did the Serks take the one I used to climb up the cliff when they took the ship?'

'I don't think so,' Roan said. 'As far as I know it's still coiled up under that tree where you left it.'

'Good,' Einar said. 'Starkad, can you go and get it? You're the stealthiest of us all. I can count on you getting there and back without getting caught.'

Starkad nodded.

'Kari, you build a secret fire,' Einar said. 'There's a chance those bastards in the tower might see some smoke but we'll just have to take the risk. The rest of us start gathering what we need. Let's get to work.'

Starkad loped off into the forest to get the rope. Sigurd and Kari started digging a pit with their swords and spears while the others gathered fallen wood and dead pine needles that would provide fuel, making sure it was as dried out by the sun as possible. That way it would produce as little smoke as possible. Einar, Affreca and Surt used knives to cut lengths of dried resin and sap from the trunks of the surrounding pines. They also cut taps into the trees and collected the fresh sap that flowed out.

Once the firepit was deep enough, Kari started on digging a tunnel about four paces away from it that sloped down to enter the pit around its base. They piled wood and dead needles into the pit and Kari set it alight using his flint and charcoal fire starting kit. The wood and needles were dry as a bone and sparked alight at once. Skar cut green branches off some surrounding trees and laid them over the top of the pit. The fire itself was below ground so its flames were invisible to any watchers. The needle-laden green branches helped to filter and disperse any smoke rising, and the tree canopy would add to this so that by the time it reached the sky there would be little more than a slight grey miasma that with luck was undetectable to any watchers. As the fire burned it sucked air down the side tunnel, using it to stay alight despite being underground.

'I will sacrifice my helmet for the cause,' Einar said, breaking up the strips of resin and throwing them inside his upturned iron head protection. 'I hope Odin appreciates the gesture.'

'It was a cheap piece of shit,' Kari said with a grin. 'Perhaps you don't understand the meaning of *sacrifice*? You're supposed to give up something you value.'

'He'll understand the meaning if someone hits him over the head later,' Sigurd said.

They put the upturned helmet over the fire and before long the resin started to melt into a thick amber goo. The rest of the company busied themselves cutting wood and stripping it into pieces that could be used to cover the holes in the hulls of the two decrepit fishing boats.

After a while Starkad returned with the rope. Einar began cutting it with his knife into several equal lengths.

By the time he had finished, the resin was melted. Kari mixed charcoal from everyone's fire-starting kits and ashes from the fire into it with a stick to make a strong, sticky gum. Then they all set to work repairing the boats as best they could. By the time they ran out of glue one fishing boat had the holes in it patched enough to be confident it would not sink. The second was at least half repaired, though there was still more to do and how long it would stay afloat was debatable.

By then the sun had set and with the fire not visible the only light they had to work with now was from the bright moon, which rose above the blackness of the sea, scattering countless diamonds of light over the waves and washing everything on the beach with its pale silver light.

'Do we make more glue to finish the second boat?' Kari said.

'No,' Einar said, shaking his head. 'We need one to be seaworthy but the other one only needs to get as far as we swam last night. We're running out of time anyway.'

'What now?' Kari said.

'Surt,' Einar said. 'You told me you knew how to make devices that could burst into flames when thrown but the trick was making a wick for them that meant you delayed the moment they exploded.'

Surt nodded.

'Could you make one of those wicks?' Einar said.

'I could,' Surt said. 'We could use the scrapings of what's left of the resin and if anyone has any candles – even stubs – we can use those to. I need a short piece of the rope too. But we don't have anything suitable to create the fire device.'

'That doesn't matter,' Einar said. 'You'll have plenty later. Just make the wick for now and show the others how they work.'

Surt set to work on this. When he was done, he explained to the others how to set it alight and how long they should burn for. Then the company gathered around Einar, and he began to lay out his plans to them.

'Some of us will get to the town by the sea,' Einar said. 'Surt: you, Affreca, Roan and I will do that. I'm betting on them recognising you from earlier and because you looked like you helped grab Ulrich they should trust you are a loyal man of the pirate emir.'

Surt and Affreca nodded.

'Ulrich has already laid the groundwork for his own rescue,' Skar said, grinning.

'Why don't we all go in by the sea?' Sigurd said.

'We need to make sure the gates are secured,' Einar said, 'and that the extra fire liquid never reaches the siphōn in the harbour. That way, once we have the ship back we can sail right out of there.'

'Once the siphōn itself has been disabled,' Skar said.

'That's what this man's task will be,' Einar said, laying a hand on the shoulder of Diogenes, who smiled in an awkward manner, not knowing a word of what was being said to him. 'Every siphōnarioi is taught a secret way to put them out of action permanently.

'This will take skilled fighting, *hard* fighting,' Einar continued. 'Which is why I need you men to take the gate. You're the only warriors who possibly can.'

He saw faint smiles appear on the lips of the Wolf Coats before him, an almost imperceptible straightening of their backs and swellings of their chests.

'You'll be outnumbered too,' Einar said. 'So victory will be even more impressive. I need you to go over the rampart, get behind it and then take the gate.'

'How are we going to do that?' Kari said. 'There's a man every twenty paces along the top. And then there's that fucking watchtower. As soon as anyone moves across the ridge, the warriors up there will spot them.'

'We'll draw the warriors off the wall and out into this part of the island,' Einar said. 'Hopefully most of the ones in the town too. And we'll make sure whoever is in that tower is too busy to worry about what we are up to.'

'And how do we do that?' Skar asked.

Einar squatted down beside the firepit. He thrust his arm beneath the covering layer of pine branches and grasped a smouldering brand from the fire. He pulled it out and stood up again.

'The same way you deal with any rats,' Einar said, tossing the glowing brand onto the forest floor amid the carpet of dead pine needles. In an instant the debris it landed on began to crackle and smoke.

'You smoke them out.'

Thirty-Six

The fire caught almost straight away. The dead pine needles that covered the forest floor smouldered for a moment then flared alight. The warm wind that blew from the sea without ceasing fanned the flames and the blaze began to creep across the forest floor with alarming speed. In moments it was licking the trunks of the trees with hungry tongues of flame.

As it built, Einar explained the rest of his plan. By the time he finished, the undergrowth was well alight and the horses were getting skittish.

'We'd better get moving,' Einar said at last. 'We don't want to be caught up in our own fire.'

They released the horses and the animals trotted off into the woods away from the growing conflagration.

Einar and the others gathered around the two fishing boats and threw their weapons and armour in. The Wolf Coats took ashes and soot from the firepit and used it to blacken their faces and arms, anywhere their flesh might be exposed. Einar did this too but did not touch his face.

When they were done, Skar turned to Einar. He held out his right hand and Einar grasped him by the wrist. The big prowman returned the gesture. When he squeezed, it felt like his fingers were made of iron. Both men locked eyes.

'Good luck, lad,' Skar said. 'We're all counting on you. Get Ulrich out and make sure that fire spout is broken.'

'I will,' Einar said. 'And I am counting on you taking that gate.'

'We will,' Kari said.

He stood to Skar's right. Sigurd was on his left and Starkad beside him. Light from the flames now flickered across all of them. They regarded Einar with gazes that held none of the animosity or challenge they had earlier. Einar hoped this meant they believed his plan would work. Perhaps now they were going into battle whatever misgivings they had about him replacing Ulrich, even for a while, had been set aside for the time being.

'See you in the town,' Einar said.

They took the one boat that they hoped was more waterproof and slid it into the sea. Einar, Surt, Affreca, Roan and Diogenes jumped in. They had cut pieces of wood to make oars and all set to work paddling away from the beach.

Einar and Surt still wore the Serk robes they had been in all day. Einar also had his wolfskin cloak and his usual dark britches and jerkin in his leather satchel.

Skar, Starkad, Kari, Sigurd, Fisk and Wulfhelm grabbed the other boat and shoved it into the waves after them. Each one of them carried over their shoulder a length of the rope Einar had cut earlier. They jumped in and began to paddle too. Their boat was soon surging ahead of Einar's, not just because there were six fit warriors rowing it but because it was already starting to leak. They were desperate to get across the stretch of tide-swamped beach at the base of the ridge before it sank.

As he dipped and hauled on his makeshift oar, Einar watched with bated breath as the other boat struggled across the water he had swum across the night before, getting ever lower as it went. He and the others kept their own boat further out from the shore. They had further to go and did not want to risk their makeshift repairs being tested by accidentally running aground.

A grinding sound from the other boat told Einar they had made it to the shore. From the little of it that now remained above the surface, it looked like they had only got there by sheer grit and brute force, but they were now on the other beach and on the peninsula without having to cross the ridge above in full view of whoever was watching from the ramparts or the tower on the hill.

There was still a chance they might be seen, but behind them the fire Einar had set was already sending flames up into the sky through the canopy of the pine trees, and those prying eyes would – Einar hoped – soon be more concerned with that than paying attention to who was sneaking up on them from the sea.

There are places a small company can walk into where an army cannot storm. Ulrich's words surfaced in Einar's memory. Tonight he hoped the little man was right, and the same rule applied to little boats and well-guarded harbours.

Skar and the others scrambled out of their boat into the waves as they crashed onto the little beach at the base of the cliffs. They turned and attacked the almost submerged boat with their swords and Fisk's axe, smashing its already frail hull to splinters that the waves took away in their greedy pull.

By this time Einar's boat was passing by. Skar raised a hand towards them, then they turned and hurried towards the path that led up to the top of the peninsula. Einar watched them go, thinking how it was up to them now how they would take the gate and get the Sea Fire, but if anyone could do it, it was those men. There were still only six of them, however.

The sound of shouts and horses' hooves above made Einar stiffen. Then he relaxed, realising that it was coming from pirates riding away from the town over the ridge. He felt heartened that his plan was working and the fire was already drawing defenders out from behind the ramparts to deal with it. On a small island like this, such fires would be a menace. They could not be allowed to get out of hand, otherwise the whole place could go up in smoke. Those in the tower would be especially worried. If they got trapped up there they would have nowhere to run to except into the flames.

Einar felt something cold around his feet. Looking down he saw there was water in the bottom of the boat. Some of his elation dissipated. He had hoped their repairs might have lasted a little longer. By his reckoning they were not even halfway there yet.

'Come on: row!' he said to the others, redoubling his own efforts as he did so.

The others followed suit, though neither Roan nor Diogenes possessed the physical power that had allowed Surt and the others to push their sinking boat onwards faster than the water could pour in. Soon they were all sweating heavily and out of breath. Einar's shoulders burned from the effort and he wondered how the others must be feeling.

Roan set his oar down. Einar opened his mouth to admonish him but stopped when the skipper lifted Surt's helmet and began using it to scoop water out of the bottom of the boat.

'My bailing will do us a lot more good than my rowing,' he said.

Einar nodded, realising the skipper, with his years of experience on the sea, was right. Brute force and ignorance were not always the best ways to fix a problem. Roan went on bailing while the others rowed and that way they were able to keep a balance between progress and sinking.

They carried on, rising and falling with the waves, keeping far enough away from the cliffs lest they be driven against the rocks and the boat be shattered into splinters. After a time they reached the far end of the island. The cliffs fell down to the edge of the town. There was nowhere to land, however. The rocks were either too steep or there was too little space to land the boat on. Einar caught sight of some people up on one of the streets that ended at the water and said a silent prayer to Thor that they were not looking out to sea.

He chose Thor to plead with and not Odin, as the red-bearded god was famous for going out in a little boat like the one Einar was in now to try to fish for *Jörmungandr*, the great beast that circled the world.

They kept going. They reached the stone quay with the tower and siphōn at the end of it. At this point they needed to get close in. If there were warriors patrolling the quay, they would be on watch for ships coming over the horizon rather than a small rowing boat right under their noses, so the closer they got to the harbour wall the better. Despite the danger of them crashing into the stones of the outside of the quay, they kept the boat right alongside it, watching upwards for any sign of movement above. Einar signalled to Roan he should stop bailing as well, lest the sound of scrape and splash alert someone.

They saw nothing, however, apart from at the town end the back of the stakes with the grisly remains of the crucified victims nailed to the other side. They passed the siphōn tower and came to the end of the quay.

Once there they made a hurried dash across the harbour entrance to the other side. As they paddled over, Einar looked around but both quays and what he could make out of the square beyond the ships that packed the harbour looked dark and deserted.

At the other side of the harbour entrance he finally saw what he was looking for: a place to land. On the outside of the other quay was a little shelf of rock just where it met the water, a remnant of the original bedrocks the quay had been built on top of.

Einar directed the others to make for it. Because Roan had stopped bailing they were already up to their ankles in sea water inside the boat by the time a wave crashed them onto the rock shelf. The wave retreated, leaving the boat sitting on top of the rock.

'Come on,' Einar said, standing up. 'We need to move fast.'

With the shift of weight the boat made a sharp tilt and Einar almost fell out into the sea. He steadied himself then reached up. At full stretch his fingers just grasped the top of the quay. He jumped, powering himself halfway up with his legs then pulling with his arms so he ended up with arms straight down, palms on the quay. He looked around but there was no one in their immediate vicinity.

At that moment the waves crashed back around the boat, swamping it and threatening to pull it back out to sea again. Affreca jumped up and threw her arms around Einar's waist, anchoring herself and through her feet the boat back on the quayside. Einar gasped and gritted his teeth. He was now not just holding his own weight but Affreca and the boat as well.

Surt clambered up onto the quay beside him. The wave receded, Affreca released Einar and the big man hauled Einar up beside him. Einar spun around and reached down to grab Affreca's outstretched arm. That way they still anchored the boat to the quayside, but in a more comfortable and sustainable way. Roan passed up the war gear from the boat then Surt leaned down and helped him and Diogenes up onto the quay.

Affreca used Einar's arm to haul herself up. With nothing left to hold it, the waves took the little boat and it washed off the ledge and out to sea. As it disappeared from sight into the darkness, it was already half swamped with water and well on its way to sinking.

For a moment they waited, staying in the dark, watching for any sign of guards or pirates on patrol at the quayside. There was no one around. As Einar hoped, what guards and watchmen there might have been on the harbour at night had been drawn out of the town to try to deal with the fires and stop them before they consumed the whole island and the town with it. There were some figures in the market square but the market itself was closed for the night and the stalls packed away under canvas covers.

Einar noted with some satisfaction the red glow visible in the sky beyond the town, towards the main part of the island. This could only mean that the fire they had set was now blazing furiously and any attempts by the pirates to put it out had so far failed.

They got up and walked down the quay, now walking as if they belonged there and had not just crept in on a little boat. As they went they scanned the ships crowded into the harbour for the snekkja.

'There she is,' Roan said, nodding towards the dragon-carved prow of the longship, which nestled alongside those of the larger Serk pirate vessels like a wolf among cows. He sounded like he had just spotted a long-lost lover.

'Get aboard and get her ready to go,' Einar said to the skipper. 'Make sure she is untied and the oars are ready. If you can unfurl the sail without drawing any attention all the better. Whatever you can do to shorten the time it will take to get out of here. When we are ready to leave we might be in a real hurry. Any time we can save could be the difference between us getting away alive or not.'

Roan nodded. 'It's a pity we couldn't go now,' he said, casting a rueful glance around the deserted harbour. 'I don't think there is anyone in that tower now.'

'We need to get Ulrich first,' Einar said.

'And my daughter,' Surt said.

'So just do what you can so we can make a swift exit when we've got them,' Einar said. 'We'll leave Diogenes with you until we come back. He doesn't fit into my plan and will get in the way.'

'I don't know what I'll do with him but all right,' Roan said.

They parted. Roan led Diogenes off the quay and across the decks of the deserted, docked pirate ships towards their longship. Einar, Surt and Affreca carried on down the quay towards the square. When they were nearly there they stopped.

'I need you to get undressed now,' Einar said to Affreca.

'I thought you'd never ask,' she said with a smile.

Einar was glad of the darkness that hid the blush that flooded his cheeks.

As they had discussed earlier Affreca stripped off the Serk warrior gear until she was only dressed in a short undershirt. Einar fought with his own eyes that yearned to stare at her now naked, long, well-toned legs and, as the warm wind pushed her shirt against her, the outline of her breasts and slim body.

Surt gave a low whistle. 'By Allah, girl,' he said in a husky voice. 'You mean to say you've been hiding all this under those breeches and heavy war gear all this time?'

Affreca shot a glare at both of them that suggested they should stop staring or bad things would happen.

'We have work to do, lads. Remember?' she said.

Einar blinked, forcing his mind back to the task in hand. He took the white Serk robe off then pulled his wolfskin cloak out of the satchel he carried. Einar put his wolfskin on with the hood down, then pulled the Serk robe back on. The garment was so loose and wide it fitted over his clothes beneath without any problem.

'I just hope I don't pass out from the heat,' he said.

Then he cut a piece of rope off one of the many that lashed ships to the quay. Affreca clasped her hands before her and Einar wrapped the rope around her wrists then tied it in a knot, making it look like she was a prisoner.

They stashed the rest of their gear in two leather satchels and hid them among a pile of barrels and chests stacked on the quay.

'Right,' Einar said when he was finished. 'Surt, lead the way to the pirate emir's palace.'

Thirty-Seven

Then they set off into the town. There were more people about there but most of them were hurrying towards the gates, presumably to go out to tackle the growing fire.

After crossing the market square, they headed down another street until they came to the end where it opened into another smaller square.

A massive stone building dominated the other side. Einar could tell by the style of it that it had been built by the Romans or similar ancient wizards. It was built of white stone and stretched all the way along one side of the square. The entrance was raised above the street, reached by a line of stone steps that were the entire width of the building. The steps were cracked and uneven, in some places worn into dips by the countless feet that had trodden their way up and down them in the centuries since they had been placed there.

A row of stone columns, each as broad as a man, lined the front of the building. Their faces were pitted and cracked, and here and there alarmingly large chunks of stone had fallen out. These supported a triangular plinth, which had carvings on it of men, women and animals so realistic that, even though some were now missing limbs or heads, they looked like actual people and creatures had been frozen then covered in plaster. Behind the columns, in the centre of the front of the building, was a tall double door.

A couple of braziers were lit, one on either side of the steps, providing light to the area. There were black-clad warriors, the bodyguards of the pirate emir, before the door.

Einar could see why Abu Hassan the pirate emir had chosen this place as his palace. It was big and made of stone. Even in a state of disrepair it was without doubt the strongest building in the town.

They made their way up the steps. As they approached, the bodyguards stiffened and came together in a line before the door. One of them began shooting questions, his voice loud and aggressive.

Surt replied in the tongue of the Serks. As planned with Einar earlier, he was saying that he had brought a new slave girl for the emir's harem as a gift. Surt said he wanted to gain an audience with Abu Hassan as he wished his permission to make a piracy venture of his own and he hoped the gift of the slave girl would help make that happen.

The Serk grinned and looked Affreca up and down, nodding in appreciation at her good looks and lovely body.

Surt then retold the same tale he had told about Einar on the quay earlier that day, that Einar had been punished by the Emir of Cordoba for piracy. This time, however, he not only said that the emir had removed Einar's finger and tongue but that he also made him a eunuch. Einar was not sure how things would play out once inside, but if they thought he was emasculated then perhaps he could get into this harem place.

The pirate frowned and said a few more words to Surt, still glancing towards Einar.

For a moment Einar thought all was lost. He prepared to pull the knife from his belt with his left hand and defend himself.

They were outnumbered but there was a chance if they were quick enough and caused enough surprise they might be able to get away.

Then Surt said some more hurried words, trying to placate whatever the pirate's concerns were. The pirate nodded and seemed mollified a little, though not completely. He gestured towards the door. Surt cocked his head at Einar who grabbed Affreca by the upper arm. The three of them moved towards the big double doors. The pirate bodyguard led them to the doors, opened them and they went in. Then he shut the doors behind them. Once inside they found themselves in a long hallway. In contrast to the heat of the night outside it was cool, no doubt due to the thick stone walls surrounding them. It was also gloomy, lit only by a couple of oil lamps.

Once the doors were closed the other bodyguards were left outside. The leader barked something to Surt and Einar then headed off down the hallway. Einar was about to follow him but felt Surt's hand grasping his own arm, restraining him. He stopped.

'He told us to wait here,' Surt said out of the corner of his mouth as the pirate exited the hall through a door at the far end.

'He fell for it, I think?' Einar said in a whisper.

'It was close,' Surt said. 'He said if you were going to take Affreca to the harem he wanted to check you really were a eunuch first. I thought it best to say you would not be going anywhere near the harem.'

Einar cursed under his breath. That potential strategy was now lost to them.

'I probably should have let him check,' Surt said with a smile. 'With a manhood the size of yours he might not have been able to tell if you were a eunuch or not.'

Einar glared at Surt but said nothing. Instead he looked around, noting how the door at the far end, indeed the wall it was in, did not match the rest of the hallway. While the walls of the hall were made of large blocks of ancient stone, the wall across the end was built from cheap clay bricks and the door was a rickety light wood. In a similar vein, looking up Einar saw the ceiling above was wood and thatch. All this work must have been recent additions and repairs by Abu Hassan.

The new work looked like it had been thrown together in a hurry – makeshift and gimcrack. Certainly not built to last. That was not a surprise. The island was populated by pirates, men who could sail ships and fight, and were no doubt good at that. Such men were seldom also great at building. They had captured the town, not created it. Perhaps someday when this island became the centre of a true emirate they would attract those with more diverse skills to come and settle there. Right now, however, they only required cut-throats and thieves.

The pirate in black returned. He said a few words to Surt. Surt looked vexed. He spoke back and from his tone of voice Einar could tell he was protesting. The pirate replied. Now his voice was angry. Einar did not like the way this appeared to be going and his hand dropped again to the knife at his waist. At that moment the big front doors opened again and the rest of the pirate bodyguards, alerted to the sound of raised voices, peered in to check on their leader. Einar saw that any action now would be futile. He moved his hand away from the knife again.

The leader of the bodyguards said a few more words to Surt, this time sounding a little more conciliatory. Then he grabbed Affreca by the upper arm and dragged her back down the hallway towards the inner door. Einar glanced at Surt who looked back, eyes wide, shaking his head with a movement that was almost imperceptible had Einar not been looking straight at him. It was clear the other man was telling him they were not supposed to follow.

Einar felt a surge of anxiety in his stomach as he watched Affreca being hauled off. Just as they got to the door she looked over her shoulder, confusion and concern written all over her face. Einar could only watch in despair. Then the pirate and Affreca were through the other door and out of sight.

The other bodyguards held the front doors open, waiting with expectant expressions for Einar and Surt to leave. Surt motioned with his eyes to Einar and they both walked out of the palace again. As they went a couple of the guards on the steps clapped Surt on the shoulder and said some words to him.

Surt led the way down the steps and back across the square. As they walked Einar felt his stomach churning. This had not been part of his plan. The idea had been to use Affreca as a ruse to get inside Abu Hassan's palace. Once inside they were to somehow slip away from whoever was with them, find Ulrich and get out. Affreca would find Surt's daughter in the harem and do the same. Now he and Surt were outside and only Affreca in.

'What happened?' Einar said in a fierce whisper once he was sure they were far enough away from the bodyguards not to be heard.

'The lead bodyguard said he went to Abu Hassan with my request to speak with him,' Surt said. 'But he said he was too busy tonight. He is working on some sort of plan with the imperial strategos. He also wants every available man out fighting the fires before they spread out of control and burn the whole island. That is where they think we are going now.'

Einar blew out his cheeks. 'Did you argue?' he said.

'Of course!' Surt said. 'I protested that I had given the slave girl to get an audience with the emir. She cost me a lot of money. He just told me to come back tomorrow when the fires were out. In the meantime Abu Hassan will test out the girl and if she is any good he might deign to talk to me.'

A chill mixed with the unsettling feeling in Einar's guts. It threatened to turn to full-blown panic. Why was everything going wrong? Ulrich's plans always worked out. Was this a sign he was not good enough to take Ulrich's place after all? Were the Norns punishing him for being so presumptuous as to think he could?

'What do we do now?' Surt said. Einar saw he was looking at him with expectation in his eyes. It was up to Einar to find a way out of this.

He closed his eyes for a moment, forcing calm to settle throughout his body and mind. One thing was sure: if he did start to panic then all would be lost for sure.

'We need to find another way in,' Einar said. 'Did you see the ceiling in the hallway? It looked like there wasn't much to it. Maybe that could be our entrance.'

Thirty-Eight

Inside the palace of Abu Hassan, his head bodyguard led Affreca deeper into the building. Once through the door at the far end of the entrance hallway, they entered a passageway that ran perpendicular to it. To the right the passageway ended in a curtain that was woven in all sorts of bright colours that shimmered in the light of multiple burning torches set into brackets in the walls. To the left the passage led past six doors – three on the left and three on the right – before ending in a blank wall. From somewhere down that way the muffled sound of raised voices and laughter could be heard.

Abu Hassan's bodyguard led Affreca to the right. As they neared the woven curtain a man stepped out from behind it. He was dark-skinned, very tall and dressed in outlandish robes that resembled a woman's dress. His height was exaggerated more by a tall, cylindrical hat that was perched on his head. Affreca noted he had what looked like a leather cudgel tucked into the broad green silk belt he wore around his waist.

Unlike every other man she had encountered since stripping off, the tall man did not stare at her bare legs or leer at her breasts that were only just covered beneath the layer of flimsy material that was her undershirt. Indeed the man seemed almost oblivious to her, giving her no more attention than a disparaging glance before turning back to the bodyguard.

From this Affreca guessed that the man was one of the eunuchs who Surt said were employed to keep order within the harem.

The bodyguard and the eunuch exchanged words, then the eunuch took hold of Affreca's upper arm, grasping her none too gently, and the pirate bodyguard returned the way he had come. The eunuch pulled back the curtain, revealing another short stretch of corridor that led to a set of double doors.

He led Affreca to the doors then drew the cudgel from his belt. Affreca tensed in case he was about to strike her with it, but instead the eunuch used its handle to rap on the doors. The door opened inwards, revealing another man dressed just like the eunuch and another curtain beyond.

The first eunuch pulled Affreca by the arm through the door then swept aside the curtain on the far side.

Affreca could not help letting out a little gasp at what lay beyond. She looked around at a large, round room. It had no windows but was lit by the soft glow of oil lamps positioned around the walls in various locations. The floor was covered with what looked like the sort of woven tapestries rich jarls and kings adorned the walls of their halls with. Those of a wealthy man in the northern realms would have depicted scenes of gods and heroes or famous ancestors; these, however, were woven to depict strange geometric patterns and the strange runes the Serks used.

The floor was strewn with large pillows and long couches. Curtains and hangings, made from rich materials, some looking like they had silver thread woven into them, adorned the walls and in some places curtained off more private areas. The air was thick with a heavy scent of perfume or incense that reminded her of the Christian church she had been in when Aethelstan had sent her to the nunnery.

The room was filled with women. Affreca counted sixteen in all. They were in various states of undress, most in just undershirts or nightwear, but all of their clothes were of the finest silks and linens.

Everything in the room spoke of comfort and luxury. There were metal tables, embossed with hammered patterns on which sat jugs of gold and silver, as well as goblets of the same. There were breads and fruits on platters decorated with jewels.

The women were from all over the world, their skins of every colour, though almost half of them were pale-skinned and blond or brown-haired.

The eunuch tapped Affreca with the handle of his cudgel. Glaring down his nose at her, he indicated to her feet. Affreca realised all the other women were barefoot so she removed her own boots. Despite the desperate situation she was in, she could not help the thrill of joy she felt as her bare feet sunk into the warm, soft woven floor covering.

The eunuch barked another order and one of the women came hurrying over. He said more words to her and she nodded, took Affreca by the hand and led her to the middle of the room. She was little more than a girl, perhaps sixteen winters old at the most, with pale white skin and long blond hair the colour of ripe wheat. She sat Affreca down on one of the large cushions then sat cross-legged before her as she went to work untying the rope that bound her wrists.

All the while the girl prattled away in a tongue Affreca did not comprehend.

'I don't speak your tongue,' Affreca said.

The girl stopped untying the rope. She looked at Affreca with narrowed eyes.

'You're *Norse*?' she said, now speaking in that tongue. The way she pronounced the word dripped with contempt. 'He said you were one of our folk.'

'You speak my tongue?' Affreca said.

'Why would I not know the tongue of the people who enslaved me?' the girl said in a bitter tone.

'You're a Slav?' Affreca said.

'Most of us are,' the girl said. She flicked her eyes around the other women. 'The Serks prize our people as slaves above all others. They think our menfolk are strong and our women are beautiful.'

'And we Norse make sure their slave markets are well supplied with your folk,' Affreca said. She felt a pang of embarrassment and pity for the plight of this girl. There were so many like her too, captured from the forests and villages south of Garðaríki or along the Dnieper and the Volga and shipped south to fill the beds, armies and servant quarters of other peoples by Norsemen like Thord who grew rich on their misery.

Not just Thord. Ulrich too. And that meant she had been part of this trade as well. This was not new to Affreca, though. Her father, Guthfrith, had been King of Dublin, one of the largest slave markets in the world. The silver from the bartered human beings had been what built his hall and had given her the privileged upbringing she had enjoyed.

'Well now you're just like one of us,' the slave girl said. 'Without your own will. I am to make you ready for the emir in case he wants you tonight.'

'What's your name?' Affreca said.

'Fejenna,' the girl said. 'I am from Belarus. The Norse from Kœnu-garðr captured me and sold me to the emir Abu Hassan.

You will need to wear something else if you are to lie with him tonight.'

She crinkled her nose.

'And you will need a bath.'

Fejenna spoke a few words in her own tongue to two other nearby women. They nodded, got up and went off towards another door in the far side of the room. As they did so they shot glances at Affreca with expressions on their faces that Affreca took to be sympathetic. She began to suspect that the experience of the first night with the emir was not a pleasant one.

'I've told them to fill a bath and find you new clothes,' the slave girl said, as she at last freed the knot in the rope that wound Affreca.

Affreca rubbed her wrists and settled back into the big soft cushion that sat behind her.

'This place is very comfortable,' Affreca said, remembering the cold, leaky wooden huts in Dublin that were the lodgings of her father's many slaves. 'My father was a king and nowhere in his hall was such luxury.'

'A prison is still a prison,' Fejenna said. 'Even if there are no bars.'

Affreca glanced at the eunuchs who stood by the door.

'What are they like?' she asked.

'They are bastards,' the slave girl said. 'I sometimes think that because they had their manhoods removed it has led them to hate all women. They are supposed to keep us from fighting each other but they delight in beating us. They're skilled at using those clubs in such a way that bruises are not left on exposed parts of our flesh.'

Affreca saw the haughty looks with which the three men at the doorway regarded the women of the harem, their arrogant stances and the ostentatious way they rested their right hands on the handles of the cudgels pushed into their belts.

'All bullies are the same,' Affreca said.

'They are not the worst,' Fejenna said. 'And there are other duties we have to perform for the emir that make me wish that I worked in the fields digging vegetables. But you will learn all this now you are one of us.'

'I would need to spend a very long time in one of these places before I became docile and tamed,' Affreca said.

'We all said that when we came here,' Fejenna said.

'There is someone worse than the eunuchs you said?' Affreca said. 'Who is that?'

'The emir's wife,' the slave girl said. She spoke in not much more than a whisper, glancing around as she did so, a fearful expression replacing one of hatred when she looked at the eunuchs. 'Rahanna. She hates us more than they do. She's very jealous. She loathes the fact the emir takes us to his bed, but it is the custom of their faith and she can do nothing about it. So she takes out her anger on us. She is a fool though. She should count herself lucky. He does things to us I'm sure he would not dare do with her.'

Affreca's mind raced. Whatever she was going to do, there was not much time to do it. If she waited too long then all would be lost. There would be too many people around and she would be in the pirate emir's bedchamber. Perhaps stuck there for the rest of her life.

Einar's plan had not worked out quite the way he had hoped but at least she was inside the palace and could do something about it. She had to find Ulrich and get them both out of that place, and she had to do it fast. Right then, this young slave girl sitting before her might be her only chance of getting any help in the task. In fact she might be invaluable as she would know her way around the palace.

She would have to take the huge risk of trusting her though. If the girl's fear of the eunuchs and pirates and her hatred of the Norse were greater than her desire for freedom, then she was as likely to betray Affreca as help her.

Affreca closed her eyes for a moment, hoping that whatever the emir demanded in his bedchamber was truly awful enough that the girl would not hesitate at the chance to escape it.

There was nothing else for it but to roll the dice.

Affreca opened her eyes and looked around too, checking that no one else was nearby. Then she leaned closer to the slave girl.

'Fejenna, what if I told you I am not one of you,' Affreca said. 'What if I said I could get you out of here? I came here with a crew of vikings. We are not with the pirates. We have a ship waiting in the harbour and if you help me, you can be on it when we sail out of here. Will you help me?'

Fejenna's eyes widened. 'You're from the company the emir's men have been hunting!' she said, aghast. 'They've been shouting about it since yesterday. The emir is very vexed his men have not captured you yet. He punished several of them. They were whipped in the market square as an example to the others to try harder.'

She stopped, then glanced at the eunuchs again.

'He has also offered a great reward to whoever can find you...' she said.

'They won't give anything to a slave,' Affreca said, her heart pounding. She could see the girl before her was thinking through the possibilities before her, weighing up what course of action she should take. Affreca needed to push her to take the one Affreca wanted.

'And even if they did reward you,' Affreca continued, 'you'd still be a slave, albeit one with riches.'

'Perhaps the emir would free me in recompense?' the girl said, a smile starting to spread across her lips. 'Maybe he would make me one of his wives. His current wife was once a slave.'

Perhaps I will kill you right now, Affreca thought, but she did not say it out loud.

'Perhaps,' Affreca said. 'But you'd still be in his bedchamber, every bit a slave to his desires as you are now. You'd still be on this island. What was it you said earlier? *A prison is still a prison, even if there are no bars?*'

The slave girl nodded. Her smile disappeared and her eyes became downcast.

'You're right,' she said. 'How do I get out of here?'

'I need to find my friends first,' Affreca said. 'They were captured by the emir's men earlier today and are somewhere here in the palace. Do you know where they are? Are there dungeons, cells?'

The girl hesitated. 'You mean you don't know?' she said. 'They were executed this afternoon.'

'What?!' Affreca said.

'The imperial strategos demanded it,' Fejenna said. 'It was part of some plan he has with the emir. They were crucified.'

The door banged open before Affreca could say anything else.

All eyes in the room turned to see a woman stood in the entrance, flanked by the eunuchs on either side of her.

She was black-skinned and dressed in a long flowing blue silk dress. She swept the room with a gaze that was both commanding and full of threat. It was the woman Affreca had seen with the emir in the square, meeting the imperial emissary earlier. It was the woman Surt believed was his daughter.

The woman spoke. Affreca did not understand her tongue but her words were full of anger.

'That's the emir's wife, Rahanna,' Fejenna said in a hushed voice. 'She says she wants to see the new slave girl so she can teach her her place. She means you.'

Thirty-Nine

Einar and Surt flattened themselves against the wall at the corner of the square. With extreme caution, Einar peeked around the corner, taking everything in then, an instant later, ducked back behind the wall again. It was a craft Ulrich and Skar had taught him and the other Wolf Coats.

Don't think, don't try to see anything in particular, Skar had said. Just let your eyes take everything in. *Your mind somehow sees it all, as long as you don't try to.*

It sounded like nonsense when they said it but somehow it worked. In one fleeting moment he had seen the palace of the emir, the buildings around it and the bodyguards on the steps.

They were the main problem. They stood in front of the doors and to get inside they would have to get past them somehow. Einar cursed himself that they had left the same way they had come. If they had taken the street parallel to the palace steps, they would now be standing beside a row of buildings alongside it. There might be a way onto the roof from there.

He motioned to Surt and they loped back down the street they had come along. About halfway down that there was a side alley. The alley was parallel to the street that ran across the front of the palace. Einar and Surt went down the alley, moving as fast as they could in the pitch-darkness. When they had gone what Einar judged to be beyond the length of the front of the palace he stopped, fumbling around in the dark until he found something that felt like a door.

'I'm going to try to find a way onto the roof of the palace,' he said to Surt. 'There might be a way in.'

'All right,' Surt said. 'Though I'm not much of a climber.'

'I'm going on my own,' Einar said. 'I need you to stay outside. It's time we raised the alarm. Go and create as much commotion as you can so the others know it's time to attack the gate.'

'If you get in,' Surt said, 'how will you get back out past those guards on the steps?'

'I'll have to work that out,' Einar said. 'If I'm still alive. Maybe I can create some sort of distraction but I don't know yet. I'm just riding my luck now.'

Surt nodded.

'Find my daughter, please,' Surt said. Einar could hear the pleading in his voice. 'Don't leave her behind.'

'I won't,' he said. 'I promise. I need you to get back to the ship as well. Tell Roan to get ready to leave and tell Diogenes to find somewhere near the siphōn tower to hide. I will need him to help me disable the siphōn or the ship won't get past the harbour mouth. He's the only person who knows the secret mechanism to do that.'

'Understood,' Surt said.

'I need to take this off as well,' Einar said, pulling off the white Serk robes so he was only dressed in his dark clothes and wolfskin cloak. 'I must be shining like the moon in those.'

He pulled up the wolf's head hood and said: 'Now hurry. We don't have much time.'

He pushed open the door he had found and entered the darkened building beyond, leaving Surt outside. If the alley had been dark, the interior of the building was pitch-black. There was a strong smell of spices though, which made Einar think he was perhaps in a merchant's storeroom or similar.

He moved across the room, using the same stealthy sweeping footsteps he used to move through a dark forest, until he felt another wall. Keeping his fingertips spread on it, he followed the wall until he found the edge of another door.

Einar opened it a crack. Peering out he saw he was now, as he had hoped, at the front of a building on the street that ran past the palace. About fifty paces to his left were the steps with the pirate guards on them. Directly opposite was a building that was part of the row of houses that ran alongside the side of the palace. It had a door that led onto the street.

Einar was counting on there being enough shadows and gloom in the darkened street for him to make it across without being spotted. He opened the door fully and scurried out, sprinting as fast as he could across the open street to the other side.

Once he got there he flattened himself against the wall, doing his best to control his breathing. Looking up the street, he saw the guards maintained their position on the steps so they had not seen him. He began sliding along the side of the wall until he found the door that led in off the street.

Opening it let in a beam of moonlight and Einar saw a short passage stretching into the house. There was another door on the left and a ladder at the far end that led up to the next storey of the building, which was exactly what he had hoped to find. He made his way with silent steps to the bottom of the ladder and began to climb.

A warm light was coming down from above, which made it possible to make out the rungs he had to climb. It also meant there was probably someone up there, so he would need to proceed with extreme caution. He was about halfway up when the sound of a man's voice above made him freeze. Then a different voice answered, which meant there were at least two men in the room above.

Moving slowly, Einar drew his knife and clamped it between his teeth, then continued on up the ladder. Each squeak or creak it made sounded loud as thunder to his ears. At every rung he ascended he expected to see someone appear above him, glowering down at this new intruder, sword ready to deal with the problem.

More words came from above. The agitated tone of the voices in the room suggested some sort of mild argument. Einar decided to take advantage of this and scrambled up the last few rungs to the top.

Once there he repeated the move of popping his head up into the room for an instant and dropping down again. In that moment he glimpsed a table with a lamp on it. Two Serk men were sitting across the table from each other over a game board of some kind. They were in some sort of disagreement about the game.

Einar grabbed the top rung of the ladder in both hands. He hauled himself up and forwards, driving with his thighs at the same time. He shot up into the room and rolled head over heels towards the table.

The men at the table looked around, eyes wide with shock. Einar was on them while they were still getting up. He snatched the knife from between his teeth with his left hand and drove it, point down, into the notch at the base of the man on the left's throat, just as the man was starting to draw his own knife. Einar's blade plunged down, cutting through flesh and bone to pierce the man's heart. He let out a strangled cry and fell sideways across the table, scattering the gaming pieces as a gush of dark blood welled up from his wound.

To Einar's consternation his knife stuck in the man's throat and was wrenched from his grasp by the weight of his falling victim. His companion was now on his feet and reaching for a sword that lay across the table. He grabbed it and took a desperate swipe at Einar.

Einar ducked, feeling the wind from the curved blade passing over him mere finger breadths above the crown of his head. Then he sprang forward, tackling the other man with both arms and driving him backwards onto the table.

Everything on the table was scattered as the two men struggled on top of it. The lamp toppled to the floor and shattered, sending blazing oil over the floorboards.

Einar was on top of the second man who in turn lay on the body of his companion. The first Serk was already dead and unmoving, his blood spreading across the table top. The man with the sword tried to strike Einar again but he was now too close to effectively use the long, curved blade and his blow ended up as little more than a thump on the back.

Einar scrambled with his left hand beneath his opponent, looking for the knife that was still sheathed at the dead man's waist. His fingers closed around the hilt and he slid it free. Einar rammed the blade into the other man's side. He cried out as Einar felt a rush of hot blood coursing from him around the knife and over Einar's left hand.

Einar shoved his right hand over the man's mouth, desperate to silence him. The Serk kicked and thrashed beneath him. Einar pushed harder with his right hand as he withdrew the knife with his left. He pushed himself up and drove the knife down, this time into the Serk's chest. The point of the blade skidded across one of the man's ribs then plunged deep between them. The Serk's back arched and he went rigid. Einar knew he had cleaved the man to the heart and he was done for. The Serk jerked twice then went limp.

Breathing heavily, Einar stepped away from the carnage on the table. Heat from the now burning floor made him skip away further and he saw the blaze from the spilled oil lamp had now taken hold of the planks of the floor.

He looked around. There was no one else in the room but if there were others in the building they must have heard the commotion. There was no sound of running feet, however.

Einar spotted another ladder at the far end of the room. This one led up to a trapdoor in the ceiling. Retrieving his knife, he sheathed it then ran to the ladder and scrambled up. Once at the top he pushed open the trapdoor and felt a rush of warm night air come in. He could see the stars above and knew he had reached the roof of the building, which was exactly where he wanted to get to.

Seeing there was no one on the rooftop, Einar pulled himself out and closed the trapdoor behind him. The rooftop was, like all the buildings in that part of the world, flat with a waist-high wall around the perimeter and seemed to be used like an open-air room. There was another table and a couple of chests, as well as some plants that grew strange foreign fruit.

He was on a building that formed part of a street that ran along one side of the palace. To the front of the buildings he was now on top of, was the side of Abu Hassan's palace. Peering down he could see the pirates still standing guard on the steps at the front. Einar withdrew to the back of the roof to a point where he could no longer see them nor they him.

All the buildings had flat roofs like the one he was on and they were either close enough to clamber from one to the other or at worst jump across.

He set off, moving from one building to the next, crossing their roofs while keeping out of sight of the men in the square below. By the time he had crossed four roofs he was right alongside the roof of the palace.

Looking across, he saw that it indeed was a hodgepodge of planks, boards, tree branches and other makeshift repairs of what had been an ancient ruin, open to the skies, when Abu Hassan had decided to make it his home.

All he had to do was get across. The gap between the building he was on and the roof of the palace was a lot wider than the ones he had crossed to get here. It would take a substantial leap to get across. If he did not make it, the drop to the street was considerable and ended in stone flags. If he fell and survived, at best he would be badly smashed up. Too broken to help any of the others.

Einar walked as far back on the rooftop as he could go. He took a deep breath, then began running. In two steps he was sprinting as hard as he could go, legs pumping as he pounded towards the edge. Reaching it, he placed his right foot on the top of the perimeter wall and launched himself into the night air.

For a few moments all he could hear was the rushing of the warm wind in his ears as he flew through the air, arms spinning like windmills in the vain hope that they would, like a bird flapping its wings, somehow carry him further. His legs kept on pumping too as if he were running on thin air.

Then he was across the gap, landing heavily on the rooftop of the palace. He rolled forward, head over heels, three times in an attempt to both break his fall and minimise the amount of noise he was making, though he knew that hope was futile. If anyone was in the room below they would hear an almighty racket overhead.

When he came to a halt he waited for a few moments,

panting. Then he clambered to his feet. He had to get moving. If anyone had heard him, he needed to get off the roof and into the building before they came up to take a look. He crouched and began digging into the wood of the roof with his knife.

Forty

Surt went running down the street back towards the harbour. Every time he came to an iron triangle on a wall or an alarm bell he stopped to set them ringing before moving on again. At the noise pirates began emerging from buildings, looking around to see what all the noise was about.

When Surt was about halfway along the street he saw a group of armed pirates running towards him.

'We're under attack!' he shouted. 'The kufaar are already in the town. The Romans betrayed the emir. The imperial navy is coming to wipe us all out! Raise the alarm!'

Urgent expressions on their faces, they started off down the street again. Surt told the same story to everyone he met. Soon alarm bells were ringing out across the town. Once at the harbour Surt ran down the quay to where the snekkja was moored and clambered aboard.

Roan and Diogenes met him with expectant faces.

'Get the ship prepared to sail,' Surt said. 'We need to be ready to go soon.'

'Not while that thing is still in working order,' Roan said, pointing at the tower at the harbour entrance that housed the siphōn. 'Or it will be a very short trip.'

As they looked, they could see figures running along the quay to the tower.

Surt grasped Diogenes by the arm. Switching to the Latin tongue he told him that his knowledge was needed to disable the siphōn, so he needed to find someplace near it to hide until Einar arrived.

The clatter of horses' hooves and rumble of wheels on the flagstones of the market square made them turn around and they saw the same wagon as earlier that day, heading towards the slope up to the town gates in the ravine.

'Einar's plan is working so far,' Surt said. 'They are going to fetch the extra Sea Fire liquid.'

He and Diogenes scrambled out of the ship and back onto the quayside as Roan began untying the ropes that kept them to the harbour wall.

A very wary-looking Diogenes went off towards the other quay to find somewhere to hide, and Surt started jogging back across the market square.

Even though a few parts of the plan had gone wrong, it looked like Einar's luck still held. Surt hoped with all his heart that it would continue to.

Forty-One

Affreca got to her feet. As she did so she felt a tugging at her undershirt. Looking down she saw Fejenna was pulling on it as she shook her head.

'You must kneel when the Mistress Rahanna comes in,' the slave girl said. 'She is the wife of the emir.'

'And I'm Princess of Dublin,' Affreca said, brushing Fejenna's hand away.

The pirate queen strode across the room, flanked by the two eunuchs. When she reached Affreca she barked out a stream of words filled with anger. She grabbed the cudgel from the eunuch on her left and brandished it in Affreca's face, her teeth bared in a grimace of rage.

'I told you not to stand!' Fejenna said in a whimper. 'Now she's really angry. She's going to beat you.'

'Tell her if she touches me with that baton, I'll smash her face in,' Affreca said. Her voice was calm and she smiled as she spoke. It was a fierce, wolfish smile, however, that bore no trace of humour.

Fejenna's eyes widened. She stared at Affreca in disbelief and wonder. Some of the other slave girls began to gather round. Whether they were eager to see the new girl put in her place or intrigued by her defiance, Affreca could not tell. They looked like Fejenna and perhaps they too understood her words.

The emir's wife drew her hand that grasped the little club back, threatening to strike.

'Tell her what I said,' Affreca said.

'No. I cannot,' Fejenna said, shaking her head vigorously. 'Her rage is terrifying.'

'Tell her what I said,' Affreca said. 'Or you will see *my* rage. And I promise you, if you think she is scary, you'll think again.'

Rahanna turned to Fejenna and shouted something at her. Affreca guessed she was demanding to know what she had said. She could see the slave girl was paralysed by fear and indecision, looking from Affreca to the pirate queen and back, fear of the consequences of obeying both their demands could bring, colliding in her mind with fear of what would happen if she disobeyed Rahanna.

Affreca met her gaze and arched one of her eyebrows, hoping to coax the girl into repeating her deliberately provoking message.

Fejenna looked down at the floor, avoiding any further eye contact and uttered a stream of words. Affreca did not need to understand the Serk tongue to know the slave girl had relayed her threat to the pirate queen. Rahanna's reaction told her that.

Utter fury took over the pirate queen's mind. Her eyes rolled in her head. She clenched her teeth as she let out an inarticulate grunt and flew at Affreca, bringing the cudgel down in a blow aimed at splitting Affreca's forehead open.

Instead of flinching back, Affreca stepped forwards. She rammed her right shoulder into the chest of the approaching woman, halting her advance. Rahanna's cry of rage stopped dead as all the air was driven from her lungs. Affreca took a half step with her left leg, rotating her body so she had her back to the pirate queen. At the same moment she reached up with both hands and grabbed Rahanna's hand that was holding the raised club. Affreca then pulled down while shoving her own left hip backwards, creating the momentum that flipped the pirate queen over Affreca's shoulder. Rahanna's legs thrashed in the air as she tumbled head over heels, landing on her back on the floor with a heavy thump that was only partly mitigated by the cushions that were strewn there.

Affreca still grasped Rahanna's right hand in both of hers. She shifted her grip, grabbing the cudgel with her left hand and giving it a vicious twist while squeezing the queen's wrist hard with her right. Rahanna gave a cry of pain and released the baton.

With a shout, the eunuch Rahanna had taken the cudgel off ran forward and grabbed Affreca, wrapping his arms around her from behind. She could feel his breath on her left cheek and his chin digging into her left shoulder. He bent backwards, lifting her off the ground and pulling her away from the fallen pirate queen.

Affreca took the cudgel in her right hand and smashed it across her left shoulder, catching the eunuch on the forehead with a crack. He let out a cry and let go of her.

She spun around to see the eunuch she had hit staggering backwards, his hands going up to a cut her blow had opened above his left eye. Affreca stepped forwards and swung the cudgel, starting with her arm straight behind her and bringing it up, using her hip to add more power. It smacked into the eunuch, hitting him on the bottom of the jaw, just below the point of his chin.

There was a sharp crack. The man's head snapped backwards

and he collapsed to the floor as if all the bones in his body had become dislocated from each other all at once. He did not get back up.

The second eunuch by now had drawn his own club and was advancing on Affreca. Acting on instinct, Affreca drove her knee into his groin. All this provoked from the eunuch was a smile. Affreca cursed herself for even trying such an attack on a man who had had his manhood removed.

The eunuch grabbed Affreca by the throat with his left hand. Holding her at arm's length he began to squeeze. Affreca swiped at the man with her cudgel but his reach was such that all she could hit was his outstretched arm. Unable to breathe, she dropped the cudgel and grabbed his hand with both of hers. His fingers felt like iron and she could do nothing to loosen his grip. Her vision began to darken and she realised that in moments she would pass out.

As if far away, Affreca heard a loud clang. For a moment she wondered if she was hearing the bell that rings at the gate of Hel's kingdom to announce the arrival of the dead. Then the eunuch's grip loosened on her neck and she could breathe once more.

Affreca saw Fejenna standing behind the eunuch, a metal tray raised to hit him around the back of the head once again.

She sucked in a deep breath, consciousness rushing back to her mind. Then she raised her leg, planted it on the eunuch's belly and shoved. The man went stumbling backwards. Fejenna hit him again with the tray. Then more of the slave girls joined in, throwing cups and jugs at the eunuch. As he staggered under the onslaught of missiles they flew at him, pushing, kicking and scratching his flesh with their nails.

The man cried out and went down under the welter of blows. Rubbing her neck, Affreca looked for her fallen cudgel, found it, and went over to the fallen eunuch, intending to use it to knock him unconscious.

She was unable to push through the throng of slave girls who now swarmed over him, venting their hatred and taking revenge for the misery the eunuch had been part of putting them through.

The man managed a few muffled cries then let out a bloodcurdling scream that made even Affreca flinch, though it was more from worry that the noise would raise the alarm than concern for the eunuch.

His cries died away to silence. The slave girls stood up, leaving the broken, battered body of the eunuch lying flat on his back. Affreca grimaced at the sight of the man's face, which was now little more than rags of torn and bleeding flesh. Both his eyes were gone. Whether he was dead or unconscious she could not tell.

She turned back to the pirate queen and saw the woman had got back to her feet and was running towards the doors.

Affreca was about to shout to the other women to stop her but realised that if they went after Rahanna they were likely to take revenge on her for the way she had treated them. Instead, she charged after the pirate queen herself, leaping across cushions and couches as she went. She caught Rahanna just before she reached the door, barging into her with her shoulder and sending her sprawling to the floor again.

The other women came running over and both Rahanna and Affreca dragged themselves up to their feet again.

The pirate queen glared around her at the circle of slaves who now surrounded her. She began shouting at them in her own tongue.

'We should kill her too,' one of the slave girls said to Fejenna, confirming to Affreca that more of them spoke the Norse tongue.

'Wait,' she said. 'This woman is the daughter of a member of my crew. We swore an oath to him we would try to get her out of here.'

'We were not part of that oath,' Fejenna said.

'If you want to be on our ship when it leaves then you will not kill her,' Affreca said. 'She must go with us.'

The pirate queen was still shouting what were no doubt obscenities and glaring in rage at all those around her. Affreca wondered why no one had come to investigate the noise and reasoned that hysterical shouting must be commonplace in the harem.

'How do you propose you will get her to leave?' Fejenna said.

'Tell her we came here with her father, Sayf al-Din,' Affreca said. 'Say we have come to rescue her. We can get her out of here.'

Fejenna raised her eyebrows but relayed the message anyway, in the Serk tongue.

Rahanna's mouth dropped open. For a moment she fell silent, looking at Affreca with an expression of astonishment mixed with disbelief on her face. Then her expression changed back to one of scorn and anger. She began to shout again.

'She says her father is a low-down bastard who left her family alone to fend for themselves years ago,' Fejenna said, translating the pirate queen's words. 'She came here a slave and is now the wife of the emir, a very rich man who one day will rule a caliphate of his own. Why would she want to leave? It seems she would rather stay here.'

Affreca sighed. There was no time for this. She smashed her fist into Rahanna's jaw. The pirate queen's eyes rolled up into her head and she fell unconscious to the floor.

'Roll her up in one of those curtains,' Affreca said. 'She's going with us whether she likes it or not. The rest of you start setting fire to drapes, cushions, whatever you can find that will burn. We need to spread chaos and maybe we will be able to get away in the midst of it.'

Affreca went to the door while some of the other women wrapped the pirate queen up in a silk hanging. The rest grabbed oil lamps or torches and began with glee setting fire to the rich tapestries, curtains and furniture that had been such grand decoration for their prison. The rich materials caught light with alarming ease and in moments the room was thick with smoke and the sound of crackling flames.

Affreca pulled the door open a crack, checked there was no one outside, then she returned to where the queen lay, now rolled in a curtain. She was still out cold.

'We'll have to carry her,' Affreca said.

'Why don't we leave her?' one of the other slave girls said. 'I don't care if the bitch burns.'

The others nodded their agreement.

'Well if you care whether you're on my ship or not, you'll pick her up,' Affreca said.

Bristling with resentment, three of the girls formed a line, picked up the rolled queen and put her across their shoulders. Affreca picked up an oil lamp from a nearby table.

'Now let's go,' Affreca said.

She led the way to the door, opened it and they all rushed out. In her hurry one of the girls stumbled, hit her toes on the edge of the door and cried out in pain.

'Quiet!' Fejenna said to her. 'We don't want anyone to hear us.'

'No,' Affreca said. 'Scream, shout, cry out in the Serk tongue. Shout about the fire. We want them to think we are fleeing it. Even if you are prisoners here no one will make you stay inside to burn. At the very least their top concern will be trying to put the fire out.'

As the women began shouting, Affreca pulled back the curtains that covered the corridor outside, let the others through, then set the curtains alight with the oil lamp. She tossed it behind her, sending trails of blazing oil in all directions as it shattered on the floor.

In moments there came the sound of running feet. One of the doors along the passageway opened and a pirate stepped out. His eyes widened at the sight of the rushing women, the blazing curtains and the thick smoke that was already billowing out through the doorway of the harem. He turned and ran back the way he had come, shouting in alarm.

Other doors banged open and more pirates rushed out. They pushed their way past Affreca and the others and ran towards the harem, no doubt intent on tackling the fire. As they did so, Affreca took a sharp left and guided the women into the passageway that led to the main front doors of the palace. She remembered the line of guards on the steps outside and hoped the ruse would work on them too.

At that moment the front door banged open and the black-clad leader of the guards stepped inside, no doubt coming to see what the noise was about. He slammed the door shut behind him then began striding down the hall. At the sight of the group of women coming towards him he stopped and shouted something.

'He wants to know what we are doing,' Fejenna translated for Affreca.

The other women shouted to him, telling him of the fire. The pirate's face turned angry. He drew his sword and shouted something back at them.

'He says we must stay inside,' Fejenna said. 'He does not care if we all die.'

Forty-Two

The big pirate stood squarely before the door, curved sword in hand, feet planted shoulder-width apart. Affreca wondered if perhaps they could all rush him at once. If they did, the first of them would die. That was for sure.

Then there came a crashing sound from overhead. Pieces of broken wood and plaster fell down from the ceiling. Everyone, including the pirate, looked upwards. The debris was followed by a man, who hurtled down from above amid a welter of dust and smashed plaster. He was clad in a wolfskin cloak and had a knife in one hand.

'Einar!' Affreca cried, recognising him at once.

The distance to the floor was quite a drop, possibly twice the height of a man. It also looked like Einar had come through the roof in a hurry. He plummeted to the floor. When he hit it he tried to roll to break his fall but ended up sprawling on his side.

The pirate commander was as surprised as everyone but recovered fast. He turned away from Affreca and the others. Seeing Einar he raised his sword to strike down at him.

Still lying on his side, Einar drove his seax knife into the pirate's left knee. The blow did not have the weight of Einar's body behind it but it still went in deep, sliding under the man's kneecap. The pirate screeched and toppled to the floor. Affreca shot forwards, wrenched the pirate's sword from his grasp and drove it into his chest. The man bucked and thrashed for a moment, then lay still.

Affreca grabbed a handful of Einar's wolfskin and helped him to his feet.

'Where did you come from?' Affreca said.

'I saw the roof was badly made when we were in here earlier,' Einar said. 'I got up there and was digging my way through it as quietly as I could. I'd just made a small hole when I saw you lot arrive and that pirate come in. I knew there was no time to be cautious so stamped my way on through.'

'I thought Odin had sent you from above to help us,' Affreca said with a grin.

For a moment they faced each other, looking each other in the eyes. Both were unsure what to do next. Einar felt a huge desire to fold her in his arms and pull her close to him. To press his lips onto hers. Before he could move, however, she pulled back from him, a look of sudden shock and horror on her face.

'Einar,' Affreca said. 'Ulrich's dead!'

'What?!' Einar said. He felt a sensation in his guts like he was falling. His head swam for a moment.

'They crucified him,' Affreca said. 'It's all part of some Byzantine plot.'

Einar fought hard to control himself. He felt panic surge into his heart. His breathing became fast and slight. His heart raced.

This was not supposed to happen. He could deal with taking leadership of the company for a time but it was only supposed to be until they got Ulrich back. Now everything really would be up to him. What would he do?

Then the pain of Affreca's nails digging into his forearms brought his attention back to the present. He locked eyes with her again.

'This is not the time to think,' Affreca said. 'We need to get out of here.'

Einar nodded.

'You're right,' he said. The panic that had flooded his heart drained away with a feeling like cold water flowing down his spine. His breathing returned to normal.

'Help me drag this body out of the way,' Affreca said, bending over to pull the dead pirate aside. 'We don't want him seen from outside.'

With a sigh Einar stooped to help her. They pulled the still-warm corpse behind the door. As they did so smoke began billowing around the corner at the end of the passageway. Shouting pirate warriors ran across the doorway in the direction of the harem. They were so intent on the fire that none paid attention to the group of women in the entrance hall or spotted Einar among them.

'So there really is a fire?' Einar said.

'It should have a good hold by now,' Affreca said. 'And they should be kept very busy trying to put it out.'

She gestured for Fejenna to come over.

'When I open the door start shouting about the fire,' Affreca said. 'Tell them the palace is on fire and the emir needs help.'

Fejenna nodded. She said a quick word to some of the other women then Affreca pulled the doors open.

Outside was like a scene from Ragnarök, the end of the world. All around the town the sound of bells and iron alarms clanging filled the air. Warriors were running this way and that, making desperate preparations for the phantom attack Surt had told them of. There were flames blazing from the upstairs window of the house across the street where Einar had overturned the lamp on his way to the palace roof. Smoke was seeping up from its rooftop. The night sky itself glowed orange from the now huge blaze outside the town. It looked like half of the hill up to the watchtower on the summit was now ablaze. The warm wind reeked with the heavy smell of smoke and burning wood.

Fejenna shouted to the line of pirates guarding the steps. The other women joined in. To add emphasis, smoke from the burning harem that had been flowing across the ceiling of the entrance passage was sucked out of the open doors and billowed up into the night air.

The pirates saw this, heard the women's cries and rushed inside to join the efforts to fight the fire. Einar pressed himself behind the door as they charged past.

'Out,' Affreca said as soon as they had turned the corner at the far end of the passageway.

They all hurried out the doors onto the now unguarded steps of the palace. Rahanna had regained consciousness but the curtain wrapped around her muffled her shouts and pinned her thrashing limbs so she could do little more than wriggle and the three women carried her out.

They hurried down the steps and across the street, heading for the harbour. As they jogged they passed groups of pirates either hurrying towards the harbour or towards the palace, no doubt going to help fight the fires there. The air in the streets was smeared with drifting smoke from the burning hillside, making the light from the torches hazy and blurred. Einar huddled in the middle of the group of women and the pirates ignored them as they passed, having more pressing things to worry about.

At the edge of the market square before the harbour Einar stopped. He turned to Affreca.

'Get them on the ship,' he said. 'Tell Roan it's time to go.'

'What are you going to do?' Affreca said.

'I'm going to meet Diogenes and put the siphōn beyond use,'

Einar said. 'Otherwise our voyage will be very short and very hot.'

'All right,' Affreca said. 'You don't need my help?'

'I do,' Einar said with a rueful smile, 'but I also need you to make sure Roan knows it's time to go and we can't do both. And I want to get Ulrich.'

'Einar, he's dead,' Affreca said.

'All the same,' Einar said, 'I can't just leave his body to rot and be eaten by the seagulls.'

'Well, good luck,' Affreca said. 'Not that you need it, of course.'

She winked at him, then turned and led the women off down the right-hand quay towards the waiting snekkja.

Einar turned and started running across the market square.

Forty-Three

Once they had landed on the beach and found some cover, the remaining six of the company – Skar, Starkad, Kari, Sigurd, Fisk and Wulfhelm the Saxon – spent a little time going over their attack plans. Then they grabbed their lengths of rope and set off up the steep path, following the same route to the top of the ridge they had taken the night before.

Once they were in sight of the rampart, which loomed dark against the starry sky, they lay in hiding for a little while, watching what was going on and taking stock of the situation.

Behind them, on the main part of the island, the fire Einar had set took hold with frightening speed. The warm winds from the sea drove the blaze wider while the forest floor, covered with dead pine needles and vegetation debris, dried to tinder-aridity by the baking sun, provided an eager roadway for it to travel by. The stunted pine trees, though living green wood, were full of flammable resin which, as the ground around them burned, caught light and transformed them into countless pillars of fire. The warm night air became even heavier with the scent of smoke and smouldering pine.

The men in the tower spotted the blaze and began to ring their alarm bell. They also sent a rider out to the town who came down the forest path and rode at a dangerous speed over the ridge to the gates in the ravine where, even at the distance they were at, the hiding Wolf Coats could hear him shouting to the men on the gate. Riders from the companies out searching the island came back to raise the alarm too.

Soon companies of riders were coming out from the gates as the pirates sent men out to fight the fires. The Wolf Coats could see these included men from the ramparts, as soon the silhouettes of the guards standing on top, one outlined against the starry sky every twenty paces, became one every forty or perhaps fifty paces along its length. They were now stretched a lot thinner, which would give the lurking attackers a better chance to make it over the wall without being detected.

'The lad's plan is working,' Surt said in a quiet voice. 'It looks like Ulrich was right. Einar is a lucky man after all.'

He turned to Sigurd and Kari.

'You two go first,' he said. 'We'll look after these while you deal with that pirate.'

He took their ropes and wound them around his own shoulders, alongside with the one he carried himself.

'I hope they hold our weight,' Kari said, casting a dubious eye at his rope as he handed it over. 'And they're long enough.'

'Well we'll soon find out,' Sigurd said, his white teeth showing through the dark as he grinned.

Then they slunk off into the night, heading for the rampart.

'Let's hope they make it,' Wulfhelm said.

'They'll make it,' Skar said.

His eyes were fixed on the rampart ahead with the palisade on it. Dead ahead there was a warrior on the fighting platform behind it, his outline visible from the waist up above the top of the palisade. The others joined Skar, focusing their attention on the lone pirate, his nearest companions fifty paces away to his left and right.

They knew that under cover of the dark, Kari and Sigurd, expert craftsmen in stealth, were creeping ever closer. There was no sound but the rush of the wind and the ever-louder crackle of flames from the main part of the island. The spreading fire was also starting to cast an orange glow across the rest of the island, pushing back the darkness and making Skar worry that it might soon be bright enough to reveal him and the others to the pirates on the ramparts and gate.

After a short while the guard on the palisade suddenly jerked forward, then his outline disappeared. For a brief moment there was another shape clambering over the top of the palisade followed by a second. Then everything returned to the way it was before, except now there was no sign of the warrior who had been guarding the palisade. The men fifty paces to the left and right remained in position, oblivious to what had occurred on the rampart between them. So swift and silent had been the taking down of their comrade that they had not even noticed.

'They're in,' Skar said. 'Let's go. If those fires on the hillside get any brighter we'll be lit up like it's dawn.'

They lifted their ropes then, keeping as low as they could, moved forward one at a time to the base of the rampart. Skar crouched down and the others used him as a step, clambering onto his back then reaching up to the top of the palisade and hauling themselves up and over it.

Once the other three had gone over him, Wulfhelm and Fisk turned around and leaned back down, dropping their arms for Skar to catch. Skar grabbed their hands and pulled himself up as they gritted their teeth, trying not to let the considerable weight of the big prowman pull them both back over the wall again.

Once Skar was at the top, they all dropped down the other side, inside the rampart of the town. For a few moments they sat, motionless in the dark, watching the guards along the palisade to the left and right to see if there was any sign their silent incursion had been detected. Both pirates continued to stand at their posts, watching outwards. Skar gestured to the others to move on.

The Wolf Coats scurried further past the rampart, going about fifty paces across the rocky ground until they were almost to the edge of the cliffs that dropped into the town. The ground was cracked and pitted with fissures and gullies, which gave them plenty of cover. They turned and began to track parallel to the rampart northwards, towards the ravine where the gate was.

The location of the gate was obvious as the light from the braziers that burned there emanated up from the ravine into the night. They still moved with caution but there was less risk because the numbers of guards on the ramparts were not only thinned out but they were concentrating on looking outwards towards the rest of the island and the growing fire.

They had not gone far when a frantic clanging of a warning alarm began to rise from the direction of the town below the cliffs to their left. This was joined by other alarms and bells, and soon shouting could be heard from the canyon ahead of them where the gate was.

'That's the signal,' Skar said in a hoarse whisper. 'Come on. We're already late.'

They hurried on and in a short while they reached the edge of the ravine. Approaching it, they stopped. Each man fastened one end of his rope around his waist then replaced the rest of it in a coil over their shoulders again. After that they dropped to their bellies and crawled forwards to get a look at what was going on below.

Reaching the edge of the canyon they poked their heads over the edge and peered down. Behind the gate was a swarm of activity. Men in the cave directly below them were hanging over the wall, helping to manhandle and lower a big lead canister out from the rectangular hole in the rock wall to its waiting wooden sled below. Others were helping from the floor of the ravine. A pirate warrior with a spear stood guard on the platform above the closed gates. He had turned around to watch the manoeuvring of the canister behind him. There were two guards behind the gate too. The whole scene was illuminated by a couple of braziers.

To the left, running into the town, the floor of the canyon fell away in a slope so sheer only a lunatic would attempt to ride up or down it. Beyond it, where the track became less steep and morphed into a street leading into the town, a wagon for the canister was rattling its way towards them.

The Wolf Coats were outnumbered by the pirates, but Einar had told them earlier that the canister contained the extra Sea Fire for the siphōn. He had predicted that when the alarms sounded, the pirates would be so busy with moving the heavy lead canister that they could be taken by surprise. Skar and the others, it seemed, had arrived at exactly the right time.

They crawled back from the edge then each man looked for something to secure the other end of his rope to. Skar found a scrub bush that might just about hold his weight and tied the rope around its gnarled, tough trunk. Starkad and Kari looped theirs over a tall outcrop of rock. Sigurd, Fisk and Wulfhelm tied knots in the ends of their ropes then jammed them into fissures and cracks in the rocks until they stuck. None of their anchors were very secure but they did not need to hold the weight of the Wolf Coats for very long.

Then Skar caught Fisk's eye and nodded. It was time for the attack to begin.

Forty-Four

Fisk got up to his knees. The vikingr-scotti already had his right arm cocked behind him, one of his two francesca throwing axes grasped in his hand. Twisting at the waist to give his cast more power, he hurled the axe towards the pirate on the platform above the gate.

The francesca shot through the air, making a whooping sound for a moment as it tumbled end over end, then hit the pirate. The blade sank itself in the man's chest with a soft thump. He flung his arms wide, dropping his spear as he staggered backwards. As he stood on a narrow wooden platform he did not go far, but instead toppled over the top of the gate, disappearing into the darkness beyond.

Fisk rose to his feet, slinging his long-handled battleaxe over his shoulder by its leather strap. At the same time, almost as one, the others stood up, turned around and launched themselves into thin air over the top of the canyon. Skar, Sigurd, Wulfhelm and Fisk held a tight grip of their ropes, using them to lower themselves in several short jumps down the rock face backwards. Starkad and Kari, heedless to whether their ropes would hold their weight or not, hurled themselves out into space, swords drawn, away from the canyon top until their ropes snapped tight and swung them back towards the cave mouth below.

All of them were screaming at the top of their lungs. The pirates below looked up, paralysed by shock, their faces masks of terror as death descended on them from above.

Starkad swung straight into the entrance of the cave. He went in feet first, colliding with one pirate and driving him backwards. Kari missed, dropping too far and thumping into the wall built to waist height across the entrance. He grabbed the edge of it, however, thrust his torso over the top and then he too tumbled inside. Starkad drove his sword into the man he had knocked aside to enter before the pirate had a chance to get up.

There were six other pirates in the cave. They dropped the ropes they held and scrambled for weapons. Outside the heavy lead canister they had been lowering dropped the last short distance, landing on the ground with a resounding hollow clang. One of the nine men outside who had been helping guide it to the ground was not quick enough in getting out of the way and the metallic boom of the canister as it hit the ground mingled with his scream as it smashed his left lower leg to a bloody pulp.

Starkad lunged at the pirates around him, slashing one across the chest while he was still trying to draw his sword. The blow nearly severed the man's right arm and gouged a deep red gash from his right shoulder to his left hip.

As he cried out and spun away, Kari was on his feet and laying into the other pirates too, slashing and stabbing with his own sword. Then the others – Skar, Sigurd, Fisk and Wulfhelm reached the cave entrance and swung inside too, adding to the onslaught. Fisk unslung his long axe and hacked a pirate down. In moments Skar, Sigurd and Wulfhelm dealt with the rest and all seven pirates inside the cave were on the floor either dead or bleeding their way fast towards it.

As they had suspected, the cave was not just for storage of the Sea Fire canister. It also served as a defensive position from which – if the gates were breached – warriors could hurl down missiles on any attackers below who had gotten through. For that purpose piles of rocks, broken masonry and a bundle of spears were stacked on the floor behind the wall built across the entrance.

The Wolf Coats seized these and began hurling them without mercy at the eight remaining pirates below, who stood around the sled and the fallen canister. The men shrieked as the missiles broke bones in their shoulders and the arms they held up in a vain attempt to protect themselves. One pirate collapsed like a scarecrow cut from its pole when a big rock, lobbed by Skar, stove in his skull, sending blood squirting from his ears and nose.

One pirate who managed to escape injury snatched up his spear and hurled it at the Wolf Coats. It was a wild cast sent in the general direction of where the rubble was coming from but went straight into the mouth of the cave, sending Wulfhelm, Kari and Sigurd diving to the floor to avoid it.

As it clattered against the roof of the cave then rattled to the floor, the pirate reached for another lying nearby. Starkad grabbed a smaller stone and pelted it at the warrior. There was a sharp crack as the stone struck the back of the pirate's outstretched hand. The man howled in pain and snatched his hand back. Hugging it close to his chest, he spun around twice, staggered a little then began to run away towards the steep slope down into the town.

Wulfhelm lifted the spear the pirate had cast into the cave and was about to send it after the running man when Skar grabbed his arm and turned him towards the gate. One of the guards who stood behind it was about to cast his own spear at the Wolf Coats in the cave. Fisk hurled his second throwing axe at the man but his aim was wide. It sank its blade into the wood of the gate with a loud bang. It was enough to distract the guard, however, who flinched sideways, delaying his spear cast.

Wulfhelm threw his spear at the guard. It caught the man on the right shoulder, sending him spinning around and dropping his own weapon.

'Out, out!' Skar shouted, shoving everyone around him towards the entrance of the cave they had just stormed. The cave was taken and there was no one in it alive or capable of providing any more trouble.

They slashed themselves free of their ropes. Starkad, Kari and Sigurd sheathed their weapons and clambered over the small wall at the front of the cave. They let themselves down until their arms were fully extended, then dropped the rest of the way to the canyon floor. They rolled to break their falls, coming back to their feet and drawing their swords again at the same time.

The others followed behind them. And a moment later they all stood in a line facing what opposition was left. Four of the remaining six who had been trying to load the canister onto the sled were nursing broken arms, shoulders or injured hands. The other two were fit to fight and had drawn their swords. One of them was dressed in the black robes of a pirate commander. He was a big man who, unlike his companions, showed no fear of the Norsemen who had descended on them so suddenly, causing so much harm in so little time.

The man spat then hurled what were probably curses at the Wolf Coats, in the Serk tongue. His display of defiance had some steadying effect on the pirates around him. The remaining guard at the gate was still in the fight too.

Skar stepped towards the lead pirate. The man in black swiped his curved sword at him in a vicious blow aimed at cutting Skar in two at the waist. With his usual surprising nimbleness, the big prowman skipped backwards, just beyond the arc the sword cut through the air. Then he sprang forward again. He planted his left boot on the pirate's right foot, pinning it to the ground. The pirate's glare of defiance turned to surprised terror as he realised he could not get away. Then Skar swung his own sword. The blade took the pirate's head off in one swipe, sending it tumbling through the air as blood fountained from his severed neck.

Skar stepped back and the pirate's decapitated corpse toppled sideways to the ground.

This was enough for his remaining companions. Nursing their injured limbs they turned and fled for the town.

'Let them go,' Skar said as the pirates skidded, slid and tumbled down the steep slope. 'We've other work to do.'

He turned to the gate. The remaining guard there was pulling up the big iron latch. He hauled it open and ran out.

'Get that gate shut,' Skar ordered. 'And make it secure. Disable the alarm bell too. We'll have all those pirates sent out to fight the fire back here soon enough. Anything we can do to slow them down will give us a bit more time.'

Wulfhelm and Kari ran to the gate. A big wooden beam lay to one side behind it for the purpose of barring it. They slammed the gate shut once more, heaved the beam up and slid it through the iron brackets across the back, holding the two doors of the gate shut.

Then they went to join the others who had by then gathered around the fallen lead canister. One corner of it was dinged by the fall but it was not split or burst. The sound of liquid still sloshing around came from inside.

'Get it on the sledge,' Skar directed, and the Wolf Coats began to manhandle the rectangular lead box onto the wooden carrier that stood waiting to carry it back to the town. It was very heavy but they were strong and it was not long before the wooden runners of the sledge were creaking under the weight of it.

There were ropes lying on the ground, abandoned by the fleeing pirates and the Wolf Coats used these to secure the lead container to the wooden runners. Then they all crouched and shoved with all their might, driving with their thighs to move the sledge to the edge of the steep slope down into the town. When it was at the edge of the drop, they halted.

'That wagon is still coming up the street,' Wulfhelm said. 'I'd say there will be more pirates coming this way very soon.'

The town itself was now ablaze with lights. Torches were lit and placed in brackets on walls. Braziers had been set alight and by their glow they could see pirates running around to and fro in the streets and market square below.

'If Einar's plan works,' Skar said, 'I wouldn't like to be down where they are soon. It will be like Ragnarök when the Fire Giant wields his flaming sword of destruction.'

He stuck the big wax plug on the top of the lead canister with his sword, shearing it off. They heard the sound of thick, oily liquid sloshing around inside and a strong smell like tar mixed with pine resin tugged their noses. Kari took the long, waxy wick that Surt had made earlier from a pouch at his belt and handed it to Skar, who slid one end into the spout the wax had sealed.

Sigurd took the last of his fire-starting kit from the pouch on his belt. He stood away from the canister and struck flint with iron until he produced a glowing piece of kindling, which he used to light a candle stub. Carrying it as carefully as he would handle a new-born baby, Sigurd handed the burning candle to Skar.

Skar took it and looked round at them all.

'Let's hope Surt knew what he was doing,' he said. 'And this takes its time to burn. Otherwise I'll see you all in Odin's Valour Hall.'

He touched the candle to the end of the wick that protruded from the spout. It sputtered alight but began to smoulder slowly rather than burn fast. The men around the sledge breathed out as one, all realising they had all been holding their breath.

'That's good,' Wulfhelm said. 'We're not dead.'

'We will be if we don't get this thing as far away from us as we can,' Skar said. 'Now push!'

They all crouched around the sled once more and heaved. The sledge slid forwards, over the edge of the top of the slope. For a moment it tottered, halfway over the edge, its front end hanging in space. Then the nose of the sledge dipped and it slid away, careering down the slope, picking up speed as it went.

The Wolf Coats stood up, watching it go. As they did so, Kari spotted a figure running across the market square below, right towards where the sled was careening with ever-increasing rapidity. He recognised who it was straight away.

'Einar's down there!' Kari cried.

Forty-Five

The lead box continued careering down the slope. It bounced and bucked but kept running on its sleds, sending showers of stones and dust in all directions as it picked up speed. In moments it was flying at a speed far too reckless for such steep terrain.

All the while the wick shoved into the spout at the end burned ever lower. The liquid inside sloshed around with the movement of the sled, making it even more unstable as it sped towards the town.

At the sight of the onrushing canister, the pirates who had been making their way towards the gate dived aside in desperate attempts to get out of its path. The men on their way to fetch the Sea Fire jumped off the wagon they were driving, abandoning the horses who pulled it to their fate.

Einar was running across the market square. He heard the cries of surprise and dismay and the scraping rumble of the rushing sled. He knew what it must mean and that he would have little time to find somewhere to hide.

There were market stalls, closed for the night, all around but he did not think their flimsy wood and canvas would give much protection from the coming fire. Then he spotted a line of stout barrels near the edge of the square where it met the back of the harbour – a ship's cargo waiting to be embarked or the stock of a merchant waiting to be sold.

He spun and sprinted for them. Legs pumping, he dodged through stalls until he got to the barrels and dived over them, putting their bulk between him and whatever was about to happen.

Once behind the barrels, Einar scrambled around into a crouch and peered back over the top of them. The thought occurred to him that the barrels might contain oil or some other such burnable materials, in which case he had just made a very big mistake.

Then the sled with the canister came hurtling down the street into the market square. It was now completely beyond control, speeding at an unstoppable pace. The left skid of the sled was off the ground, the other letting out a horrific scraping sound as it slid over the flagstones. Einar realised it was going so fast it could shoot straight across the square and into the harbour.

A stream of dark liquid, Sea Fire, being expelled from the open spout on the canister by the hectic jolting of the sled, was trailing behind. Halfway across the square the sled plonked down level again, then the right skid hit a broken flagstone. The back of the sledge rose into the air in the start of a crazy somersault. It had just got to the point where it was almost perpendicular when the whole thing was obliterated in a blinding flash.

The centre of the market square was consumed in a huge fireball. Einar flinched at the sight as a hot wind blasted around him. Blazing liquid shot in all directions, setting ablaze market stalls and the unfortunate pirates in the square who had been taken by surprise and could not get out of the way in time. Some splattered across the fronts of the houses at the edge of the square. The awning at the front of the tavern Einar and the others had been in earlier and the chairs and tables outside it ignited straight away.

The initial ball of fire subsided, fading into the air, but what had been the market square was now a lake of burning fire. At its centre was the twisted wreckage of what remained of the canister and sled, while all around market stalls blazed. Men, cloaked in fire, ran screaming this way and that through the inferno.

Einar stared in horrified amazement at the destruction. He had never seen anything so powerful. He did not have time to stand and stare, however. The conflagration in the market square would keep the pirates busy enough that the Wolf Coats' longship could get away. They would not have long, however, and if he did not put the siphōn out of action they would not be going anywhere.

He got up, raising a hand to protect his face at the intense heat of the blaze. There was something else he had to take care of on the way as well.

Einar jogged towards the left-hand quay that ran out to the harbour mouth where the tower that housed the siphōn brooded. A knot of dread twisted in his gut at the sight of the line of crucifixion stakes. The last time he had seen them, the first five bore corpses that were little more than bird-pecked skeletons. Now the first two had been replaced by much fresher meat.

Araltes was nailed to the first one. His hands were up above his head, an iron spike hammered through both wrists. Another transfixed his ankles to the bottom of the stake. He was stripped to his undershirt and his arms and legs were covered with bruises, showing he had suffered a ferocious beating before being crucified. Dried blood, black in the light of the flames, coated his arms and feet.

He was dead – there was no doubt about that. His head was thrown back and his eyes were closed. The twisted expression on his downcast mouth told of the pain he had endured in his last moments.

Einar took a deep breath and moved to the next stake. As he had feared, Ulrich was nailed to it. Einar stared in disbelief, hardly able to take in the sight of the little Wolf Coat leader, his arms pinned like Araltes, blood all down his arms and legs. His body dangled, arms fully outstretched, knees bent. He too had been beaten before being crucified. His head lolled to one side. What was left of his receding hair was matted with dried blood, either from a wound on his scalp somewhere or from that which had run down his arms from his wrists transfixed above. Unlike Araltes, Ulrich's face seemed somehow serene.

Einar's eyes stung with tears of sorrow. How could Ulrich be dead? The thought was incomprehensible. They had never seen eye to eye but for the last few years Ulrich had been the star that guided Einar's life. Not just Einar but the whole company. What did this mean for them all now? Could he really lead the úlfhéðnar? They were Ulrich's úlfhéðnar, not Einar's.

He gritted his teeth in frustrated rage. His fingers itched to draw his sword, run into the blazing market square and slaughter as many of the bastard pirates as he could. In his heart he knew that was futile, however. He would just be wasting his life, a life Ulrich had paid such a high price to preserve.

'Well I'm not leaving you here,' Einar said, his voice cracking. 'The least I can do is raise a burial mound for you to rest in.'

He drew his knife and worked the blade into the long iron spike that was driven through Ulrich's ankles. When it came free he started work on the one that pinned his arms above his head.

'Einar?'

Einar froze. The voice was cracked and faint, but it was Ulrich's. He looked at him. Ulrich's right eye was closed, caked shut with a thick swathe of dried blood, but his left was open and it was looking at Einar.

'You're alive!' Einar cried.

'Of course I am,' Ulrich croaked. 'Do you think I'd let myself be killed like the Christians' God?'

He grunted, his face twisting in a half-smile. Einar realised this was the most literal display of Ulrich's gallows humour he had yet witnessed.

'I knew sooner or later one of my crew would come for me,' Ulrich said. 'I've taught you all well. I thought it might have been Skar though.'

The same half-smile told Einar that Ulrich was as usual, even in this most extreme of situations, needling him.

'Skar is busy causing all that,' Einar said, nodding to the blazing carnage behind him.

Ulrich's smile disappeared as his face twisted into a grimace of agony. Einar could see the little wiry man was in bad shape. The torture he had undergone must have been extreme. Not just the beatings but then he must have been hanging, impaled, bleeding and in agony, all day in the baking sun. It had been too much for Araltes, but somehow Ulrich had endured until now. How much longer he could manage too was unclear. Einar cursed himself for not getting back to the town earlier.

He worked at the nail faster. Ulrich gasped in pain with every jolt and twist.

'Odin's blood, lad,' Ulrich said. 'You're as gentle as a bull elk.'

Einar felt a rush of admiration for his leader that he could still joke in this situation. Then again, that was the viking way. Ragnar Loðbrók had chanted poetry as the snakes came to kill him. Gunnar the Burgundian had laughed in the face of death. It was what every one of them aspired to. Einar hoped when it was his turn he could do the same.

'It was all statecraft, lad,' Ulrich rasped as Einar worked at the nail. 'We got caught up in some stupid Byzantine plot. Surt was right: the Romans' greatest enemies are themselves. They are forever scheming, conspiring to kill each other so they can get ahead and place their own arses on the imperial throne. Araltes there and his strategos were on the wrong side of one of these plots. The Romans we saw arrive today are on the other. Strategos Aleksander is part of some plot to depose the emperor. It's a conspiracy led by the emperor's own uncle for fuck's sake. That's how slippery these folk are. Aleksander took great pleasure in telling Araltes this before he demanded the pirate emir execute us.

'The biggest threat to their plot was Strategos Theoktistos who commands the loyalty of most of the navy. And his right-hand man Araltes, of course. They needed something to lure them into a trap and knew the prospect of a Sea Fire siphōn falling into the hands of the Serks would be too great a threat for men as loyal to the emperor as those two to ignore. So the conspirators did a deal with the pirates here.'

'They gave their greatest weapon to their enemies?!' Einar said, shaking his head as he continued to dig at the wood. 'They really must hate each other so much.'

'It's a risk, but not a reckless one,' Ulrich said. 'I've had time to think about this while hanging around here with nothing else to do.'

He made a derisory grunt.

'These pirates are rebels, breakaways from the caliphate,' Ulrich continued. 'These Roman plotters did not give the Sea Fire to their main enemy. They probably mean to wipe them all out when their purpose is fulfilled. Or else that siphōnarioi they lent them to work it could put it beyond use. Either way, they won't leave it here when they've got their own man on the imperial throne.'

'That second siphōnarioi,' Einar said. 'Surt told us that the Romans threaten to kill a siphōnarioi's family if they let one fall into their enemies' hands. How did they persuade that one to work with the pirates?'

'Simple,' Ulrich said. 'They threatened to kill his family if he didn't.'

At that moment the nail came free.

'Prepare yourself,' Einar said.

He pulled the nail swiftly from Ulrich's flesh. Einar had expected Ulrich to scream but to his further astonishment all Ulrich did was make a sharp gasp. He slumped down, unable to support his own weight. Einar caught him before he fell.

'You're quite the *drengr*, Ulrich,' Einar said, using the utmost compliment that could be given to a man. If a man was a drengr he stood up for his principles and beliefs. He was like a rock in the sea, unmoved by the tides of opinion, challenges, fashion or kings. To be a drengr was to be admired.

'It didn't hurt as much as it did going in,' Ulrich said, attempting to grin again but not quite making it this time. Einar could see he really was in a great deal of pain.

'Einar,' Ulrich said after a moment. 'I thank you for getting me down. It was fucking sore to be nailed up there I can tell you. But I'm done for. I can't walk and my arms and legs are destroyed. I am no use to anyone now. I don't know how long I can hang on anyway. Leave me here and get away. Make sure the others all escape. I can die here in peace now I'm not nailed up.'

'I can't leave you here,' Einar said. 'You're Odin's greatest follower. You can't be killed in the same way as the white Christ!'

'Araltes consoled himself with that thought as he died,' Ulrich said. 'He screamed out to his God, thanking him for the "gift" of being able to share the same doom as him. But Odin too hung on the tree of pain, his side impaled with a spear. He sacrificed himself to himself. Through that he learned much wisdom. The same happened to me. In the depths of agony I realised much. I learned many things both about myself and the world. Don't mourn for me, lad. This was indeed a gift. I can die content. Now leave me.'

'I'm not going to leave you,' Einar said.

'I can't walk,' Ulrich said. 'What are you going to do? Carry me?'

'Yes,' Einar said.

He picked up Ulrich's shattered body and heaved him over his shoulder. Then he headed towards the siphōn tower.

Forty-Six

Einar had not gone far when a figure jumped up from behind a stack of cargo that sat on the quay. Einar froze. With Ulrich over his shoulder he was not able to fight off an attack, so he would have to drop him. In Ulrich's present state that could very well kill him.

Then he relaxed, realising the person approaching him was Diogenes. The Greek let out a torrent of words Einar did not understand but he gleaned that in general he was pleased that Einar had finally arrived.

Einar cocked his head towards the siphōn tower. Diogenes nodded, his expression turning to grim resolution, and they set off again. When they reached the end of the quay, they were further away from the fires ravaging the market square and there were more shadows and dark areas. They were perhaps thirty paces from the door of the tower when Einar spotted two warriors on guard at the bottom of the four wooden steps that led up to the door.

One of the defensive barricades they had manned earlier when the imperial dromon had arrived was nearby. Einar went behind it, followed by Diogenes. He set Ulrich down carefully, then he and Diogenes crouched, peering over the top at the men outside the tower.

Einar's mind tumbled as he tried to work out how to overcome this obstacle. He cursed himself, realising he had put so much effort into working out all the other problems they had to solve that he had not thought about how they would get into the siphōn tower. His hope had been that all those guarding it would have gone with the wagon to fetch the extra Sea Fire and were now dead, their corpses burning in the market square. This did not seem to be the case.

He cursed himself further, realising he had been relying on what he hoped would happen, rather than planning for everything that might.

Perhaps he could sneak up on the guards at the door, but then it would be two against one: Diogenes would not be much use in a straight fight. And what then? Who knew how many more pirate warriors were inside?

Then Einar felt the same prickling sensation he had felt on the beach earlier. He looked back down the quay. It was almost imperceptible, but he swore he saw a hint of movement, a mere instant of what could have been a head popping up from shadows by the wall, then it was gone again. It was the sort of thing most folk would then dismiss as a trick of their imagination. Einar had been trained not to ignore such tricks, however.

He cupped his hands to his mouth and made the owl call. A moment later an answering call came from the shadows near the wall. Einar's heart soared. His companions had arrived.

A few moments later Skar, Surt and Kari arrived, wreathing through the shadows like cats, so stealthy the warriors at the tower did not spot them.

'Ulrich!' Skar exclaimed in a hoarse whisper as he stared in horror at the broken and battered body of his old friend lying behind the barrels. 'What have they done to you?'

'Never mind me,' Ulrich gasped. 'The lad needs help here.'

'You got him, Einar!' Skar turned to Einar. 'Well done, lad. We're here to give you a hand.'

'Where are the others?' Einar said.

'They've gone to the ship,' Surt said. 'I told them to get it underway while we came here to help you make sure the siphōn is put out of working order.'

'That,' Kari said, 'and the fact that we thought we might have killed you by accident in that fireball and we would have to break the siphōn ourselves.'

'There's two men guarding the door,' Einar said. 'I was thinking maybe we could sneak up on them somehow and take them by surprise.'

'We'll take them by surprise but there's no time for sneaking about,' Skar said. 'It's only a matter of time before more pirates arrive. We passed a bunch of them who looked like they were mustering to come this way. You bring Ulrich. We can't leave him lying out here. Ready?'

He looked at the others. They nodded and drew their swords.

'Go,' Skar said.

The Wolf Coats got up and ran at the tower. The guards at the door, startled to see someone approaching out of the dark, the fire behind them, did what all guards do and shouted a challenge. While they were still trying to work out if they were under attack or not, Skar and the others kept on coming. By the time the guards realised they were, the attackers were already upon them.

The guard to the left of the door drove his spear towards Skar who danced to the side. The point of the spear head went past him instead of into his guts. Skar then brought his sword down, severing the shaft of the spear and turning it from a deadly weapon into a stick.

Kari ran in close and stabbed the guard through the chest. He collapsed to the ground, making a loud groan. Surt attacked the second guard. He too thrust his spear at Surt who parried the blow with his sword. Steel rang as the iron head of the spear met Surt's blade and they rasped across each other. The guard went to strike again but Surt and Kari turned on him at the same time. Surt rammed his blade into the guard's throat as Kari shoved his blade into the guard's guts. With a strangled gurgle he dropped his spear and fell to his knees, both hands going to his throat in a vain attempt to staunch the hot blood that gushed from it. Then he toppled over onto the quay, dead.

Einar, with Ulrich over his shoulder again and Diogenes following behind, ran to the tower door. As he arrived, the door at the top of the steps flung open and the same man as they had seen there earlier in the leather headdress and apron – the siphōnarioi – glared out into the night, no doubt coming to see what the commotion was outside the door.

His eyes widened at the sight and he started to slam the door shut again. Surt reached up, grabbed the handle on the outside and wrenched the door open again, even wider than before. The big man's strength was such that the siphōnarioi, who still grasped the inside handle, was hauled out of the tower with it. He let out a yelp as he sprawled into the night air, tumbling down the steps face first.

The inside of the tower was gloomy but there was enough light from it to see through the open door that there were other Serk pirates inside. Surt, Kari and Skar charged up the steps. Einar passed Ulrich to Diogenes, then ran after them. He had no time to secure his sword into his fighting glove so drew his seax with his left hand as he ran up the steps.

Inside the tower were three more Serk warriors. They were

dressed in black like the emir's bodyguards. The first lunged at Surt with a sword as he came up the steps. Surt dodged the blow and brought his own blade down, severing the man's outstretched arm at the elbow. He screamed in horror. Surt drove his shoulder into the man's chest, knocking him out of the way so he could get inside the door. The others poured in after him.

Skar swung at a second pirate and Kari took on the third. The pirate parried Skar's attack and for a moment they locked blades. Then Skar head-butted the pirate, sending him staggering backwards, blood gushing from his shattered face. Skar swept his legs from under him with a scything kick of his own left leg then finished the pirate off with a sword thrust to the chest.

The last pirate struck at Kari with a desperate swipe aimed at taking his head off. Kari ducked and it passed over his head. As he did so Einar ran forward and drove his seax into the pirate's side. The man cried out as Kari came back up and drove his sword into his belly.

The fight was over almost as soon as it had begun. For a few moments the Wolf Coats stood panting, their hearts racing. The only sound was the final groans of the dying men on the floor.

Einar looked around. The interior of the tower was lit by a single oil lamp that was set on a shelf in the wooden wall. On the wall facing the harbour entrance was the great brass tube that sprayed the Sea Fire. It was raised up on a wooden scaffold to about twice the height of a man where it poked out through a slit in the wall of the tower. A long, snake-like hose, wondrously constructed of what looked like countless metal rings connected one on top of the other to form a flexible pipe, trailed down into a large metal box that sat on the floor. This had no top and Einar could see it was empty. Beside it, on a raised platform, was a big lead tank identical to the one the

Wolf Coats had sent careering down the slope into the market square. There was a long metal lever on the right-hand side and something that looked like huge leather blacksmith's bellows with a wooden lever attached on the left. The air was filled with the metallic stench of spilled blood and a heavy smell like strong pine resin so strong it made Einar's eyes smart and his throat catch.

There was a cry of anguish from outside.

Einar ran to the door and looked out. Ulrich lay on the ground. Diogenes was on his knees beside him, both hands clutching at his chest. He looked up at Einar, his face a mask of anguish and gasped something in his own tongue.

Further down the quay, fleeing at full sprint, Einar could see the other siphōnarioi.

Surt came to the door beside Einar. Seeing the incomprehension on Einar's face Diogenes said something to Surt in another tongue Einar did not understand either.

'He says the other siphōnarioi grabbed one of the fallen pirates' swords,' Surt translated. 'He stabbed him with it and ran off.'

Einar cursed the fact that he had been right: Diogenes was indeed not much use in a hand-to-hand fight.

'He'll be going for help,' Kari said.

More shouts erupted from the far end of the quay. Figures were moving against the firelight. Swords and spear heads glinted. They were coming towards the siphōn tower.

'It looks like he won't have far to go to get it,' Skar said.

Forty-Seven

'Get them inside,' Einar said.

He, Surt and Skar ran down the steps and lifted Ulrich and Diogenes and carried them back into the tower.

'Get the door shut,' Einar said once they were back inside. 'See if you can bar it. We need some time to get this siphon disabled.'

'But we'll be stuck in here!' Kari said.

'We can go out up there.' Einar pointed to the opening above where the siphon poked out through the wall. 'We'll be high enough to jump into the harbour from there. But if we don't get this thing put out of working order that other siphōnarioi can still incinerate us and the ship as we try to sail past.'

They propped Ulrich and Diogenes up, sitting with their backs to the wall. Einar was dismayed at how much blood was leaking down the Greek's torso. His wound was deep and in the lamplight his face looked ghastly.

Skar slammed the door shut. There was a beam behind it which he slid into place to lock it shut.

'Ask him what we need to do,' Einar said to Surt.

Surt spoke to Diogenes, who responded through gritted teeth now stained with blood.

'He says we need to pull the metal bar on the right back

until it clicks, then push it as far forwards as it will go,' Surt said.

Einar went to the siphōn and grabbed the lever. He yanked it back. It was not easy and he had to lean back himself, adding his body weight to the strength of his arms. There was a loud click and the lever became a lot looser. Einar pushed it forward until it was level to the ground. A gushing sound came from inside the canister and the open-topped metal box began to fill with dark, viscous liquid. The smell like pine resin got even stronger.

Diogenes said something else.

'He says to now pump the wooden handle on the bellows a few times,' Surt said.

Einar did that and a sucking, gushing sound began in the metal tube that ran up to the siphōn head. The level of liquid in the open metal box dropped a little, then returned to its previous level with a gurgle.

Diogenes provided further instructions.

'Now he says there is a small wheel at the bottom of the siphōn that you need to rotate all the way to the left,' Surt said.

Einar peered up at the underside of the metal tube above. He frowned, squinting in the gloomy light, looking for the wheel.

'Get me that oil lamp,' Einar said over his shoulder. 'I can't see a thing.'

Kari lifted the lamp from its shelf and began to walk over to Einar with it. Diogenes became very agitated and shouted something. Then he grimaced, clutched the wound in his chest and his head slumped into his chest.

'He says not to bring the lamp near the siphōn,' Surt says. 'He says it's now primed full of Sea Fire liquid. The slightest spark could set it ablaze and the whole tower with us in it as well. This is the time of most danger.'

Kari halted halfway across the floor.

'Hold it there then,' Einar said. 'I'll see what I can do.'

He clambered up the wooden scaffold that surrounded the siphon until he reached the top. Running his hand under the brass tube, he felt a small metal wheel and turned it all the way to the left until it would go no further. A hissing sound like a strong wind blowing through a narrow mountain pass began to emit from the brass tube.

Einar began clambering back down to the floor.

'Now what?' he asked as he climbed.

Diogenes did not reply.

'Now what?' Einar said, louder this time. 'Come on. We don't have much time.'

Skar crouched beside Diogenes. He felt his neck and looked in his eyes.

'He's dead,' the big man said.

'Shit!' Einar said. He jumped down the last part. 'What do we do now?'

A wild hammering started on the door. It bucked and rattled against the bar that held it.

'The pirates are here,' Kari said.

'I don't think that door will hold long against them,' Surt said, pointing at how the bar was bulging with every thump from the outside.

'Let's get out of here,' Skar said. 'We'll go out the top of the tower as Einar suggested.'

'That other siphōnarici is with them,' Einar said. 'He knows how to operate this thing. Not only that but we've even made it ready for him. They'll burn us to a crisp as we try to get out of the harbour.'

'Diogenes said a spark from the oil lamp could set the whole place alight,' Kari said. 'That would destroy the siphōn and let the ship escape.'

'But we'll all go up with it,' Surt said. 'You saw what happened in the market square.'

'So what do we do?' Skar said.

All eyes turned to Einar.

Einar opened his mouth but did not know what to say. If they ran they would die. If they stayed they would die. The choice was really only which death they preferred.

'We'll fight them,' he said, gritting his teeth.

'Don't be an idiot, Einar.'

Ulrich's voice made them all turn. The battered Wolf Coat leader still sat with his back to the wall, head back, one eye still closed over with caked blood.

'*A corpse is no use to anyone,*' Ulrich said. 'Those are the words of Odin. Get yourselves out of here.'

'What about the Sea Fire?' Einar said.

'Set fire to it, like Kari suggested,' Ulrich said.

'We can't do that and get away,' Einar said.

'You can get away,' Ulrich said. 'I can set it on fire.'

'No,' Skar said. 'We're not leaving you.'

'Skar old friend, I'm already as useless as a corpse,' Ulrich said. 'My legs are broken. My arms are skewered. I've been bleeding all day. I'm going to die anyway. I won't recover from this and even if I did, I don't want to live the rest of my life a cripple. At least this way I choose my own fate and I can help you get away. Now get out of here. Go.'

No one moved.

'Go!' Ulrich said in as close to a shout he could muster. 'This is my last order to you. This is not the time to start disobeying me.'

Skar heaved a heavy sigh. He nodded.

'I will see you in Odin's Valour Hall,' he said. His voice cracked and his eyes glittered in the wan light.

'I'll have a horn of ale waiting for you,' Ulrich said. 'Einar, give me that lamp. The rest of you get out of here.'

Einar took the lamp from Kari and went to Ulrich while the rest nodded their farewells to Ulrich and began scrambling up the wooden scaffold around the siphōn.

Einar crouched beside Ulrich and handed him the oil lamp.

'I don't know for sure,' Einar said. 'But my guess is that if you throw this into the open metal box that's filled with the Sea Fire liquid, the whole thing will go up in flames.'

Ulrich grunted. He grasped the handle of the lamp in his painful, stiff fingers.

'Will you be able to throw it from here?' Einar said.

'I'll manage,' Ulrich said, his voice fading to no more than a whisper.

Then he reached out with this left hand and caught a handful of Einar's wolfskin cloak. The grip was slight and only two of his fingers had any real power. His open eye, however, which had seemed dull and almost sleepy, was now bright and alert with the old energy of Ulrich.

'Einar, take the crew home,' he said, his voice full of burning intensity. 'We do not belong here. Odin walks the forests and mountains of the north, not these hot realms. Lead the company back. Make all of them as rich and free as jarls like I planned to. If anyone can do it you can. Odin blessed you with gifts. He led you to us. Now it is your time to lead them.'

Einar nodded. Tears stung his eyes. He was at an utter loss as to what he should say.

'One more thing,' Ulrich spoke again. 'They took my fighting sword, but my good one should be still on the ship. That is, if the bastards didn't find our secret hiding places. You know the one I mean?'

Einar nodded. It was one of the swords they had taken from

the grave mounds above Gandvik a few winters before. Its hilt was decorated with elaborate decorations of twisting beasts, outlined with gold thread. Ulrich treasured it.

'Take it with you back north,' Ulrich said. 'Give it to my son.'

'Your son?' Einar's mouth gaped open. Ulrich had never mentioned he had a son, or any child.

There was a crack of splintering wood as a blade came through the door, hacking a sliver from it.

'Now get out of here if you don't want to share my funeral pyre,' Ulrich said. 'And remember: until now only Odin watched you from Valhalla. From now on I will be watching as well. Don't let me down.'

Einar ran to the scaffold and began climbing. The others were already up and through the slot in the wall above. As he climbed he heard the sound of more splintering wood below him, and then a crash as the door finally gave way.

At that moment Einar reached the top of the siphōn. He planted a foot on the opening in the wall and looked down. He saw many pirate warriors pouring through the open doorway. Ulrich sat facing them, the oil lamp held up in shaking hands.

'Good evening,' he said. 'So good of you to join me for my funeral feast. I hope you like roast meat.'

He tossed the lamp into the Sea Fire liquid in the tank at the base of the siphōn.

Einar threw himself through the opening in the wall. He was about halfway through when he felt as if a warm wind picked him up and blew him through the air out into the night beyond. Then he was flying through the night as the tower behind him dissolved in a huge blossom of fire. Splintered wood flew in all directions as Einar fell, arms and legs spinning into the harbour.

With a huge splash he hit the water below. He sank deep then, lungs bursting for air, he kicked himself back to the surface.

Sucking in a deep breath, Einar began treading water as he looked around. The others – Surt, Skar and Kari were doing likewise nearby. The siphōn tower was now little more than a blazing stump with a heap of twisted, unrecognisable metal within. Burning Sea Fire liquid ran down the harbour walls as pirates, caught in the blast and splattered with Sea Fire, ran screaming in all directions or leapt into the sea, desperately trying to extinguish flames that would not go out and burned even under water.

Coming towards them, sail full and oars undulating up and down like the wings of a dragon, was the Wolf Coats' snekkja. Affreca stood at the dragon-carved prow, dangling a rope for Einar and the others to climb up.

Einar waited in the water as the ship approached, secure in the knowledge that, at last, they would soon be free of this cursed island where Odin was a stranger.

Forty-Eight

The Imperial Palace, Constantinopolis

The room was stunning. Each of its four walls were equal in their width and height, making each one a perfect square. Joined together, they formed another perfect square of the room. The ceiling above rose into a point to form a pyramid. One wall had a huge window through which the sea and the main harbour of the city could be seen, sprawled below the palace in the legendary Golden Horn, the crescent-shaped estuary that divided the greatest city in the world, Constantinopolis, from the ancient town of Byzantium where it had begun.

The floor and the walls of the room were hewn from a wondrous marble, purple in colour with flecks of white as if sand had been sprinkled over it. The room, known in the tongue of the Greeks as the *Porphyra* Chamber, was fit for an emperor. Not just in its luxury but in the most literal sense too: purple was the imperial colour. For half a millennium only Roman emperors had been allowed to wear garments of that colour.

In the centre of the room sat a man swathed in a purple cloak. He nestled among luxurious cushions on a gilt chair, his chin resting on his fist, elbow on the chair arm, as he surveyed the magnificent view of the harbour through which most of the wealth of the world came and went. This wealth was the lifeblood of the empire he ruled and made

Constantinopolis the richest and largest city on earth, and its ruler the richest man.

Named Constantine, he was the seventh emperor to bear the name of the founder of the city. He was also named *Porphyrogenitus* because he had been born in this very room: son of an emperor who had arrived into the world in a room whose very walls were built of stone of the imperial colour. He had ascended to the throne when only two years old, a position he had held onto until now, when he was in his mid-thirties. This was no mean feat in a place where the normal running of the state was riddled with violence and treachery and changes of ruler were frequent and bloody.

In so many ways Constantine was the epitome of the imperial figure at the heart of this great empire. However, even his apparent long and firm grip on power was as febrile as his forebearers. His imperial lineage was in fact a sham. His mother had been his father's fourth wife – illegal in the eyes of the Church and God. It had been in a desperate attempt to legitimise him that she had staggered into this very room, heavily pregnant, to give birth to him. Ever since he had been at the mercy of a series of powerful, ambitious men and women who had competed for influence over him so as to get their hands on the reins of power through him. At any time, he was well aware, if their own grip on power had become strong enough, they would have done away with him.

But he was still on the throne. He was still alive. All those ambitious people who had fought to control him had killed each other instead of him. They had been so busy keeping their eyes on their rivals that they had ignored the studious young man who appeared more interested in books than statecraft. They saw no danger in him, and that was their mistake.

Despite his increasing years, Emperor Constantine's long,

curled hair and beard were both still a lustrous black and his eyes that rested on the harbour view were bright and surrounded by only a few faint lines, though their whites were tinged with red and showed signs of strain.

There was a table near the window. It was piled high with scrolls and parchments. Writing tools were scattered across it. There were splashes of ink on the tabletop too, as well as on the fingers of the emperor, evidence of the studies he had been engaged in until a short time before.

He had been reviewing the latest volume of a compendium of agricultural lore he had been working on for some time. That morning he had found himself engrossed in the study until a short time before, when his stinging eyes and a sore head had alerted him that it was time to take a break.

A large, rectangular box, covered with a lid, sat on the floor near the throne. The emperor glanced at it, grimaced at the thought of what was inside, then returned his gaze to the harbour.

The tall double doors of the Porphyra Chamber crashed open.

Constantine swivelled in his chair to see a man standing in the entrance. He was around the same age as him, and dressed in almost as grand robes, though lacking the purple cloak of an emperor. At the sight of Constantine, a malevolent grin spread across the man's face.

'Stephanos,' Constantine said, rising from his throne to face the newcomer. 'To what reason do I owe this visit from my brother-in-law?'

Stephanos strode into the purple room. Still grinning, he walked around the emperor, looking at him and taking full enjoyment of what he clearly regarded as a moment of triumph.

'Your time on the throne is at an end, Constantine,'

his brother-in-law said at last. He spoke in a thundering, commanding tone. 'I am here to tell you that.'

'No doubt you are taking my place?' Constantine said.

'I will take on the burden of imperial power, yes,' Stephanos said. 'For the sake of the empire and the good of the Church, someone responsible must take command.'

The emperor looked at his brother-in-law, an expression of sadness mixed with pity on his face.

'Stephanos, you are an ambitious man,' he said. 'And a capable one. But sometimes it is not enough that you should get something just because you *want* it. You cannot just announce you are emperor and expect the world to believe it.'

'You think me a fool?' Stephanos roared. 'We have been working on this strategy for some time. Strategos Aleksander supports me and he brings with him the entire Eastern Themes and their soldiers.'

'Do you think Strategos Theoktistos will go along with this plot?' the emperor said. 'I doubt it. And he commands the navy and holds the loyalty of half the army.'

'We have dealt with that fool,' Stephanos said, his voice holding a note of glee. 'And his barbarian lapdog Araltes. They will not be able to help you. Your own personal bodyguards, the *exkoubitores*, are on our side too.'

'And what of my sister, your wife?' Constantine said, raising one eyebrow.

'She knows you are too weak to command an empire,' Stephanos said. 'The imperial throne needs a strong man on it. A determined man with a firm hand. Not some weakling who is more interested in books.'

'Sometimes, Stephanos, we can learn a lot from books,' the emperor said. 'Especially history books.'

'I care nothing for old lore!' Stephanos said. He was shouting again. 'Your days are over, Constantine. I am here to give you the opportunity to fall on your sword now. To die like a true Roman. The alternative will be long, painful and undignified. I am here to give you the gift of a dignified death, even though you do not deserve it. You can thank your sister for that.'

'And I thank you for such a generous offer, brother-in-law,' Constantine said. 'And in return let me give you a gift.'

He walked to the large box, picked it up and brought it to Stephanos. At the sight of it his brother-in-law's expression changed from righteous anger to puzzlement.

'Is this some sort of trick?' Stephanos said. 'I will not take it. Come no closer! Set it down before me. Open it.'

The emperor did as he was told. Setting the box on the marbled floor he pulled the lid off and stepped back.

Stephanos blinked. Then blinked again, as if unable to believe what his eyes were telling him.

The skin of the severed head inside the box was dry and leather-like. It had been mummified with various ancient herbs and spices in the manner the ancient Egyptians had used and the hair was like twisted wool. However, the features were still easily recognisable as those of the Strategos Aleksander.

Stephanos opened and closed his mouth but no words came out. He glared in disbelief at the severed head and at the emperor who he had until that moment regarded as a harmless fool.

'We found out about your plot, Stephanos,' Constantine said. 'All your fellow conspirators – if they have not already been arrested – are being rounded up as we speak. Including now, my sister I am sorry to say. You confirmed her guilt yourself.'

His eyes, which had been soft and appeared full of sorrow, now had a hard look in them.

Stephanos finally managed to make a noise; however, what

came from his mouth was an inarticulate scream of frustrated rage. As his hand went into his robe to grab the knife concealed in it, the sound of running feet came from behind him. Ten imperial warriors in full ceremonial armour came charging into the room. They swarmed around the emperor's brother-in-law, pinning his hands behind him, wrenching the knife from his fist and taking him prisoner.

'Blind him,' the emperor said as the warriors dragged his horrified brother-in-law out of the room. 'Then send him into exile on some godforsaken island.'

When he was gone, the tall figure of Strategos Theoktistos strolled into the room, his hands behind his back, his usual haughty expression on his face. Beside him was a bearded Norseman wearing imperial army uniform. An axe rested on his shoulder and his long blond hair was braided.

'So, Theoktistos,' Emperor Constantine said. 'It seems what these wolfskin-clad Norsemen told you was correct.'

'Indeed it does, *Kyrios*, my Lord,' the strategos said, a smile spreading across his lips. 'This was a most insidious conspiracy. We almost lost a siphōn, Sea Fire and its siphōnarioi to the caliphate as part of it too. Thankfully that also was averted.'

'I am sorry it cost Araltes his life,' the emperor said. 'He was a most capable and loyal soldier.'

He turned to the Norseman.

'He was your brother, I believe?' the emperor said.

The Norseman nodded his head in respect.

'And what is your name?' Constantine asked.

'My name is Bjorn, Kyrios,' the Norseman replied.

'Well, Bjorn,' the emperor said, 'your brother and your fellow Norsemen have done me great service today.'

Bjorn bowed his head once more.

'And the exkoubitores? My sentinels?' Constantine said, turning to Strategos Theoktistos. 'They were really part of this plot?'

'Yes, Kyrios,' the strategos said. 'Unfortunately that is also true.'

'Have their commanders executed,' the emperor said. 'The rest will be moved from those rather comfortable quarters at the city gate and stationed in some godforsaken, remote, dangerous part of the empire where they will be too busy to worry about the barbarians who surround them to have time for conspiracies or plots.'

He looked at Bjorn for a moment.

'Perhaps I would be better off with a company of these axe-bearing fighters to guard me,' he said. 'I am sad to say foreign mercenaries appear to be more trustworthy than my own soldiers.'

'It is worth considering, Kyrios,' the strategos said. 'Men who fight for gold tend not to be swayed by the rivalries and politics of the empire.'

'I shall think about it,' the emperor said. He turned to the Norseman. 'In the meantime make sure your countrymen are well rewarded for their part in saving my throne. Perhaps you might even persuade them to stay here? Their service would be most welcome.'

'I'll see what I can do, Kyrios,' Bjorn said.

He bowed his head and withdrew from the purple-walled room.

Forty-Nine

Einar, Affreca and Skar waited at the huge gate of the imperial palace.

The gate itself was like a fortress, though the most beautiful one any of them had ever seen. The walls of the passageway through it were lined with marble, not purple this time but white, green and red. The ceiling was covered with pictures of strange men looking down, their images made up from countless little tiles that sparkled in places with gold or gemstones. Beyond the gate they could see glimpses of gardens, dotted with pools and fountains, which led up to the palace itself.

In the blazing sunshine it looked like paradise on earth. However, this impression was marred by the maelstrom of activity that swirled around it. Soldiers ran this way and that, rounding up men in official robes, clerks with ink-stained hands and even contingents of other soldiers: anyone implicated, accused or even just suspected of being part of the plot against the emperor. The soldiers shoved, punched, kicked and marched their prisoners off at spearpoint to what were no doubt grim fates.

Through the chaos Einar spotted Bjorn, Araltes' brother, approaching. He carried a leather, iron-bound chest before him. From the stiff way he walked, Einar could tell it was heavy.

When he reached the group of Wolf Coats, Bjorn set the chest on the flagstones that lined the road into the palace. A satisfying rattle of metal came from inside.

'There you go, lads and lasses,' Bjorn said. He flicked open the lid, revealing a king's wealth of gold and silver coins, jewellery and other treasures. 'Your reward for your part in keeping the emperor on the throne.'

Einar stared at the wealth laid before him. The bright sunlight reflected dapples of gold and silver across his face. Affreca let out a low whistle.

'That's enough to buy a kingdom,' she said in a hoarse voice.

Skar looked unimpressed. 'It is the price of Ulrich's life. If I could, I'd gladly exchange it to have him back.'

'It's the cost of my brother's life too,' Bjorn said, his face becoming grim.

'We should get back to the ship,' Einar said.

'I will walk with you,' Bjorn said. 'At least some of the way.'

Einar and Skar picked up the chest between them and they set off into the city. As they left the great marbled gate, a tremendous roar filled the air like a great rushing wind. It was the unmistakable sound of many voices all crying out at once. Einar flinched a little at the sound. He had not heard such a sound since the last time he had been charging into battle in the middle of an army. Frowning, he looked to Bjorn to see how he reacted.

'That's the sound of the Hippodrome,' Bjorn said, a faint smile playing on his lips. 'It's a place where the Greeks go to watch horse and chariot races and where they execute criminals. A lot of those conspirators against the emperor will end up there over the next few days. The sands of the Hippodrome will be red with their blood.'

'People will watch the killings?' Affreca asked.

'Executions are one of the most popular pastimes in the city,' Bjorn said. 'Next to the chariot racing that is. The Hippodrome has seats for a hundred thousand spectators.'

'A hundred *thousand*?' Einar shook his head. 'Surely there are not that number of people in the whole country?'

'My friend, half a million people live in this city,' Bjorn scoffed.

Einar blinked. The thought that he was surrounded by such multitudes of people made his head spin. It was unbelievable. Then, as they left the street that led to the palace gate and entered the *Mese*, the grand Middle Street of Constantinopolis, he really could believe it.

The street was over thirty paces wide and paved the whole way. Both sides were lined by walkways shaded from the sun. These were flanked by lines of stone columns on the outside and their interior filled with merchant stalls and markets where everything from cheese, fruit, bread, fish and clothes to tools, jewellery and slaves was on sale. Beyond the hawkers in the porticos, huge stone buildings – mansions of the rich, churches, libraries and other state offices – towered. All along the length of the Mese were stone statues, images of emperors and heroes so lifelike they looked like real people who been turned to stone by the spells of witches. Here and there carved stone figures spouted fresh, flowing water that people could drink. The street thronged with so many people it seemed like the whole world had gathered there.

Einar remembered being so impressed by Aethelstan's city of Wintanceaster but compared to this, it was just a hamlet in a backward country. Even there shit and the detritus of the houses had flown down the sides of the streets in foul ditches. There was no sign of any of that here.

'What's it like to live here?' Einar asked.

'Unbelievable,' Bjorn said. 'It's hard for me to find the words that would be adequate to explain it to someone who has never been here or seen anything like it. The Hippodrome is the largest stadium but it's only one of hundreds of places to relax here in the city. There are theatres, libraries, bathhouses, taverns, shops, even in the streets there are conjurors and jugglers. There is always something happening. Life here goes past at such a fast rate. It's exciting beyond words.'

'I can see how that could be,' Einar said. He felt like his head was spinning and his voice was a little breathless.

Affreca looked askance at Einar, her brows beginning to knit into a frown.

'Folk like you could do very well here,' Bjorn continued. 'The empire needs capable fighters and if you've a head on your shoulders and a bit of craftiness in your heart all the better. The emperor now trusts foreign fighters more than his own Greeks. Warriors like your company would be perfect for the marines. You'd all be welcome. Even your friend the Saracen from the caliphate. There is a place here for everyone.'

Einar looked around at the myriad of faces that passed them in the wide street. They were of all colours, not just pale white like himself or black like Surt but every shade in between too. The people wore all sorts of clothing made in widely different styles. This truly was the hub of the world, the meeting place of all the nations.

'Surt is too busy trying to make sure his daughter doesn't run away,' Skar said. 'He would not even leave her on the ship in case she was gone when he came back.'

'She's a grown woman,' Affreca said, shaking her head. 'Perhaps he should let her make up her own mind what she does?'

'She's certainly something,' Einar said with a smile. 'I think Surt is trying to make up for many years of absence, perhaps.'

'Good luck to him with that,' Affreca said. 'It looks like she was perfectly happy where she was until we burned down her home and kidnapped her.'

The Mese led downhill towards the harbour and for a time they walked in silence through the crowds thronging the street. The noise around them was an almost deafening cacophony of different tongues, the rattle of wagons, the clip of horses and the splashing of the water in the many fountains they passed. Eventually they came to the edge of an area of narrow, dark alleys that ran between towering buildings, which Bjorn explained were either mansions of the rich or tenement blocks where hundreds of people all lived crammed in one on top of the other. Their height made Einar's head spin and his stomach lurched at the thought of trying to sleep on one of the upper floors. They cast their shadows on the thoroughfares between them that led from the Mese to the harbour. Compared to the majesty of the great middle street, these alleys – lined as they were with taverns, stables, warehouses and brothels – were dingy, dark and strewn with all sorts of trash.

'Then there is the other side of the city,' Bjorn said. 'This is where I will leave you. I must be getting back to my duties. You'll need to be careful carrying that gold through that area though.'

'I think we'll be all right,' Skar said.

Bjorn nodded. 'Right enough,' he said with a smile. 'I'd pity the thief who tried to rob you lot. Are you sure I can't persuade you to stay?'

Einar stopped. He looked around, back up the wide street, taking in the crowds, the statues, the grand buildings and all the dazzling sights and sounds of Constantinopolis, the greatest city in the world, the very centre of civilisation.

He sighed.

'No,' he said. 'We're going home.'

'You're sure?' Bjorn asked.

Einar's maimed right hand fell to the hilt of the sword he wore at his waist. His fingers played across the elaborate decoration that covered it.

'Yes,' he said. 'I made a promise to someone.'

Bjorn nodded. 'Very well. You're maybe right. There's enough gold in that chest for you to live like kings back home. Here it might just buy you a room in one of those tenements. Good luck. And if you ever change your mind, come back and ask for me.'

He saluted them, turned and headed back up the street through the crowds.

'So we will take Ulrich's sword home, as he wished,' Skar said, a look of satisfaction and approval on his face.

'Aye,' Einar said, his fingers moving once again over the silvered twisting beasts that decorated the weapon Ulrich had so treasured.

'You say he wanted us to give it to his son?' Affreca said. 'I've never heard him say he had one.'

'Nor I,' Einar said. 'I heard him talk of a wife but never a child. What about you, Skar? You of all people would know if he had a son or not.'

The big man shrugged.

'Perhaps it was just the wishful thinking of a mortally injured man,' Einar said with a heavy sigh. 'Ulrich went through agony that day. Perhaps his mind broke so he no longer knew the difference between real life and dreams.'

'Ulrich was the hardest man I ever knew,' Skar said. The edge to his voice betrayed his irritation at the very suggestion. 'There is no way that could have happened. If Ulrich said he had a son then he spoke the truth. I did not know him all his life. He could have sired several children before we met.'

Affreca and Einar exchanged glances.

'Very well,' Einar said. 'Then let us go and find him.'

'How do we do that?' Affreca said.

Einar looked around, squinting and grimacing a little at the bright sunshine.

'I don't know,' he said. 'But we won't find him here in this heat and sun. We will sail northwards.'

'Northwards and netherwards,' Skar said with a bleak grin.

Einar and Affreca smiled too, recognising his dark humour. They both recalled the ancient lore Skar's words had come from. They were the words of the old witch who foretold the end of the world and the doom of the gods. Northwards and netherwards were the directions Odin would take on his ride to the kingdom of Hel.

'*Urðr er fullráðinn,*' Einar said. 'So be it. Let's go.'

About the Author

TIM HODKINSON grew up in Northern Ireland where the rugged coast and call of the Atlantic Ocean led to a lifelong fascination with Vikings and a degree in Medieval English and Old Norse Literature. Tim's more recent writing heroes include Ben Kane, Giles Kristian, Bernard Cornwell, George R.R. Martin and Lee Child. After several years in the USA, Tim returned to Northern Ireland, where he lives with his wife and children.

Follow Tim on @TimHodkinson and www.timhodkinson.blogspot.com

The Whale Road Chronicles

by

TIM HODKINSON